Roommates

Jackie Calhoun

Bella
BOOKS

2008

Bella Books, Inc.
P.O. Box 10543
Tallahassee, FL 32302

Printed in the United States of America on acid-free paper

First Edition

Editor: Cindy Cresap
Cover designer: Stephanie Solomon-Lopez

ISBN-10: 1-59493-123-2
ISBN-13: 978-1-59493-123-9

To Madeline and Danielle, who remind me of my youth.

Acknowledgments

Thanks to the following people:
Joan Hendry, always my first reader;
Diane Mandler, for accuracy;
Madeline Snedeker, whose suggestion was the seed for this book;
Linda Hill and the staff at Bella Books for their excellent work;
and my new editor, Cindy Cresap

About the Author

Jackie Calhoun is the author of *The Education of Ellie*, *Obsession*, *Seasons of the Heart*, *Abby's Passion*, *Woman in the Mirror*, *Outside the Flock*, *Tamarack Creek* and *Off Season*, published by Bella Books; *Crossing the Center Line*, printed by Windstorm Creative; and ten books put out by Naiad Press. Jackie lives with her partner in northeast Wisconsin. Look at her Web site at www.jackiecalhoun.com or contact her at jackie@jackiecalhoun.com. She would love to hear from her readers.

Part I
1990

I

Peg

Peg leaned against the doorframe, attempting to look cool as she watched her roommate unpack her bags. This had to be Julie Decker who came from Chicago. They'd exchanged letters in August after Peg's best friend Cassie became pregnant and married Brad—thus ending their plans to room together.

Cassie's sudden marriage betrayed a long friendship. Peg had been so sure when her gaze met Cassie's over the heads of the other girls in the cabin on the Chain of Lakes after graduation that the zing of joy she felt was shared. They'd been more than friends, calling each other morning and night, spending time together every day.

Cassie had been dating Brad, but she hadn't seemed tied to him by the invisible thread that attached other couples. Peg swore she was never going to be chained to someone like that. Not her.

Her roommate turned toward her and a dazzling smile transformed her from being simply beautiful to drop-dead gorgeous. With ash blond hair, eyes like smoke and a figure to die for, she rendered Peg temporarily speechless. For years Peg had lived in a state of anticipation, expecting to meet someone exciting around every corner, and here she was. The grievance she carried against this girl because she wasn't Cassie vanished.

"Hey," the girl said, big smile in place, taking a step Peg's way, "are you Peg Kincaid?"

Nodding, she found her voice. "And I guess you're Julie? I hope it's okay that I took this bed." She gestured at her unopened luggage.

"No problem," Julie said. "There's an orientation downstairs in half an hour. Want to go?"

"Sure. I'll just start putting things away first." She sidestepped toward her bed.

When Julie glanced at her watch and said it was time to go, they ran down the stairs and entered a large room off the entry hall. With all the chairs taken, they sat on the floor with their backs to the wall.

"I'm glad you're here. I don't know anyone," Julie said in her ear.

"I don't either." She snuck a look at her. Julie had piled her hair on top of her head in a sort of ponytail. She gave Peg a crooked smile along with a quick lift of eyebrows, and something moved in Peg's chest. Gratitude? Admiration? Envy?

That night, she lay in bed watching the moon course its way across the sky. At home the only light at night came from the heavens. They didn't even have a dusk-to-dawn light, because her mom said it would hide the stars. Here the stars disappeared in the glow of streetlights.

She'd put down her book and switched off her light when Julie had turned her back and said goodnight. They'd been reading in a charged silence, although Peg thought only she felt the crackle of electricity. She was so wound up she feared she'd be awake all night, but the events of the day quickly overtook her and she fell into an exhausted sleep.

She woke to the sound of the clock radio. Sunlight flooded the room. Julie came in fresh from a shower, wrapped in a towel, her hair glistening with drops. Turning her back, she dropped the cover and quickly put on panties and a bra. Peg stared at her perfect backside, the tan outlining a bikini swimsuit.

Mumbling a good morning, she grabbed her shower bag and towel and headed for the bathroom down the hall. When she got back, Julie was gone. She dressed quickly and clambered downstairs for breakfast, her backpack slung on her shoulder.

"Over here, Peg." Julie waved from a table near the buffet line.

She set her backpack on the floor next to her chair.

"Hey," Julie said with a smile.

"Hey," she replied, wondering how anyone managed to look so good first thing in the morning. She sported a zit between her eyes. It was that time of the month. Her mom always said how lucky she was to have wavy hair, but her waves defied style. Julie's hair and skin glowed under the fluorescent lights, the same lights that made Peg appear sickly.

Their table filled as Julie waited patiently, while Peg ate rubbery eggs, chewy bacon and cold toast. The girl on the other side of her introduced herself and pushed her plate away.

"I'm Annie Waite. Has anyone got English Composition this morning?" They had classes already, although shortened ones. Yesterday they had picked up textbooks.

"I do," Peg said.

Julie wasn't in any of her classes, but she walked with them as they wove through the crowds of students. Excitement hung in the air. Some of them, like Peg, were living away from home for the first time.

In the creative writing class she bent over her blank legal pad and filled the page with words that sprang from a sentence on the board—"The swollen river roared under the bridge, lapping dangerously at its underpinnings."

She thought they'd be listening to a lecture instead of jumping right into action. Professor Alexander said he wanted to find out if there was any talent in the class, which immediately gave her writer's block. For a couple of minutes, she sucked her eraser, and then she began to scribble furiously.

She wrote that a huge tree, uprooted in a downpour, hit the bridge like a battering ram—again and again. The bridge began to break up just as a car with a girl driving alone sped toward it. Momentum drove the vehicle halfway across before it began to fall along with the concrete and steel. The girl jumped out before the car hit the water. She scrambled onto its roof as it slowly filled and began to sink.

One of the people gathering on the shore, another girl, dove into the wild water, towing a rope with two life jackets someone had thrust at her. Nearly swept away, she grabbed a floating limb that had caught on the car and made her way, twig by twig, to the stranded girl. The two young women, connected by the rope and buoyed by the life jackets, bobbed off downstream. They reached shore a mile away, exhausted and cold, and huddled close together for warmth until they were found.

The gist of her story, that *she* saved Julie instead of some guy, pleased her. She'd given herself an armchair getaway, just like reading a book. A brief crazy thought crossed her mind that maybe she could fill the empty space stretching before her with writing—books, articles. She'd absorbed as fact her parents' assumption that she'd go to college. No ambition pursued her here.

Professor Alexander said he'd read their papers aloud on Wednesday and let the class critique them, making her afraid that what she'd written was incredibly stupid. She hurried out of the room.

"Wait up." Annie chased after her. "Where are you going next?"

"Calculus." Math was her least favorite subject but a requirement.

"Too bad. I've got biology. See you later." Annie's brown hair brushed her shoulders and her dark eyes shone against alabaster skin. Had she spent most of her summer days inside? Studying? Reading?

After abbreviated classes where they were assigned homework, she went to the university bookstore and stood in the long lines of students who hadn't already purchased textbooks. So many kids knew each other that she felt out of it.

"Hey, what did you think about English Comp? I'm Mr. Schmidt, a.k.a. Charlie, and you're Ms. Kincaid," he said, jokingly referring to the formal way Professor Alexander addressed them. He stood in the line next to hers.

"Peg," she said, trying to place the dark curly hair and tiny mustache that quirked upward.

"This is Joe Danforth." He thrust a thumb at the tall, lanky guy behind him.

"Hey." Joe stuck out a huge hand and tossed yellowish hair out of his eyes.

"We're roommates," Charlie said.

Julie grabbed her arm, startling her. "There you are. I've been looking all over for you."

She turned, flustered. Julie's shining hair curled around her shoulders. Peg stared for a moment, remembering Cassie's pug nose that she once thought so adorable. "I have to get a book on grammar. Hey, meet Joe and Charlie. Charlie is in my English Comp class. My roommate, Julie Decker." She felt ridiculously proud introducing Julie and warned herself not to get too attached again to a straight girl. She should be looking with interest at these guys instead of Julie.

Julie repeated their names. "I'm pre-med," she said, although all freshmen took core courses.

They stared at Julie as Peg had at first, then Joe said, "I'm pre-law and Charlie here is going to be an author."

Peg had no burning desire to be or do anything. She read voraciously, always fiction, escaping into a good story. A hobby, not a vocation, she reminded herself. But no one asked about her ambitions. Julie had unwittingly claimed Joe's and Charlie's attention. No big surprise. She had Peg's too. As they shuffled forward in line, Julie stuck to Peg's side talking to Joe and Charlie.

"Want to go out?" Joe asked. "I know this awesome little place outside of town. We could make a foursome."

"Sweet," Julie said. "Maybe later." At his obvious disappointment, she caved. "On the weekend, if we don't have too much work. Okay, Peg?"

Peg's heart flip-flopped at the inclusion.

Julie possessed looks, brains and a quick wit. She also took an interest in everyone, which drew people to their door. Annie and her roommate, Shari Brooks, lived across the hall. Shari partied nights and slept during the day, so Annie practically moved in with Julie and Peg. They studied in group-mode, throwing questions at each other.

Peg rode high those first six weeks. Alexander gave her an A- for her first effort in Creative Writing, the one about the girl (Peg) rescuing the other girl (Julie) from the flooded river. After that, she bent to the task of writing imaginatively. English was a snap for her, and Annie, who planned to major in physics, helped her understand calculus. She'd thought she'd love American Lit, because fiction was her only real passion outside of horses, but they read books by Richard Wright and William Faulkner and John Steinbeck, which depressed the hell out of her.

Charlie and Peg ran their essays and short stories and character sketches past each other. He challenged her because he was so good. She wrote one story about a gay guy after reading *Giovanni's Room* by James Baldwin. Her main character tried to commit suicide when his boyfriend outed him but changed his mind at the last minute. She deleted the whole thing. Who would understand? She was deep in the closet.

Gays and lesbians fascinated her. They'd hung together in high school. A girl in her lit class walked around campus holding hands with another girl. One evening she came to their room with her girlfriend.

"Hey," Julie said. "Come on in. Peg, it's Tammy and Chloe. We've got chemistry together." Julie laughed at the obvious chemistry between the two girls.

"I know you. You're in my lit class." Tammy pointed at her. "Don't you think James Baldwin is the coolest?"

"Yeah." She thought Tammy was the coolest and the bravest to flaunt herself. Her close-cropped hair sported a ducktail, and she wore a wide leather choker.

Tammy put an arm around Chloe and kissed her cheek. "Peg's the quiet one in the second row."

She looked away. She didn't want to be known as the quiet one.

Chloe's large eyes and anorexic body reminded Peg of a Dr. Seuss character. Her smile was almost as wide as her face and her teeth looked huge.

"Let's get at it before everyone shows up." Julie plopped down and patted the mattress. The other two sat side-by-side, facing her. There was hardly room on the single bed for the three of them.

She took her algebra problems to Annie's room and returned as Joe and Charlie arrived. Tammy and Chloe were leaving, hand in hand, laughing. She trembled inwardly. With longing? With curiosity?

"Hey, that cool place outside of town that I told you about?

They serve you, no questions asked. Want to go?" Joe asked.

"Awesome," Julie said. "Maybe on Saturday." She winked at Peg. "Want to go, girlfriend?"

"Wouldn't miss it," she said, turning away before anyone saw her skin burning. For God's sake, she thought, get a grip. It was just a wink. Cassie was a shadow lurking in the back of her mind.

The Roadside turned out to be a log bar on an access road. Joe and Charlie picked them up in Joe's rusted Chevy Blazer. Peg briefly wondered how Charlie felt about being stuck with her in the backseat. Julie was the star around which they all orbited.

They walked into a smoke-filled room packed with kids drinking beer and reverberating with music that even shouting failed to override. Elbowing his way to the bar, Joe ordered Miller Lite, which they drank out of bottles. When Joe and Julie began to dance, Charlie and Peg followed. They made a foursome, each moving to her or his own version of the beat, facing each other in a square dance gone spastic.

Peg saw Tammy and Chloe locked together, swaying out of sync with the music. Shari, Annie's roommate, was across the room with some guy. Peg waved and someone else waved back. No one she knew.

They stopped to drink another round of beers. Peg caught a few words and tried to piece them together by reading lips. The smoke settled over everyone, a noxious cloud. Her head began to throb.

Charlie leaned over, his beery breath tickling her ear. "I've got better stuff than beer and cigarettes."

She nodded vigorously in answer.

In the parking lot, she gulped mouthfuls of air. Julie coughed violently, and Joe patted her back before opening the passenger door for her. Peg glanced at Charlie, and he winked at her as they slid into the backseat.

Driving to the end of a dirt road, Joe shut off the engine. Through the open windows, crickets chirped. A sweet smell floated her way, and Charlie handed her a tightly rolled joint. She sucked on it, coughed and passed it up front to Julie, who did the same before handing it to Joe. Several puffs later, Peg stumbled out of the car to escape the cloying odor.

The stars flung across the dark sky blurred and moved. The waning moon rose in the east. Cricket chirps pulsed in her veins. She began to sing softly a nursery song from her childhood.

Charlie lurched out of the backseat. "Hey, you all right?" He put his hands against a tree on either side of her and looked at her so seriously she began to laugh. He laughed with her. They held each other up, howling like hyenas with about as much reason.

Joe leaned over Julie and yelled out the open window. "Let's go get something to eat. I'm starving."

She was too she realized when they slid into a booth at a roadside restaurant. Across the table Julie's pupils had taken over the color in her eyes. One of them snorted a laugh, and they all began to giggle like fools.

When the food came, they fell on it as if famished. Afterward, she blinked under the fluorescent lights and told Julie she was beautiful. Later, she doubted any of them remembered what was said.

When she and Julie got back to the dorm, Julie told her that she wished people would see her mind rather than her body. She wanted to be admired for her brain and liked for her wit. And then she laughed. Pretension was not her strong suit. It was one of the things Peg liked best about her.

September turned into October and October into November. On some clear weekend days, she and Julie played touch football with Joe and Charlie and Tammy and Chloe and sometimes Annie. Others joined in. On weekend nights, Peg and Julie went out with Charlie and Joe. During the week they often studied with them. Peg took it for granted that to be with Julie she'd have to share her with Joe and Charlie, and she always wanted to be with Julie.

Julie went home with her for Thanksgiving. She wanted to see the horses and meet the family, or so she said.

Peg's brother Cam picked them up. Five years older than Peg, Cam had a degree in agriculture and hired himself out to local farmers when they went on vacation. He trained and showed other people's horses as well as his own. When he graduated from UW-Madison, he'd moved into an apartment above the garage.

Around six feet tall, he had the same coppery colored hair and dark brown eyes she did. He ducked his head when she introduced him to Julie, making her realize how stupid it was to be crazy about someone who was such a magnet for men. On the drive home he said little as if tongue-tied.

Into the silence Julie announced, "I took riding lessons for years."

She and Julie sat in the back of her mother's Taurus wagon. Bert perched on the edge of the passenger seat, his nose sticking out of the partially open window. Whenever Cam hit the brakes, the dog slid off onto the floor and scrambled back onto the seat. Bert had shown more enthusiasm upon seeing Peg than Cam had, but that wasn't unusual. She could be gone half an hour and Bert would go into a tail wagging spin all over again when she reappeared.

"No kidding," she said. "Did you ride western or hunt seat?"

Julie looked puzzled.

"Did you post or sit a trot?" she asked.

"Both," Julie said.

It didn't matter how Julie rode. The fact that she rode at all was what counted. She could use Peg's horse, Cosmo, a five-year-old gelding, or her mom's sorrel, Red. Both were well broke and gentle.

When Cam turned onto the gravel driveway, she noticed the sign out front—*Cam Kincaid, Horse Trainer*. "So it's official, huh? Where are you going to put all the horses?" She was half-joking but he answered dead serious.

"I go to the owners' places and work with them right now. When I'm established, I'll add on to the barn."

She envied him his choice of careers. Maybe if she couldn't find a job, he'd let her work with him.

Her mother, home from teaching that day, came out to greet them. Peg introduced Julie.

"Peg made your place sound so awesome I had to see it," Julie said, managing to sound sincere rather than gushing.

Peg's mom, who had just embraced Peg and now held Julie's hand, glanced Peg's way. A wry smile lit her face. She suspected her mother had guessed her sexual orientation long ago and was just waiting for her to own up to it. "We're always happy to have Peg's friends. Come inside."

It was like walking into a Hallmark card. Pumpkin pies cooling on racks, a bowl of cranberries on the work island, soup simmering on the stove. Peg took Julie through the house and up the stairs to her room where they dropped their backpacks on the double bed. Julie went to the window that overlooked the barn behind the house and the pasture beyond, and she followed. The horses were turned out. Cosmo and Red and Buck, Cam's seven-year-old gelding, grazed close together.

Julie's eyes shone. "What a cool place."

Peg was thinking the same thing. It hit her that she would be leaving here probably for good four or five years from now. She thought about how she'd always wanted to be with Cassie and her other friends in high school. Home had been where she slept and ate and took care of the horses. She never got out of cleaning stalls and feeding. She guessed she had to go away to appre-

13

ciate the place.

When Joe talked about being a public defender and Charlie hoped for a career in writing, Julie said she planned to join the Peace Corps. Peg despaired that Julie would be on her way to a third world country in Africa or some other place when she graduated. With no aspirations of her own, maybe she could go with her and build houses or dig wells or something. She banished these thoughts. Four or five years seemed light years away.

Downstairs, the smell of onions simmering in butter overwhelmed the odor of the pies cooling on a rack. Peg's mom glanced at them. Her coppery colored hair sported some gray. Her brown eyes, so like Cam's and Peg's, lit with pleasure.

"Need some help?" Julie asked.

"Later. Why don't you show Julie around, Peggy?"

"Is Dad at work?" she asked. As an accountant for the county, her father got about half as many vacation days as her mother did.

"Yep." Her mom cut through stacks of bread, making cubes for the stuffing. "You can make the rolls later, Peg. You do such a good job."

"Oh, sure. Almost as good as you do. Come on, Julie."

They headed out back with Bert on their heels. She and Julie leaned on the fence behind the barn, watching Cam ride in the outdoor arena. When their arms accidentally touched, the hairs on Peg's rose in response.

"Whose horse?" she asked as Cam trotted past them.

"Mine," he called over his shoulder. "He's a two-year-old. Why don't you saddle up Cosmo and Red?"

"Okay." She envied him again, temporarily forgetting what it was like to clean stalls and feed in the cold of winter when they sometimes had to break the ice out of buckets and thaw out the hose just to get water to run through it. Days this late in November weren't usually sweatshirt weather like this one.

Cool without the sun, the barn smelled of hay and grain and

horses, odors she'd grown up with. Putting some grain in a small bucket and grabbing two halters and lead ropes, she went out to the pasture with Julie.

"This is so exciting." Julie danced alongside her. She'd taken gymnastics as a kid and was incredibly agile. Peg loved to watch her move.

She caught sight of Cam sitting on his new horse and staring at Julie, and she laughed.

The horses eyed the bucket of grain and came running. They milled around Peg, trying to nose the pail. Julie hugged her side, now fearful.

"It's the grain they're after, not us," she reassured her, slipping a halter around Cosmo's gray head. Handing the lead rope to Julie, she put the other halter on Red, a sorrel gelding with a white blaze. Dumping the remaining grain on the ground for Buck, she started toward the barn.

Julie tried to keep a few steps ahead of Cosmo, but all the horses had been trained to walk next to the handler. "He's so big," she said.

"He won't step on you, Julie."

Cross-tying Cosmo and Red in the aisle, she got a currycomb and brush for each. "Don't worry about hurting him. Rub hard. He'll love it."

The horses grunted with pleasure. Both stood still for the pad and saddle. Peg removed the halters, slipped the bits into their mouths and pulled the headpiece over their ears. "You go ahead and get on. I'll lead them out to the arena."

She unlatched the gate, and Julie rode into the arena. By now Red knew he had a novice on his back. He pulled on the bit, snatching at the dead grass under the fence. When Julie shortened the reins and put her heels in him, he walked lazily around the ring.

"Looks like he needs a reminder," Cam said and began coaching. "Put your heels down, sit deep in the saddle and make him pay attention. He should work on a loose rein." When Red continued grabbing at grass, Cam moved his horse between the sorrel and the rail. Red pinned his ears and Cam's horse shied. "Do what I do," Cam told Julie.

Peg rode behind them also doing what they did. She wanted to take her horse out of the pen and through the pasture to the creek that ran along the back of the property, but Julie clearly wasn't ready. She urged Cosmo into a canter.

Running a hand along his long neck, she talked softly to him. "You're the best horse here even if you are a hairy beast." When Cosmo's coat felt damp, she brought him to a halt and walked him out. Cam was still coaching Julie who was laughing. Opening the gate, Peg started off across the pasture toward the creek.

"Can Red and I come, Peg?" Julie asked.

She pivoted Cosmo, ready to go back and re-open the gate, but Cam was doing that. He let Julie and Red out and followed, latching the gate behind him. The three of them headed toward the creek at a walk. Buck followed.

The swiftly flowing trout stream created eddies in its wake. Shining through leafless trees, the sun turned the water golden. They had to go through another gate to reach it. Once there, they gave the horses their heads so that they could drink. Red waded in and Julie let out a little screech. Cam and Peg urged their horses close to her, each grabbing a rein, although they both knew that Red always walked into the stream.

Back at the barn, Cam turned on the overhead bulbs. The day was fast turning into night. Peg and Julie helped him clean stalls and fill water buckets, and left him there to feed. When they walked to the house with Bert following, light from the house windows spilled across the ground.

Peg's dad was about as tall as Cam but not as lean. His light brown eyes glowed warmly as she hugged him and introduced Julie. His hair had more gray in it than any other color.

After dinner, Peg made the dough for the rolls. She and Julie and Bert were alone in the kitchen, her parents in the other room watching *The Lehrer Hour.* Cam had gone back to the barn.

Sitting on a stool at the island, Julie patted the dog that waited patiently for something edible to drop. "Does Cam spend all his time in the barn?"

"Just about. He lives above the garage now. Horses are his life."

"His passion," Julie said. "Books are yours. I wish I had one."

Peg stared at her. "I thought yours was medicine."

Julie graced her with a faint smile. "Did I ever tell you my older sister and brother are doctors? One's a gynecologist, the other is a pediatrician. They're in practice with my parents." She sighed. "I'm expected to join the family clinics."

Covering the dough, Peg put it in the fridge to rise overnight. Hope swelled in her heart. Maybe she wouldn't lose Julie to Africa. "I have no idea what to major in. You don't make any money reading books."

"You could write a novel."

She scoffed. "Oh yeah, like I have anything interesting to say."

When they climbed the stairs to her room, all Peg could think about was getting into her double bed with Julie. She'd always taken up the whole bed. If she rolled against her in the night, Julie might not want to sleep with her.

A cool breeze crept in under the slightly open windows as they burrowed under the quilt. "I'd give anything to have a home like this, Peg." Julie faced Peg, so close that Peg felt her breath on her face.

"You must live in a pretty fancy place." She hoped her breath smelled like toothpaste too.

"Downtown Chicago, along the lake. You can walk anywhere. It's great for culture and shopping and jogging on the beach, but it's so totally different from this. Be nice if we could trade homes for a while."

"Maybe we can go to yours some weekend."

Peg turned over and hugged the edge of the bed. Drifting off in mid-sentence, she awoke in the night to find Julie tucked up against her, spoon-like. Breaking into a sweat, Peg tried to lie still, to enjoy the intimacy of the moment, but Julie's soft exhalations on the back of her neck created an itch she had to scratch.

"I'm lying all over you," Julie murmured, rolling away. "Sorry. That's why nobody wants to sleep with me."

"Hey, I don't mind. Bert used to do the same thing till Dad found out. Now he's banned from my room at night."

Julie laughed softly, sending chills up Peg's spine. "When we went on trips as kids, my sister and I had to share a bed. She was always shoving me away. Violently."

"I won't do that."

Shadowy branches from the maple outside the window moved over the wall. "I know. You're nice."

"I'm not nice," she said. If she were a guy, she'd have a boner. She laughed nervously.

"Hey, it's okay. Whatever."

Still curled in a ball, she stayed in place. Sweating. Tense. Uncomfortable.

Julie snuggled up to her again. "You're so warm," she said, her breath once more hot on Peg's neck.

Peg thought she'd never sleep, but she did. Finally.

The days flew by, sweetened by Julie's presence. She learned to relax when Julie pressed against her and even opened the windows wider so that Julie would seek her warmth in bed. On the last night of vacation they played cards with Peg's parents and went upstairs after eleven.

"I hate to leave," Julie said as they undressed, backs turned.

They'd ridden every day, helped Cam in the barn and Peg's mom in the kitchen like the perfect family.

"Me, too." She'd never leave if Julie stayed.

She was nearly asleep when Julie kissed her on the cheek. "Thanks for sharing."

Her hand stole up to touch the spot. "Thanks for coming."

"Speaking of coming, do you want to?"

Startled, she turned toward Julie who kissed her on the mouth.

Stunned by the unexpected, the only imagined, she closed her eyes and inhaled Julie's scent, intending to memorize it in case this never happened again. She briefly wondered if she was an experiment. But when Julie's mouth moved over hers, tongue warmly probing, Peg stopped thinking. Julie fingered the hem of the large T-shirt Peg wore to bed, and Peg reached shyly for hers.

The feel of skin, warm and smooth, electrified her, just as the kissing caused her to lose all sense of place and time. Although short-lived, the pleasure that followed was almost painful in its intensity. As their breathing slowed in the aftermath, her last thought before sleep was that this would be very hard to give up.

They awoke later to begin again. Already more experienced, more confident, more needy.

The next morning Cam yelled up the stairs, startling them awake. They quickly moved apart. To be safe, Peg tore the sheets off the bed and remade it while Julie showered. Then she showered and stuffed her laundered clothes in her backpack.

Her mother's eyes searched her face when she entered the kitchen with Julie. Peg flushed, and her mom gave a slight nod. Had she heard them? Did she know?

"We've got to get going." Cam stood by the kitchen door.

"We'll take them back," her dad said. "It seems like they just got here."

The look on Cam's face would have made her laugh had she

not known how he felt. He inclined his head slowly. "Okay. You want to come out and say good-bye to the horses, Julie?" His face reddened.

"Sure."

Her mom pushed the coffee cake toward Julie. "Take some breakfast with you."

She grabbed a piece. "Thanks. You coming, Peg?"

"In a minute." She would give Cam his time alone with Julie. Believing that Julie was now hers, she savored a tired joy.

The drive back was a quiet one. She and Julie fell asleep as Peg's parents talked quietly up front.

II

Peg

In January, Peg trudged up the stairs to her dorm room carrying a note she'd found in her mailbox scheduling a meeting with the Assistant Dean of Women the next day at ten thirty. Her grades were the issue.

Julie turned as Peg closed the door and leaned against it. She held a similar note. "You too?" Peg nodded. "Want to blow this place?" Julie asked.

They had blown everything else. It seemed impossible that they had managed to fall so far in such a short time. She experienced a momentary rush of guilt. Her parents, who believed she would be ultimately successful despite her pitiful performance to date, would be forced to face the fact that she had nearly failing grades in all but English Comp and Literature. If they didn't know by now, they would in a few days.

"Where would we go?" She had no money.

Every night, they'd climbed into a single bed together and slept with arms and legs entangled in an intimacy Peg had never known, even more personal than the sex that preceded it. She wasn't about to give that up. She'd follow Julie anywhere and do whatever it took to stay with her.

"Milwaukee. We'll use my credit card till we get jobs." Julie's eyes glowed with a smoky fire.

Peg gave a soft snort of disbelief. "What will I tell my parents? What will you tell yours?"

"I'll tell them I need time to get my shit together, that I don't want to waste any more of their money."

They stared at each other until a slow smile grew between them. "What about Joe and Charlie?" The guys had attached themselves to them. They studied together. They played together. They drank and smoked weed together.

"What about them? They're entrenched. They're not going to leave."

She knew Joe at least would have trouble letting go of Julie. "What if they want to come with us?"

Julie threw up her hands, and the note fluttered to the floor. "They'll find other girlfriends. It'll just be us, making it on our own."

After dozing off over every text, it was a relief to climb into bed with a good book. Peg found, though, that she could neither concentrate nor fall asleep. She turned to Julie whose ankles entwined with hers.

"Hey, Jule," she whispered, kissing her on the ear, the cheek, the neck.

Julie shifted, wrapping her arms around Peg and murmuring, "Hey yourself. I can't concentrate either. I keep wondering what Brennan is going to say tomorrow. I think we're going to be put on probation."

"The next step to being kicked out."

"I know. My dad's advice on most things is don't throw good

money after bad. We're definitely a risk. Once we're on our own, we can do anything we want."

Peg shifted uncomfortably under Shirley Brennan's unwavering gaze. The woman appeared troubled. "You were doing so well at the beginning of the semester," she said as if mystified.

"I know. I just don't know what I want to major in." She took a deep breath. "So, I'm not going to spend any more of my parents' money."

"Many students don't choose a major their first year, and you have a scholarship."

"It's pretty small. I don't want to waste that money either."

Brennan played with a pen on her desk. "Maybe it would be better if you and Julie didn't room together. You seem to think along the same lines."

She misinterpreted. Had Brennan talked Julie into staying? No way did she want to leave if Julie was going to stay. She said nothing.

The woman sighed and seemed to give up. "Okay. Talk it over with your parents."

She left Brennan's office with wet armpits and an aching jaw. Julie waited outside the door, and they ran up the wide steps.

"What did she say to you?" Julie asked.

Peg told her. "You are leaving, aren't you?"

"*We're* leaving. Together."

When Julie told them, Joe and Charlie looked disbelieving. "You're what?" Joe said.

"Our grades suck. We're taking off before they kick us out."

"When?" Charlie asked.

"Before the next semester starts."

"That would be this week." Joe's hands clutched the table.

"I know." Julie's brows arched. She had done all the talking.

"We could go with you. Work for a year and come back," Joe

said.

"I can't." Clearly distressed, Charlie glanced at Peg. "Are you coming back next fall?"

Her answer caught in her throat. She shrugged.

When they returned to their room around ten, Annie was sitting on Peg's bed, studying. Annie had one more exam. Looking up, she asked, "What did Brennan say?"

"We're leaving," Julie announced.

Looking stunned, Annie asked, "She kicked you out?"

"No, not yet," Peg replied.

"Then why are you going? And where?"

"We'll send you a card when we get there. Maybe you can visit." Julie began dragging her bags out of the closet. "We're not waiting for the verdict." She emptied her drawers methodically.

Guilt flooded Peg. During her last phone conversation with her parents over the weekend, she'd mostly listened to a pep talk from her dad.

Annie asked, "Who am I going to hang with?" Her grades were awesome.

"Maybe Joe and Charlie," Julie said. "Don't tell anyone, Annie. Better start packing, Peg. We're getting out of here first thing tomorrow morning. The bus leaves at eight."

The phone rang and Peg reached for it, only to have Julie's hand close over hers. "What if it's your parents, or mine? They must know by now that we're on probation."

"I'll tell them we're leaving."

"Do it after we're gone. Otherwise they'll drive here tonight."

"Where will we stay?"

"I've got a cousin. He'll take us in till we find our own place."

"We're just going to show up on his doorstep? Won't he tell your parents?" The ringing stopped, and she exhaled.

Julie dug through her desk and came up with an address and phone number. She left a message when the cousin didn't answer. "It'll be okay. He's the black sheep in the family." She giggled. "He won't have that sole honor anymore."

When the phone rang again, Julie talked Annie into answering it. "Sorry, Peg's not here. I'll give her the message." She hung up and said, "Guess who?"

"My parents," she answered, feeling terrible and excited at the same time. She and Julie were starting a new life together.

Peg was still awake when someone knocked on the door. Leaping out of Julie's bed, she rumpled up her own before taking the chair out from under the doorknob. They never ran the risk of getting caught in the same bed. The door opened and the dorm counselor, a graduate student, stood framed in the opening.

"Put the phone back on the hook. Your parents have been calling," she said. "Some people around here want to sleep."

Julie had taken the receiver off before they went to bed. Peg's heart thudded as she hung it up. When it immediately began to ring, she flinched.

"Answer it," the girl snapped and left when Peg picked up the phone.

"Hello," she said in what she hoped was a sleepy voice.

"Peggy, we've been trying to reach you for hours. We heard from the dean today," her mom said.

"Did you take the phone off the hook?" Dad asked, on the other line and clearly upset.

"Not on purpose," she replied, glancing at Julie who was sitting up looking at her.

"What's going on?" Dad barked.

"I'm sorry." She wanted to cry but for them not herself.

"We better come get you," her mother said.

"Not yet, Mom." They *would* have to be understanding rather than angry. It made her feel even shittier.

"Come back to bed," Julie said when she hung up. "It'll be okay."

Burrowing into Julie, Peg tried not to think about the panic her sneaking off to Milwaukee would generate. Convinced that this was the only way she and Julie could remain together, she felt she had no choice.

"Go to sleep, sweetie," Julie murmured. "We have to get up early."

The endearment warmed her but didn't bring on sleep. She read until she dozed off around quarter to four.

Julie shook her awake. "Come on, Peg, get dressed. The taxi will be here at seven thirty."

With their luggage at their feet, they shivered outside the dorm lest the driver show up and blow the horn. The wind gusted around them. Peg's ears and nose had lost all feeling by the time the cab rattled around the corner.

The driver got out and loaded their bags in the trunk. They climbed into the warm taxi that smelled of oil and gasoline and garlic. Leaning back against the torn seat, her mind as numb as her body, Peg felt neither remorse nor excitement.

A cigarette dangling from his lips, the cabbie studied them in the rearview mirror. Of Middle Eastern descent with black bushy eyebrows and hair, he spoke with an accent. "You girls running away?"

"Nope," Julie answered and stared out the window, avoiding his piercing gaze.

Was going off without telling anyone brave or cowardly? Peg thought maybe both. It was certainly disloyal. She felt nauseated and hungry at the same time. Before leaving the room, they'd split a package of stale Twinkies Julie had found in her desk drawer.

At the bus station, Julie bought the tickets while Peg stood over the luggage outside the door. The bus idled at the curb in a cloud of diesel fumes. She tried to breathe in as little as possible.

When Julie came out with the tickets, the bus driver tossed their bags in the lower compartment. With their backpacks at their feet, they sat together next to a window away from the station.

The bus slowly took on passengers—a tired looking mother with a kid in a carrier on her back, several chattering older women, two men in uniform, an incredibly heavy man who took up the entire bench behind the driver. Two young black guys, talking loudly, earphones plugged in, danced their way down the aisle. The driver climbed inside, took his seat, pulled a lever and the door hissed shut.

"We're off on our big adventure," Julie whispered and squeezed Peg's thigh.

Peg's heart leaped as the bus pulled away. First chance she got she'd call home. And say what? She'd run off with Julie?

It was still early when the bus stopped at the Milwaukee station. The wind howled down the street, and they hurriedly climbed into the first waiting taxi. Julie gave the driver the address while Peg stared at the dirty snow piled along the side of the street. She'd lost track of her feelings.

The taxi sped north through the gray city. She watched the passing scenery without much thought. Julie hadn't talked to her cousin. There was only the message she'd left to warn of their impending arrival.

Bumping her luggage up the steps to the porch of the old three-story house, Peg thought if she had to lug this stuff any farther, she'd toss all but her toothbrush and a change of underwear.

The bell with Jim Decker's name under it jangled inside the house, but no one appeared to let them in. Julie opened the storm door and turned the inside knob. Locked.

"Now what?" Peg asked.

"We wait." Julie thumped down on her suitcase and set her backpack between her legs. "I know what you're thinking, but I'm not going back."

Actually, Peg hadn't considered that option. She'd been daydreaming about sitting down in a warm place with some food.

"Hey, it's going to be okay." Julie took Peg's hand and heated it between hers. "We just have to hang together."

They were still hanging together, shivering, nearly two hours later when Jim sprang up the porch steps, two at a time. Julie looked at him from her perch on her suitcase. "Where you been, cuz?"

Tall, thin and shaved bald, Peg thought he resembled a bowling pin. His deeply set eyes were the same gray as Julie's.

Julie stood and stretched. "Isn't it kind of cold to be going around without any hair?"

"Don't be rude. I thought you were coming tomorrow." He unlocked the door, grabbed the suitcases and carried them up two flights of stairs.

Unlocking that door, he let them into the apartment. Peg sank into a beat-up easy chair next to a worn sofa, which shared an ancient floor lamp between them. A bookcase made of warped boards held up by bricks and filled with tattered paperbacks stood under a window that looked out on another house about ten feet away.

A kitchenette with a short counter and two stools, a small fridge and stove, a few cupboards and a tiny microwave occupied the other end of the room. On the counter sat a computer and printer.

Jim pointed out his bedroom and the bathroom. "The couch opens up into a double bed."

"We'll be out of here as soon as we both land jobs," Julie said.

Jim raised an eyebrow. "What kind of jobs? Management?" He laughed at his joke. "Why aren't you at the university anyway?"

"They were about to kick us out. Don't tell my parents I'm here, okay?"

"If you don't tell them I'm here." He laughed again.

Peg desperately needed to use the bathroom and said so. The room was so tiny she could have brushed her teeth while sitting on the toilet. Water stains streaked the small shower and sink. Two towels were thrown over the shower rod and two toothbrushes poked out of a coffee cup on the small counter under the mirror above the sink. Someone else lived here, too.

"If we go get something to eat, will we be able to get back in?" Julie asked.

"Take the key by the door." He nodded at a nail, holding one key. "There's a restaurant and a gas station with a little food mart attached a couple blocks east. Not much room in the fridge, though. Don't buy a ton of stuff. Pete and I need some space."

"Pete?" Julie said.

Jim smiled wryly. "You're not the only one with a roommate."

Outside, bits of snow, dry leaves and litter scuttled ahead of the wind. Peg wrapped her jacket tightly around her. They increased their pace almost to a run.

A corner restaurant called The Diner drew them into its shabby, warm interior. The booths and chairs and stools were clad in faded red vinyl, the walls painted a dingy off-white. They sat at the counter. A waitress, wearing jeans and a long-sleeved shirt with UWM printed over her left breast and a nametag with Lisa on it over the other, looked them over.

"Coffee?" she asked, and they turned their cups upright for her to pour.

"Is it too late for breakfast?" Julie asked.

Lisa turned and yelled the request. A young guy with a bandana around his forehead appeared in the opening behind the counter and placed two plates with sandwiches and chips on the sill. "What'll it be?" He looked right at them.

"Pancakes, hash browns and bacon," Peg told him.

"Denver omelet, American fries and wheat toast," Julie said.

Lisa wrote the orders on her pad and handed them to the guy, then took the plates to a couple of girls in one of the booths.

"You okay, Peg?" Julie asked.

"Yes. No. Are you?" The truth? In addition to being tired, she was scared and unwilling to admit it.

"We better buy a newspaper and start looking for work. What have you got for money?"

"A hundred and two dollars. I'll buy the food."

"Hang onto it for now. I may as well use my Visa till my parents axe my credit line." The waitress put their plates in front of them, and Julie asked, "Are you hiring, Lisa?"

The girl turned her head and loudly echoed the question.

The guy's head appeared again. "Either of you cook?"

"I do," Julie volunteered. "I make your basic foods."

Peg figured she meant macaroni and cheese out of a box and frozen pizza and an occasional hamburger.

He nodded. "You don't have to be a chef extraordinaire. You just need to know how to fry stuff—eggs, burgers, fish and fries. Can you do that?"

She flashed her winning smile. "Hey, no problem."

"Why don't you start tomorrow? It's always busiest on Fridays. What's your name?"

"Julie. Peg here is a good waitress if you need someone else."

Outside of setting and clearing at home, she'd never waited tables, but she figured it'd be a no-brainer. That is, if she could remember who ordered what.

"Not at the moment. We'll keep her in mind, though. Come in around six thirty tomorrow morning. What's your phone number?"

Julie dug out the note with Jim's name, address, and phone number and copied it.

"I'm Hal Burton and this is Lisa Williamson."

Lisa refilled their coffee cups and Julie asked, "How do you like UWM?"

She shrugged. "It's okay. I go part-time, work part-time and live at home. Not very exciting."

Julie nodded. "That's what we're going to have to do now."

Peg stopped wolfing down her food and looked at Julie. If that's what she had in mind, they should have put their efforts into studying and stayed where they had a free ride. Anyway, she wasn't ready to go back to school. She needed a breather, time off from deadlines and other people's expectations.

The door opened, letting in a gush of cold air along with two students, backpacks slung over their shoulders. Lisa went to their booth.

They finished eating in silence and left a tip they couldn't afford. Julie stuffed her pockets with packets of ketchup, salt and sugar. They left The Diner and crossed the street to the food mart.

Outside near the sidewalk, stood a phone booth. "I'm going to call home and leave a message." Peg closed the door against the sound of traffic.

Not expecting anyone to be there on a workday, she panicked when her mother answered on the first ring. "Hi," she stammered, "It's me."

"Where are you?" her mom demanded, desperation behind her words.

"I'm fine, Mom. Don't worry. I'll call again soon. I'll find a job." She talked fast, adding, "Trust me." As if she was trustworthy after running off without telling anyone.

"Come home, Peggy. You can live here and work."

"Let me do this, Mom."

Her dad took the phone. "At least tell us where you are."

"I'm in Milwaukee, staying with friends. I don't remember the address. Tell you later. I've got to go." She hung up, sweating despite the cold, and hurried into the food mart to find Julie.

"Maybe I can bring home leftovers from The Diner. Stuff they're going to throw away anyway," Julie said as they walked hurriedly toward Jim's, heads down against a cold wind.

No one greeted them at the apartment. No note lay on the counter. They stuffed their purchases—milk, butter, tuna, bread, coffee—in the fridge and cupboards.

Julie turned to her. "How about a quickie?"

She hesitated even as a spurt of desire shot through her. "What if Jim or Pete shows up?"

"We won't take anything off. Besides, we'll hear them coming up the stairs."

The ratty sofa smelled like it had spent years in a basement. She disliked even sitting on the stained cushions, but when Julie beckoned, she never thought to say no.

After fumbling with zippers on tight jeans, they finally wriggled their hands into position where Peg's promptly went to sleep. She was trying to revive it when someone bounded up the steps and thrust a key in the lock.

Tearing the offending hand out of Julie's pants, ripping her skin in the process, she leaped to her feet and managed to straighten her clothes as the door flew open. She wrapped the hand in a napkin she found in her pocket and shot a glance at Julie who was fastening her jeans.

A dark, hairy guy stood in the doorway, staring at them, his mouth slightly open in surprise.

"Hi," Julie said brightly. "Are you Pete?"

"I'll let you know when you tell me who you are." Stepping into the room, he shut the door. His black brows knit together in a fierce frown.

"Jim didn't tell you we were coming, did he? I'm his cousin and this is Peg," Julie said.

"Are you staying here?" he asked, incredulity in his voice, confronting them with hands on hips.

A nervous giggle gurgled up Peg's throat, and she glanced at the tired carpet to hide her face.

"Only till we get jobs and find a place to live. I start work tomorrow at The Diner. It's just a fill-in till I find something else. Know of any job openings?"

"Depends on what you want. Have you got a degree?"

"One semester of higher education," Julie said, chin high.

If failing grades counted, Peg thought, clearing her throat to cover another giggle.

"We're applying to UWM," Julie added.

Pete sat down on the couch and wiped a hand across his face as if to erase them from view.

"Are we taking your bed?" Peg asked, thinking perhaps he and Jim were only roommates.

He guffawed. "That's rich, girl. Are you for real?"

She flushed. "Sorry. Maybe we should go, Julie."

Julie looked at her like she was nuts. "Where?"

"It's not every day you come home and find a couple of strange girls fucking in your apartment. Wouldn't you want to know what's going on?" Pete asked.

"We weren't—" Julie began indignantly.

"Yeah, sure, and I'm Santa Claus."

Peg broke into laughter. Every time she managed to stop, she looked at Pete or Julie and started all over again. Finally, she sat down on the couch with Pete to catch her breath.

Julie asked, "What's so funny?"

Close to tears, she gasped, "Nothing." It was all so absurd.

Another bitterly cold day was beginning as she walked Julie to The Diner. Julie nervously confessed she was no cook.

"Why did you tell him you were then?" Peg asked.

"We need the money, honey." The "we" part gave Peg a little thrill, as if they were a real couple.

The previous night they'd watched a basketball game. Mind numbing. Peg had fallen asleep in the chair. Apparently, Pete and Jim were big sports fans. She and Julie couldn't make the sofa bed till after eleven because the guys were sitting on it. Then they listened to their lovemaking till Julie rolled on top of Peg, setting off their own brand of sex. "Let's finish what we started earlier," she'd whispered as if they could be heard over the grunts and the rocking bed in the other room.

After leaving Julie at The Diner's door, she crossed the street to the food mart and asked the blond woman at the cash register for a job application. Filling it out by the coffee machines, she took it back to the woman who scanned it.

"Looks good to me. You're hired. I'm the manager. Brenda Martin. The pay is six dollars an hour. Can you work nights? We're sort of hooked to the gas station hour-wise."

She nodded. "I can start right now."

Brenda's blond came out of a bottle, her flesh-stressed buttons and zippers, and her tired blue eyes floated softly in red-veined whites. When she smiled, she lit up and looked almost motherly. She was old enough to be Peg's. "Okay. Stock those shelves over there." She pointed with her chin to some boxes in the aisle. "Then I'll show you how to run the register."

Brenda let her leave when someone else came on shift, telling her to come back at three the next day. She'd be on till ten. Shrugging into her jacket, she crossed the street to The Diner. Lisa let her in. Julie and Hal were just finishing up in the kitchen.

She and Julie walked to Jim's apartment. Wet with sweat, Julie was soon shaking with cold. "Next time I'll layer. That kitchen is a furnace."

Tiny, almost sleet-like flakes fell, covering the dirty slush and turning everything white. Peg had always loved snow. A wave of homesickness washed over her as a clear mental image popped up of Cosmo shoveling the stuff with his nose and snorting it out.

Julie hooked her arm through Peg's. "Isn't this awesome?" she asked.

"You're awesome." Julie was the reason she was here. Having watched girls fawn over their boyfriends, she'd sworn she'd never lose herself to anyone, but that was before she met Julie. Now she understood.

Jim and Pete lay on the sofa in each other's arms, watching TV. Maybe this was how they planned to get rid of Julie and her. Sleep deprivation would force them to move. Peg sank into the chair and drifted off in the middle of another basketball game.

Julie shook her awake later. Streetlight filtered through the dirty window. Wind rattled the glass. They snuggled under the blanket, both of them wearing sweats. Julie put an arm around Peg and drew her close. Jim turned the heat down at bedtime.

"You smell like a french fry," Peg whispered.

"Yeah, well I'm not getting the ketchup." Julie yawned in her ear, and she wiggled closer.

When Julie got up in the morning, Peg slept on in the cooling vacuum. Next she knew, Julie was leaning over her.

"See you later."

"I'll walk with you." Her tongue was thick and slow, almost as sluggish as the rest of her. "Give me a minute."

"You'll have to hurry."

She pulled on jeans and a sweatshirt while Julie put the bed together. They ventured into the dark stillness of pre-dawn. It seemed as if they'd just walked the other way, except it was no longer snowing and the cold was the kind that froze nostrils together. Streetlights illuminated the fresh snow on the ground and cars and trees. The door to The Diner jangled as they stepped into the warmth and breathed in the stale odor of used cooking oil. Not even the smell of coffee covered it.

"Lock the door behind you," Hal called from the kitchen. "We don't open till seven."

"Where's Lisa?" Julie asked.

"She's taking today off. Don't worry, kiddo, it won't be busy like last night. I can manage the food if you can handle the cus-

tomers, unless maybe your friend here would like to wait tables."
He looked as if he hadn't changed clothes or looked in a mirror.

"Do you sleep here?" Peg asked.

"Yep. There's a bed in the room behind the kitchen and a shower."

"Can I use the bathroom? I have to brush my hair and wash my face." She hadn't even put on a bra.

"You own the place?" she asked when she came out. She'd had to wet her hair and use his comb to tame it. She'd considered using his toothbrush but instead rubbed toothpaste on her teeth with a finger.

"Hell, no. My Uncle Scrooge does. He pays diddlysquat. The dishwasher needs emptying." An industrial size, huge and hot, awaited her.

The TV on a high shelf at the end of the dining room was muted on a morning news station. Desert Storm was in progress. Troops and tanks moved across the barren landscape. A helicopter hovered overhead. She watched while she gobbled down pancakes and bacon. Hal said they couldn't work on empty stomachs. She'd come every morning if he served her breakfast.

After, she set the tables and booths, turning cups upside down on saucers and placing them next to empty water glasses. She put the tableware, wrapped in a napkin and fastened with a little paper tab, on top of a paper placemat. The windows fogged over inside as the coffee and cooking oil heated up. Julie scuttled around the kitchen doing Hal's bidding.

When Hal unlocked the front door, The Diner filled up quickly. Steam rose off the puddles on the floor. The noise level swelled. Peg stood near the counter, wondering who to wait on first.

Until somebody yelled, "Do we have to get the coffee ourselves?"

Grabbing a pot and a water pitcher, she took them around the room. That finished, she started scribbling orders on a pad.

36

Most of the customers were UWM students and called out what they'd ordered as she brought the steaming plates out to distribute. She apologized about fifty times for setting dishes down in front of the wrong person or forgetting to bring ketchup or spilling coffee or water. She felt like a dope, but no one seemed to mind. She kept saying she didn't really work there, that she was filling in for Lisa. That got her off the hook.

Hal gave her a quick lesson on how to keep track of who ordered what. He told her to number the tables and always write orders down clockwise. It helped with the lunch crowd. When the last one slipped out the door around two, letting in a swirl of frosty air, she cleaned up, reset tables and collapsed on a stool at the bar.

"I have to go to work at three," she said, pouring a cup of coffee. "Want to split the tips?" She'd picked up thirty-six dollars.

"Share them with Julie. You earned them," Hal said. "Want a burger and fries?"

"I'll fix them," Julie said. "How do you want your meat, Peg?"

"Hot," she replied, flickering her eyebrows.

"So, that's how it is? I wondered," Hal said. "I'll have mine medium."

Julie laughed.

Peg smiled. "Then I have to go."

"Hey, thanks for pitching in," Hal told her. "You'll get a check for seven hours. Two thirty an hour. Wow!"

"Plus eighteen in tips." She went out the door into the cold where the only smell was exhaust.

III

Peg

Brenda stood behind the counter counting out change. Her hair looked blonder, the tired lines beneath her eyes smoother. She laughed at something the customer said and spotted Peg standing inside the door.

"Hi, Peg, come on back here. You can work the register."

At first she was nervous with Brenda watching, but the older woman was easy with the criticism. "We all hit the wrong keys when we start. You'll catch on quick."

Brenda left at nine and said she'd be back before ten. By then Peg had gotten the hang of handling charges and ringing up sales. The machine told her the amount of change to return. She didn't have to be a math whiz.

Her heart jumped, hot and charged with guilt, when Joe and Charlie came in. She never expected to see them again, certainly not here. "How?"

"We stopped for gas and saw you through the window," Joe said. "We were on our way to see Julie's cousin Jim." He lifted his brows and smiled smugly.

"How did you know where to look?"

"Julie's mom," he said.

"Julie will appreciate that." If Julie's mom knew where they were, some day soon she'd no doubt look up and see her mom and dad standing where Joe and Charlie were.

"Where is Julie?" Joe asked.

Of course they came to see her. "Across the street at The Diner."

"I'll hang around here," Charlie said.

She told him if he went across the street he could get something to eat.

"I already ate." When customers came up to pay, he walked around the store or stood silently nearby. When alone, they talked about what they'd read. Under his unzipped Columbia jacket, he wore a UW hooded sweatshirt. She wanted a sweatshirt like that to remind her of where she'd been, like one of her horse show trophies.

As promised, Brenda showed up just before ten. "You did good, honey," she said after checking out the register. Peg felt ridiculously proud. "I'll take it from here. See you at three tomorrow."

"Okay." Zipping her jacket against the damp, cold night, she shouldered out the door with Charlie behind her. A car idled out front with some guy sitting behind the wheel, smoking and waiting for Brenda. They crossed the street to The Diner. Through the window she saw Joe sitting on a stool and Lisa setting up for the next day, like some scene out of a play.

"Hey," she said, sitting next to Joe. Charlie grabbed a stool on her other side.

"Why did you sneak out on us?" Joe asked plaintively.

"We told you we were leaving." Julie's raised voice came from the other room.

"Yeah, but not where you were going." Joe still sounded aggrieved.

"We didn't tell anyone." Julie appeared at the kitchen door.

"We could have helped." His eyes held a desperate hope that Peg just as desperately hoped would never be realized.

"There's no room for you where we're staying," Julie said bluntly and tripped Peg's heart with a smile. "How's the new job, Peg?"

"Okay."

"Why don't we go for a drive and talk?" Joe said.

Lisa's back was turned as she set up the coffee for the morning. She pretended to ignore them, but Peg knew she was listening, trying to put two and two together.

Hal emerged from the kitchen. "Good idea. It's closing time."

"You want a ride home?" Julie asked Lisa.

"I'll take her," Hal said.

They climbed into Joe's Blazer and drove to a parking lot that overlooked the lake. Joe cranked the heater and radio, and Charlie got out some weed and cold beer from a cooler. A full moon lit the gray choppy waters of Lake Michigan.

It was like old times. Joe talked about school. Charlie rattled on about books. She slowly drifted off in the warming vehicle. When Julie said they were going to enroll at UWM, the tone changed and Peg jerked awake.

"Why? You can find jobs like yours in Madison. Come back and go to school part-time," Joe said.

"Where would we live?" Julie asked edgily.

"With us," Joe said. "You could live with us."

"At the dorm. Yeah, sure, like you've got room for us."

"Marry me." Joe sounded desperate. "They have housing for married students."

Peg feared Julie would take the easy way. Her heart pounded anxiously. All three honed in on Julie as they waited for her response.

"No, Joe. Peg and I are going to stay here."

She exhaled, not even aware that she'd been holding her breath.

"I'll move here and go to UWM too then," Joe said.

"I don't have time for a boyfriend." Julie's voice sounded flat, final. If Peg hadn't been so relieved, she'd have felt sorry for Joe, but then Joe began whispering, pleading, kissing Julie on the neck, the ear, the eyes. Between the seats, Peg saw his arm cross the space between them, and she knew he was giving her a hand job. Julie shifted toward him, and her arm appeared under his as she returned the favor. Peg's chest hurt. Was this how to tell him she didn't want to be with him?

Charlie put his arm around Peg and gently turned her face toward his. It wasn't the first time he'd kissed her, but it was the first time she really returned it. His mustache tickled her nose. He put her hand on the hardness in his jeans and groped with her zipper. Hesitating, she heard Julie moan as she had moaned for her and she tugged on Charlie's zipper, releasing the thing within that quivered in her hand. She knew this meant Joe and Charlie would come back, but at the moment, she was both desirous and furious.

Later, she fell asleep on Charlie's shoulder, his head on hers, thinking as her eyes closed that he was a friend she might need one day.

Joe and Charlie dropped them off at Jim's apartment around five in the morning. Joe said they'd be back next weekend now that they knew where she and Julie lived and worked. Conflicting emotions swept through Peg, one following the other as she staggered up the stairs and into the bathroom with Julie. She was as guilty as Julie. They'd betrayed each other.

"Are you taking a shower, too?" Julie looked surprised.

Squeezing into the tiny stall under the falling water, Peg leaned forward to kiss Julie, their lips and bodies as slippery as their relationship. Sliding a hand between her legs, she tried to take her back. She hadn't known how fragile it was between them, how they could dissolve as if they'd never been. Next weekend they'd be back in Joe's Blazer, probably doing the same things. She had to make Julie want her, not Joe.

Julie pushed her away gently. "It's okay, Peg. It just happened. You did it too."

"Because you did," she said. "I wouldn't have otherwise."

"Don't always follow me, Peg. Do what you want to do."

The words pierced, little knives slicing into her self-confidence, making her unsure of where she stood with Julie. She looked down, so Julie wouldn't see the same desperation that had been on Joe's face on hers. Tears washed off in the falling water.

"Hey, stop that. I don't love Joe." But Julie didn't say she loved her.

"I love you," she whispered.

"Me too," Julie said. "Now I have to wash my hair and get out of here."

Peg washed it for her.

They walked to The Diner together, their hair freezing in place. Peg was dizzy from lack of sleep, but she couldn't let Julie go alone. Snow fell thickly. Passing cars whirred by. Sound was as muffled as a padded room.

Peg fell asleep on the counter and Hal told her to lie down on his bed in the back room. Julie joined her during the break between breakfast and lunch. Just before three, she brushed her hair with Hal's brush and crossed the street to the food mart, still tired but no longer dizzy.

Brenda already had her jacket on. "See you later."

Peg went behind the counter and checked in. A few people

came in to buy stuff off the shelves—milk and bread and chips—after filling up their cars next door. The hours passed slowly. Before nine, Julie showed up to say she was going back to the apartment.

Peg watched her walk across the wet pavement and disappear down the street. The fallen snow was already dirtied from traffic. She decided she'd not get up with Julie the next morning but then remembered The Diner closed on Mondays.

It was cold walking to Jim and Pete's. Her feet and pants legs soaked up the snow on the sidewalks. A few people were out shoveling. Plows with flashing lights left hillocks of snow along the curbs, covering driveway entrances and at times splashing as far as the sidewalk. One of them sprayed her as it went by.

Jim and Pete were snuggled together on the couch while Julie slept on the chair. She started to say something, but Jim pointed at the TV, silencing her. "This is about us."

Hanging her wet jacket on one of the hooks on the back of the door, she sank into the computer chair. Somebody was interviewing gay couples on the tube. They wanted to marry and raise kids and own a house just like straight couples. Actually, their goals and lives sounded pretty much like everyone else's. Boring.

"Do you want to get married?" she asked Jim and Pete during a commercial break.

"I want the right to marry, don't you?" Jim responded.

She imagined being married to Julie, coming home to their house. When she got to the part of visiting their parents, she snapped to. What kind of a wedding would they have anyway? Who would wear the tuxedo? Who would they invite? Who'd come? Julie would probably marry Joe and ask Peg to be her maid of honor. She wouldn't do it. She'd tell everyone that they were lovers instead.

"Well?" Jim arched an eyebrow.

"Of course," she said, "but it's not going to happen."

"It will someday," Jim said. "We have to work toward it."

43

"Not in our lifetime, Jimmy," Pete said.

"You're such a cynic. Aren't you tired of getting the short end of the stick? Married couples have special rights and benefits, not us. I can't even be on your health insurance or you on mine," Jim said.

"You sound pretty cynical yourself," Pete retorted. "Anyway, I don't want to get married. That's a straight thing."

"You want equal rights, don't you?"

"You're cute when you get all worked up." Pete yawned. "I'd like to see the long end of your stick. Let's go to bed. Peg looks like she's going to drop dead." He wriggled his eyebrows.

"Put your earplugs in, kiddo," Jim told Peg, dropping his impassioned stance, which had even aroused her.

"Will do." She brushed her teeth and pulled the sofa bed out. The mattress was a hammock. Even if she and Julie tried to stay on their own sides of the bed, it would have been impossible. They rolled into a heap in the middle as soon as they lay down.

"Hey, wake up," she murmured, touching Julie's shoulder.

"Hey yourself," Julie answered, falling in bed fully dressed. Peg took off her shoes and crawled in with her, pulling the cover over them. "Let's look for a place to live tomorrow." Julie curled close.

"Okay." She'd already studied the classifieds and found nothing they could afford.

The next morning, Peg woke up only when Julie slid a hand in her panties. She turned over to reciprocate, almost feeling that Julie was hers again. While drinking coffee in the empty apartment, Julie made several calls. Two were answered. They showered, dressed and walked to the first place, an attic room under the eaves on Murray Street.

A flat, gray sky hung over the city like a pall. It pressed on the buildings and turned everything into a dirty reflection of itself.

Even so, she felt lighthearted as they hurried through the chilly day. They were joining their finances to rent a room together. She thought no further.

The woman who answered the door looked them up and down. "Students?" she asked. She was older than Peg's mother and a little on the heavy side with the head of a doll, a Cupid's bow mouth, rosy cheeks and dyed curly hair.

"Part-time," Julie answered. Although it wasn't true, if you said it enough, you almost believed it. "We've got jobs too. I'm Julie and this is Peg." She held out her hand and the woman shook it.

"I'm Mrs. Matthews. The kids call me Mrs. M." She gave Peg a limp grip.

The stairs hugged the wall and were lined with a faded carpet. The place smelled ancient as if the dust had settled into the floors and walls. Mrs. M. opened a door to a bathroom, revealing a tub with shower, a sink and toilet.

"You share this with the second floor people. Keep it clean," Mrs. M. said, leading them up a narrower stairway with no carpet to the room at the top.

Two side-by-side little windows looked out on the street. Advertised as a furnished efficiency, the room came with a microwave, a mini-refrigerator and a toaster oven. A sofa bed lay under the sloping roof. There were also a sink, a small table and two rickety chairs in an alcove. The house, like Jim and Pete's, was three stories tall with only about ten feet between it and the next one.

Despite a tall register, the room felt cold. "I turned the heat off, so as not to waste it," Mrs. M. said as if reading Peg's mind.

Julie glanced at Peg, who guessed she was about to say they had another place to look at and would let Mrs. M. know.

Mrs. M. glanced at her watch. "A young man is coming to see the room at eleven." It was close to that now.

"We'll take it," Julie said, arching an eyebrow at Peg in an unspoken question mark. "That okay?"

"Sure." They could live here. Now that they were decided, the room transformed itself from shabby to homey.

Julie paid cash for a month's rent, two hundred fifty dollars that included utilities and heat. Peg forked over the deposit, which was a hundred dollars. She'd emptied her savings account. A special student rate, Mrs. M. said. It about cleaned them out and they still had to buy linens and dishes.

"Go to Goodwill. You can get what you need there cheap. That's what the kids do," Mrs. M. told them. "There are some rules here. No loud music, no underage drinking, no parties. You can have a few friends over if you keep the volume down."

Peg thought of Joe and Charlie who would want to spend Saturday nights here. Would Julie say no?

"We'll go get our stuff," Julie said as Mrs. M. gave them each two keys—one for the front door and one to the room.

When they were back on the street, Peg said, "Let's not tell Joe and Charlie where we live. They can drop us off at Jim and Pete's and we can walk here."

Julie didn't answer. Instead, she poked Peg playfully in the ribs and ran backward in front of her, keeping just out of reach. "We better get going if we're going to sleep there tonight."

She ran after her. "No more listening to loud sex. No more basketball games." No TV either, she realized.

Jim helped them move. He piled their suitcases and back-packs in his trunk and drove to the new place where he helped carry them up the stairs. Then he took them to a Goodwill where he bought most of his clothes. They strolled the aisles, picking up a set of sheets and two blankets along with two coffee cups, eating utensils and a can opener, two small bowls and one large one, all mismatched. On the way back, they stopped at the food mart and bought cereal and soup, peanut butter and paper cups and plates.

After Jim helped carry their purchases upstairs and then left,

Peg made a peanut butter sandwich before setting off into the cold for work. Julie was staying home—she thought of it that way already—to make the bed and put things away. She said she'd come to the food mart later, maybe. What would she do? Peg asked. What you do, she replied, holding up a book.

Sometimes Peg would be stopped dead by images so real she almost believed she was there watching. She pictured Cosmo galloping off when first turned out. Who would ride him? Who would show? A thought crossed her mind that she couldn't shake, not even when she got to the food mart. Would her parents sell her horse?

Horses were expensive and labor intensive. Her dad made sure she knew how much. In addition to hay and grain, there were vet bills and blacksmith costs. She'd heard her dad say a horse should earn its keep. What he meant was it should be used. No horse earned enough showing to pay for its maintenance. It took lots of money to show—show clothes and tack, a truck and horse trailer and gas, entry fees. No winnings pay for all that. Earning quarter horse points makes the horse more valuable.

She imagined a kid and her parents coming to look at Cosmo. Of course, they would want him. It made her frantic, worrying about this while taking people's money and saying, "Have a great evening." She worked alone now. Brenda picked up the money at ten when she locked up.

"Want a ride home?" Brenda asked after breezing in the door.

Peg did. Walking home alone after ten scared her. Every time she passed a dark alley, she expected someone to leap out and jump her. The streets were pretty much deserted, especially during the week.

Brenda locked up and got into the big Lincoln her man friend drove. "This is Peg, Sam," she said as Peg climbed into the backseat.

Sam assessed her in the rearview mirror and nodded. The car, the dark eyes and hair plastered to his scalp and the big diamond ring on his little finger convinced her he belonged to the Mafia. She gave him her new address, and he eased the Town Car onto the street.

First they stopped at a nearby bank and Brenda slipped the money and charges into a night deposit slot, while keeping up an easy chatter. "You know what I thought when you first walked in the door, Peg?"

Of course, she didn't.

"I thought you were a runaway. You look so young. What did you do in your former life?"

They were nearing her place. "Went to the university."

"Ah, I thought that too. You caught on so quick."

Sam parked outside the frame building, and she slid out of the car, thanking them for the ride.

Julie flung open the door as Peg stuck the key in the lock and pulled her inside. "I'm bored out of my mind." She dragged Peg toward the sofa, which had been made into a bed. Candles burned on the windowsills and table. "We're going to buy a TV tomorrow, a little one."

"You have to work tomorrow," Peg said, glancing at her watch as Julie unzipped her jeans and pulled her sweatshirt over her head. She should have called her mom from the pay phone. She told Julie her worries about Cosmo as Julie pushed her on the bed and fell on top, catching herself with her hands. Julie's thick hair hung in Peg's face, and Peg buried her fingers in it and looked at her.

"What?" Julie asked.

"I have to find out about my horse."

"Your horse is more important than me?"

"I can't get rid of this idea that they're going to sell him."

"Do you really think they'd sell your horse out from under you? Not your mom and dad. Maybe mine."

Peg started to cry.

"Hey, hey, hey." Julie wrapped Peg in her arms and rocked back and forth which made Peg cry harder. When she stopped, Julie wiped her face with the sheet, kissing the spots she dried.

Peg forgot Cosmo and kissed her back. Her fingers tangled in Julie's hair and her tongue played with hers as they pressed against each other. When someone banged on the door, they jumped apart.

"Who is it?" Julie asked as she pulled on her sweats and Peg wriggled into her jeans and sweatshirt.

For a wild moment, Peg thought it might be Joe and Charlie, but Jim answered as she quickly straightened the bed.

"Hah," Pete said, coming in and looking around. "Caught you in the act again."

Jim held up a big bottle of red wine. "Don't say I didn't ever give you anything." When Peg and Julie looked at each other searching for some explanation, he added, "Housewarming gift."

They'd never offered them any liquor at their place. "That was so you didn't get too comfy," Jim said when Julie mentioned it.

"Besides, you're underage," Pete added. "This is the exception, not the norm."

Peg thought of Mrs. M.'s rule of no underage drinking. "Better keep it quiet or we'll end up back at your place."

Julie got some paper cups and Jim unscrewed the wine cap and poured. Peg gulped gratefully, no matter the taste. She and Julie sat cross-legged on the bed. Jim and Pete took the two chairs by the small table.

"It's small but sort of cozy," Pete said, looking around and raising his cup. He laughed. "I'm amazed at what they get for these places."

Peg laughed with him and slugged back the rest of her wine, holding out the cup for more.

"Take it easy," Jim said, but she drank deeply again, feeling the wine flowing like a drug through her veins and into her head. She leaned back against the pillow.

Julie broke open a box of crackers and put them on a paper plate. They wolfed them down and shook out more.

"Have you talked to your mom?" Jim asked Julie.

"Once or twice. I think she's written me off."

"Nah. Aunt Viv? She wouldn't do that, not after all those years of grooming."

Something flashed in Julie's eyes. "Parents do that when you don't follow their rules. Peg thinks her mom and dad are going to sell her horse, but I don't."

Peg frowned, worried again.

"You've got a horse?" Pete asked.

Picking at the thin threads on the blanket, she said, "Yeah. Cosmo."

"No kidding. Are you a cowgirl or what?" Pete poured her more wine.

"Sometimes I ride hunt seat, but mostly I ride western."

"What do you do with your horse? Ride him around the field and down the road or what?"

"We show the horses. My brother trains and shows for a living."

Both Jim and Pete stared at her, and she saw her world as unimaginable to them.

"I'd like to meet your brother," Pete said. "Is he a stud?"

"Yeah. A heterosexual stud." Julie put a hand over hers. "Don't make a hole in the blanket."

"What's it like, showing a horse?" Pete asked.

She shrugged, sad now. Setting the cup on the floor, she told them as best she could. "You work as a team when you show. You have to be in tune with each other. The horse responds to the cues you give. Either of you can blow a class." It was true, but it was the wine talking.

"And what do you and the horse do?" Jim asked.

"Depends on the class. If it's western pleasure, he walks, trots and canters on a loose rein in an arena with other horses."

"How many people and horses go to these shows?" Pete was eyeing her as if she were an oddity.

"At the really big quarter horse shows there are hundreds of contestants. Kids, amateurs, professionals. At the smaller shows, you might have less than fifteen in a class. I showed in 4-H and in open shows too."

"Does your brother win?"

"He used to, not all the time but enough. I don't know how he's doing now. He just turned professional last year." She looked down at the blanket, sensing their interest waning.

"Hey," Julie said, lifting her chin. "You can go visit, you know."

Her eyes swam. She blinked and shook her head. "This is supposed to be a party." Picking up her cup, she drained it.

"I grew up in a trailer," Pete said. "We didn't even have a dog. We had a cat. Nice cat but not show quality." He laughed.

She smiled. She knew how she looked to him—spoiled, rich—and her family probably was rich compared to his. She'd always done her share taking care of the horses, though.

"Come home with me sometime, meet my mom and my step dad. Mom waits tables. My step dad is on disability. He stays home and keeps an eye on the TV." Again he laughed.

Jim said, "My dad makes big bucks, but he's never home. When he is, he and Mom indulge in their hobby—fighting. They shake the fucking house. I used to hide under the bed with my little brother."

"Are you making that up?" Julie said disbelievingly. "I never saw them fight." They were her aunt and uncle.

"They're lovebirds around anybody else. Phony as hell." He made a face. "What are yours like when no one's around but the kids?"

"They're workaholics, curing the sick and making big money

doing it."

"What do they say about you being here? Do they know about Peg?" Jim raised his eyebrows, causing his forehead to wrinkle and his shaved scalp to move.

Julie said, "Mom called to express their concern and tell me they'll be there when I come to my senses. They don't know about Peg." They hadn't cut her off, though. She still had credit on her charge card. "Do your mom and dad know about Pete?"

"Nope."

"He didn't take me home for the holidays," Pete said, holding up the bottle. "We killed it. Time to go home."

They carried the empty bottle with them, and she and Julie crashed. As she drifted off, Julie muttered in her ear, "You should take a day off and go home."

"How would I get there? Hitchhike? Besides, I'm not going without you."

"Why?"

She feared Joe would take her place if she left for long, but she said instead, "I'd miss you."

She called home Saturday afternoon. When her mom answered, she went straight to the question. "I know you're mad at me, you and Dad, but you won't sell Cosmo, will you?"

Misconstruing the pause that followed, she jumped in again, "I'll send money for his keep." It was an absurd suggestion since she didn't have any to spare.

"No need. We wouldn't sell Cosmo for any reason, but it's funny you asked because Ginny Carver needs a horse to take into 4-H. I said I'd have to talk to you."

Relief swept through her followed by the familiar surge of guilt. They were going to ask for her permission to let Ginny use Cosmo after what she'd done? Julie had been right. Not her mom and dad. They wouldn't sell her horse. "Thanks, Mom."

"How are you anyway?"

"Good. And you?"

"Busy. When will we see you?"

She hadn't been home since Christmas break. "I don't know, Mom. I work weekends."

"Well, maybe one of these days you'll get homesick."

"Yeah." As soon as it warmed up, she would. Maybe it wouldn't be five years before she left home for good. Maybe she already had. A depressing thought.

She watched the door while at work Saturday night, waiting for Charlie to walk through it. When Brenda showed up at ten to take the charges and cash, Peg crossed the street to The Diner. Behind the steamy windows, Joe sat at the counter. She waited a moment for Charlie to come out of the bathroom or wherever he was. When he didn't, she went inside.

Joe swiveled on the stool and said too loudly, "Hey, Peg. Charlie had a big exam coming up. He'll be here next week."

Terrific! She sat down next to him. From the kitchen came the sounds of Hal and Julie batting words back and forth as they cleaned. Lisa was setting up the coffee and turned to say hello. Peg answered absently, wondering how this was going to pan out. Would Julie go off with Joe alone? No way would she tag along, but she knew what they would do if she wasn't there.

Julie pulled her apron over her head and shook her hair loose from its bandanna as she came out of the kitchen. She met Peg's eyes, gave her a slight smile and said, "Hey, I've got an idea. Why don't the five of us go out?"

Joe looked up from zipping his jacket, his face a study in dismay. "Where?"

Julie turned to Hal for an answer.

"Um. There's this little place on the south side. Good music. I can drive."

"But I've got beer in the car," Joe said.

"We don't need it," Hal told him.

"I've got some weed too," Joe added.

"Bring that." Hal grabbed his jacket off the coatrack. He shrugged into it and helped Lisa into hers.

"You sure?" Lisa asked.

"I'm sure," Hal answered. "We'll have a great time. A little smoking in the car, a little dancing, then we'll go home."

Peg laughed with relief. The conundrum was solved, at least for a few more hours.

Hal took one puff off the joint and waved off the second one when it came around. Lisa sat up front with him. Peg and Julie and Joe crowded into the backseat. Julie held Peg's hand tucked under their thighs out of sight. Joe slid an arm around Julie's shoulders. She said nothing, but she didn't lean into him either.

By the time they entered the dance club, everyone felt pretty mellow. They had to pay five bucks apiece at the door. It was a barn of a place with a band of young people in one corner, chairs and tables around the walls and a dance floor in the middle. They took the bunch of empty stools at one end of a long bar. The menu on the wall listed only snacks and pop. Bowls of popcorn were spaced out along the counter and on the tables. This was an underage place. No alcoholic drinks.

Peg sat on the end next to Hal and Lisa. "Salsa music. Hear that Latin beat?" Hal slid off the stool. "Either one of you want to dance?"

"You first, Lisa," she said. She'd never danced to music like this. Neither had Lisa apparently, but she followed Hal's lead pretty well. Peg had once seen a ballroom dance contest on public TV. The couples had made dramatic teams. With hair slicked down, the men in tuxes, the women looking like Barbie dolls ready for the prom, they'd danced intricate routines in perfect sync.

Hal grabbed her hand and pulled her out on the floor for the next dance, a fox trot. She managed to stay off his feet as he led her through the steps. She'd always wanted to be a good dancer.

"I took ballroom dancing in my younger days," he said. He smelled of sweat and fries. She supposed she just smelled of sweat. This was strenuous exercise.

"You're pretty young now."

"I took my first lesson when I was fifteen."

She told him about the public TV program.

"I watch it every year. I used to compete." He laughed. "Then someone found out. The boys pegged me as queer, and I quit."

She leaned back to look at him.

"Keep your head to the side and lean back into my arm. That's the girl."

"Are you?" she asked.

"Yeah. I like to dance too."

People were always surprising her. She hadn't guessed he was gay nor imagined he'd be so agile on his feet. "I'm impressed," she panted.

Next he led Julie onto the floor. They moved like a couple of pros. People stopped dancing to watch them. Hal had found someone almost as good a dancer as he was, and Joe looked glum. Peg smiled to herself.

"You want to give it a try?" she yelled at Joe, who was on the other side of Lisa. She apologized when Lisa covered her ear.

"Warn me next time," Lisa said.

Joe shook his head. "I can't."

"Sure you can," Peg said, taking his hand. "Anyone can waltz." She dragged him off the stool. His cheeks flushed with embarrassment, his jaw clenched. With his eyes on her feet, he tried. Peg had to give him that.

The next dance was a jitterbug, and she and Lisa took to the floor, while Hal continued to dance with Julie. Joe watched from the stool. After a while, he went outside. She figured he was smoking a joint.

Everyone was kind of quiet on the way back. Hal dropped Lisa off at her house and drove to The Diner. She and Julie rode to their room with Joe. He climbed the stairs behind them and looked around the place, no doubt wondering where he would sleep. So much for keeping him out of their room, she thought.

"We have an extra blanket," Julie said.

"That's okay. I've got a sleeping bag. I'll get it." He looked hangdog tired, his eyes bloodshot.

While he was gone, she and Julie changed into sweats. He unrolled the bag next to Julie's side of the bed and climbed in with all his clothes on. Peg turned her back to Julie, thinking there'd be no fooling around tonight.

She woke later to Julie saying, "No way, Joe."

He'd crawled into the bed but soon slithered back into his sleeping bag.

Peg lay awake for a few minutes, till she heard him begin to snore. The next time she awoke it was morning and Julie was snuggled up against her, one arm flung over her waist.

"I won't be back," Joe said, looking down at them. She nodded, and he quietly let himself out.

Julie stirred and stretched. She'd been faking sleep. "That was fun last night." She looked at her watch and jumped out of bed. "Too bad he left. I could have used a ride to work."

He was waiting for her, she told Peg later, sitting in his running car. He told her he loved her. She said she liked him. He asked if she and Peg were lovers. Peg wondered if she'd admitted it.

"I told him to find another girlfriend," Julie said.

Peg had mixed feelings about letting go of Joe and Charlie. It seemed as if they'd let go of everyone. They'd never sent Annie a card. They were estranged from their families. Their friends consisted of Hal and Lisa and Pete and Jim. It was a small world they lived in, one hampered by lack of money. Truth told, they couldn't do anything they wanted. Julie's parents had cut off her credit when she'd argued with her mom over the phone. She'd recounted the conversation.

"Live on air," her mother had said. "See how you like it."

"I've got a job," Julie had shot back. "I don't need handouts."

Yeah, sure, Peg thought. Between them, they barely managed to pay the rent. They shopped at Goodwill for everything but food. Microwaveable dinners were expensive. Lots of time they ate cereal or peanut butter sandwiches or leftovers from The Diner.

Julie and Hal started dancing every Saturday night after work. That was their social life. Peg tagged along, as did Lisa, even after Peg was fed up with sitting and watching Hal and Julie sweeping around the floor. Julie's agility and grace failed to move her anymore. She was jealous of Hal for the time Julie spent with him instead of her. No matter that he claimed to be gay. Every third dance he would choose either her or Lisa as a partner, or some other guy would ask, or she and Lisa would jitterbug.

February had turned into March. Pete and Jim invited them over for pizza on a Sunday. They were sitting on the sofa and chair, eating off paper plates on their laps and drinking red wine, when Peg's mom called. She'd given her Jim's number for emergencies.

Jim handed her the phone after a moment of, "Yeah, yeah. No problem. She's right here." Then, "Your mom."

"Hi," she said, and the small world she'd helped create shattered like a fragile lie.

A young horse had fallen on her brother. In addition to a broken pelvis and leg, Cam lay hospitalized in a coma. Stunned, she wondered if this was punishment for her behavior. She'd have to leave Julie and go home. The fact that she even hesitated shamed her.

IV

Julie

Not wanting to be left behind on Murray Street, Julie suggested she go home with Peg. She told Peg she could do the necessary things. Take care of the horses, run errands, cook. But Peg seemed not to be listening.

In bed that last night on Murray Street, Peg clung to her. The comfort Julie meant to convey turned into desire, after which Peg murmured, "Do you think we should be doing this?"

"Why not?"

"It seems like we're celebrating or something."

Julie leaned back to look at Peg better. "I thought we were saying good-bye."

"He's in a coma and we're having sex." Peg began to cry, tears sliding down her cheeks.

"That's pathetic. Why don't you flog yourself?" Feeling rejected, she choked back her anger.

"Why do I feel like I'm being punished?" Peg asked.

Julie said, "You weren't even there."

"I know it's stupid. Tell Brenda for me, will you?"

"No problem." Already Julie felt alone and resentful. "Are you coming back?"

"Of course." Peg wiped her face on the sheet. "Will you be here?"

She hesitated. She wasn't sure she could afford to keep the room or if she wanted to. She asked flat out, "Don't you want me to come with you? I could help."

Peg said, "Of course I do, but it's better I go alone now."

"When do you think you'll be back?"

"When Cam wakes up."

"That could be a long time." They started over, trying to cross the physical borders that separated them and meld into one.

"You're not going to wait, are you?" Peg asked. "You're going to see Joe, aren't you?"

"If he comes, I will." Why not? Peg wouldn't let her go with her. "I might have to live with Jim again." Or go home. It depended on how much time passed.

"I'm going to miss you terribly."

"Take me with you then," she said.

"Let me see what it's like first."

They made one final attempt to join, even as they were separating. Something to remember, Julie told herself.

Julie rode with Jim and Peg to the Budget car rental. She stood next to Peg while she filled out the paperwork, while Jim walked around the lot looking at the vehicles. They hugged good-bye, both red-eyed and exhausted. Peg got into the Dodge Neon and drove away.

Hands in her pockets, Julie watched Peg's car disappear in traffic till Jim took her by the shoulder and walked her toward his beater.

"Come on, girl. You're shaking." She hadn't noticed till then.

"She'll be back," Jim said reassuringly as he pulled out on the street and joined traffic in the opposite direction.

Looking at the houses a few feet apart, the slush at curbside, she wondered what the hell she was doing here.

"Want to stay with us a while?" he asked.

"Nah. I'll be okay."

"If you get lonely, come over."

Yeah, she thought, and watch basketball. She usually ran up the stairs to the room, but not today. When she unlocked the door and stepped inside, she saw the place as it was—a cramped, impersonal space. She and Peg had failed to make it their own, and she didn't want to be there.

Going back down the stairs, she walked to the food mart. Customers were paying for gas and buying groceries. She waited to talk to Brenda.

"Tell her I'm so sorry," Brenda said over a noisy background. "There's a job waiting for her when she comes back. Is she coming back?"

After trying to convince herself and Brenda that Peg would return, she walked back to Mrs. M.'s and noticed the new phone in the hallway on the first floor. There was a note beside it. Mrs. M. had it installed for her boarders use. Elated, she dialed Peg's number. Peg should be home by now. She left a message with the pay phone's number on the answering machine.

The phone rang while she slept. Someone called up the stairs, and she stumbled out of bed and nearly fell down the steps in her hurry to get there. The receiver hung by its cord, banging lightly against the wall. "Hey," she said into it.

"Hey yourself. I'm calling from the hospital. Cam is still in a coma. Mom and Dad are here and my grandma. I have to go to the airport tomorrow morning and get my other grandma and grandpa. There are flowers everywhere." Peg took a deep, shaky breath. "Cam doesn't look good, Julie. He's the color of the sheets. I can't talk long."

She told Peg what Brenda had said and asked when she'd call again.

"When I can. I have to use the phone in the kitchen or living room or call from the hospital."

"I miss you." She never would've guessed how much, and it was only the first day. "This is a pretty lonely place without you."

"For me too."

"You're not alone."

"Sometimes that's worse. I gotta go. Here comes Dad."

"Wait! Did you ask your parents if I could come help?"

A hesitation. "They think it's better to be just family for a while."

"Aren't we family?"

"They don't know that. Love you." Peg hung up. Gone. Unreachable.

"What happened?" Hal asked Tuesday when he saw her red eyes and whipped demeanor. "Did Peg leave you or something?"

Julie hadn't slept much after Peg's call. "Yeah. A horse fell on her brother. He's in a coma."

"Wow. How did that happen?"

"He rides horses for a living," she said.

Lisa came to the doorway. "Is he going to be all right?"

"I don't know. Nobody knows." She put everything out of her mind, concentrating instead on what had to be done—helping Hal make breakfast, lunch and dinner for the people that crowded into The Diner. When Hal drove her home, she invited him in.

"I've got some beer in the fridge." Pete and Jim had left a six-pack behind last time they'd been there. For next time, they'd said.

It was Hal's first visit. She watched closely but saw no dismay in his face when he looked around. They sat at the small, battered table across from each other.

"I need a little comfort," she said, opening two Miller Lites.

Hal took a swig and said, "Dancing helps."

She must have looked as blank as she felt.

"Exercise. Helped me sleep at night when my boyfriend vamoosed."

"Sorry about the boyfriend." Had Peg known he was gay?

He took a swig of beer. "He couldn't dance anyway."

"Most guys can't or won't. I actually used to like this room." She sighed. "It was cozy with Peg here. You know what she thinks?"

He shook his head.

"She's got this idea that she's being punished. As if there's some vengeful god who would hurt her brother to punish her. Is that crazy or what?" She felt terribly disloyal, but she had to talk to someone.

"Makes sense if she thinks being a lesbian is unacceptable."

She had expected him to side with her, to be as dismayed as she was. "She didn't act like that when we were together."

"Hey, have you told your family?"

She hadn't, unless she counted Jim. "But I don't think I'm going to be punished by some higher being. I'm not sure there is a god, and I'm not sure I'm a lesbian."

"You think you're bi?"

She shrugged. "Maybe. I never did anything like this before Peg came along."

He studied her for a moment. "If you want, you can stay in my room. I've got a TV and a cushy mattress pad that could go on the floor." He looked around again. "What do you do here at night?"

"Read, listen to the radio. It's depressing as all hell." They'd never gotten around to buying a TV.

"I know. It's pretty damn lonely when your lover leaves." He slugged back the rest of the beer. "I've got to go, sweetie. See you tomorrow."

After a two-day bout of insomnia, she drifted off almost immediately at night. Sleep rescued her from thinking about where she was, from considering where she would go from here. That's what Peg and sex had done for her up till now, kept her from contemplating her future.

On Saturday she and Hal went to the dance club. Lisa opted out. They danced till her side ached, which took less than an hour. "We need to come during the week to whip you into shape," Hal said, as they stood on the edge of the dance floor while she caught her breath between a rumba and a fox trot.

"Wednesdays and Saturdays," Hal said on the drive home.

A message tacked to her door read that Peg had called three times and said Julie should call no matter how late. She thought Cam had either died or woken up. As it turned out, Peg only wanted to talk. Cam's condition remained the same. She sat on the steps and whispered.

"You must have been sitting by the phone."

"I took the portable to bed with me. Were you dancing? God, I miss you. It's so hard to talk when you don't have a phone. I can only call late at night when everyone's gone to bed."

"This one in the hall is a hell of a lot closer than the one by the gas station."

"I'm beat. I clean stalls twice a day, feed twice a day, turn the horses in, take them out. Run over to the hospital three or four times a day, do laundry, shop for groceries. I don't have to cook, though. My grandmas do that. Besides, no one eats much. How was the dancing?"

Julie bit her tongue and said nothing about Peg refusing to let her come help, nor did she point out that it wasn't exactly a piece of cake working at The Diner either. "Okay. We're going Wednesdays and Saturdays now. Did you know Hal is gay?"

"Yeah, I think he told me. Can't remember why. Hey, I got a

letter from Annie. She misses us."

"I miss everybody."

"Wish you hadn't left school?"

Did she? "This being alone took the fun out of it."

Peg said, "You're all I think about at night."

Julie made her case again. "I could take care of the horses and do stuff around the house."

"The house is running over with relatives who want to help. Mom said to wait till everyone goes home."

She sucked back her disappointment. "You still think you're being punished?"

"Stupid, huh? I love you. Don't go away."

"I can't wait here forever."

"Don't leave without telling me. Promise?"

"I'll talk to you later."

Disappointed and hurt, she climbed the stairs. She thought with nostalgia of her large bedroom at home with a TV and computer and windows that looked out at the city and lake.

Hal closed early Sunday nights, at seven instead of nine. He drove her to Pete and Jim's where a party was brewing. The apartment overflowed with mostly young men, smoking weed and drinking beer and wine. The TV was tuned to the Sweet Sixteen or Final Four. She wasn't sure which and didn't care. Hal stopped to talk to someone, and she pushed her way to the counter where she poured a large bottle of white zinfandel into a plastic cup.

A girl appeared at her right elbow—cropped hair, emaciated body and huge eyes. She looked like a refugee from a concentration camp. At first Julie thought she was Chloe.

"Hey. What's your name, pretty girl?" the girl asked.

"Julie. You remind me of someone."

"Daphne," she said in a voice that sounded like Chloe's echo. "I have a twin."

"The Chloe who goes with Tammy?" Daphne nodded. "What a tiny world it is."

"And I'm all alone in it right now. Want some company?"

Julie shrugged. "Sure. Do you go to Madison?"

"Our parents thought it would be good if we split up. We're bad news together."

"I have to make a call. Be back in a minute." She found Jim and forced some money on him. "I need to call Peg."

He stuffed the dollars in his pocket. "Tell her she's missing a good party," he shouted.

Daphne followed her to the bedroom where they stood in the doorway staring at the naked threesome on the bed. "Goddamn," Julie said. She took the portable phone into the hall and sat with her back to the wall, which vibrated with sound.

"Hey," she said when Peg answered. "I dreamed about Cosmo last night." He'd chased her across the field, blanket flapping, hooves thundering, ears pinned. She'd run screaming in terror, calling for Peg who'd stood calmly talking to Cam by the fence. "He tried to kill me, and you just watched."

"Cosmo wouldn't hurt anyone," Peg said with a soft laugh. "Sorry about the nightmare."

Daphne leaned against Julie's shoulder, her ear against the back of the receiver. "Say hello," she whispered.

"You'll never guess who's here."

"Where's here?"

"Jim and Pete's. They're having a party."

"Who?"

"Chloe's twin sister."

"Lemme say hello?" Daphne grabbed the phone. She reeked of marijuana and wine. "Hey. This is Daphne. Is Julie your girl-friend? She's gorgeous. I wouldn't let her out of my sight."

Great, Julie thought, snatching the receiver back. "Peg? Daphne's a little out of it. She doesn't mean it."

But Peg laughed. "Daphne and Chloe. Does she look like

Chloe?"

"Yes. All eighty pounds of her." The door opened and a flood of sound flowed out. Someone quickly shut it.

"Wow! Must be a lot of people."

"Mostly gay men. How'd today go?"

"Daphne's not going home with you, is she?"

"Of course not."

"Everyone's on edge here. Mom sits for hours next to Cam's bed and talks to him. He's out of ICU. Sometimes he squeezes her hand."

"He'll wake up."

"Soon, I hope."

"Me too." She paused. "Peg, what's going to happen when he does? Will you be okay with coming back?"

"Do you remember when you were a kid, how you didn't step on a crack or you'd break your mother's back?"

"I bet you avoided every crack."

"I'd like to play with yours," Daphne whispered loudly.

Julie leaned away and pressed the phone tighter to her ear. "Answer my question."

"Who's going to take care of the horses till Cam can?"

"I could be at your place tomorrow," Julie said.

Peg whispered, "Dad said maybe later, not now."

That was it then. She hung up shortly afterward and went back inside to get wasted. Heading toward the wine on the counter, she poured another cup and downed it in two gulps. Daphne stayed with her.

"Is your girlfriend cheating on you, honey?" Daphne asked, slurring her words. "Because I can help."

"Get me some weed. That'll help." A thick-necked guy handed her a half smoked toke. "Hey, thanks."

"No problem. Share it," he said.

"I'm amazing in bed." Daphne blinked a couple times as if for emphasis.

She inhaled deeply, and Daphne undulated before her eyes. "You're too skinny." It would be like banging a bag of sticks. She handed Daphne the weed.

"What? You like 'em fat?"

"I like them with their bones covered."

Another guy pushed between them and took Julie's hand. "I'm Allen and you're beautiful."

She pulled away from him. "And I'm private property."

"Yeah? Well, I want to make an offer." He handed her a cup of wine. Daphne took it from her and dumped it in the sink. "He put something in that. I saw him."

"Hey, I thought we could just have a some fun." He staggered a little.

Hal stood at her shoulder. She wondered how long he'd been there. "This girl's seriously impaired. She's off limits to everyone. You too, Allen." He turned to her. "Come on, honey, I'll take you home."

"Don't butt in, you fag. What do you want with her?" Allen shoved Hal, who sprawled against the guy behind him, setting off a domino reaction.

Suddenly everyone was yelling. "What the fuck's going on?" "Who the fuck?" "Hey, shut the fuck up." Guys came running out of the bedroom, pulling on jeans over bobbing pricks.

"Fuck" was the word of choice. Julie took the opportunity to pour more wine, now glad to have Daphne fastened to her side.

Pete helped Hal off the floor, while Jim shoved Allen out the door. "Who let that hetero in here anyway?" he said. Voices fell to a normal level.

Did she want to go back to the room alone? Not really. Sitting in the easy chair, she shared what was left of the weed with Daphne and watched the muted basketball game. Daphne settled on the arm and played with Julie's hair.

&

How she got home she didn't know. She woke up with a screaming headache and lurching stomach. Next to her lay Daphne, mouth open, skin gray as the sheets. She'd been sick in the pail next to the bed.

Julie got up and staggered under the immensity of her head. She grabbed the pail and tottered down the stairs to the bathroom. After throwing up, she dumped and rinsed the bucket and took a quick shower. The water battered her skin, tender as if she were sick with the flu. Back upstairs, exhausted, she drank two glasses of water and sat at the table. Placing her head on her arms, she fell asleep.

"Hey girl, come back to bed."

The voice startled her. She'd forgotten Daphne and frowned at her as if she were an intruder. "What happened last night?"

"I don't remember. Do you?"

"Look, Daphne, I'm with someone."

"She's not here, though, and I am. Think about it."

"I don't want to think about it. Why don't you go home, and we'll talk about this later?"

"I can't go anywhere. If I move, I'll barf." And to prove it she threw up in the pail.

Defeated, Julie put her head back down. She wanted to fast forward to tomorrow when she'd surely feel better. The phone rang several times during the day. No one must have been around, because it seemed to ring forever. She just couldn't drag herself down the stairs.

After dark, when her behind was so sore from sitting on a hard chair, it rang again. Mrs. M. called up the stairs, and she went to the door. "I'm coming." She was surprised to see it was only seven.

"Hey, where you been all day?" Peg said.

"Asleep. Recovering." She ran a hand through her hair and down her face. "I feel like I've got the flu."

"Hangover?" Peg gave a soft laugh that made Julie miss her desperately. "What happened to Daphne?"

"She went home, I guess." She had left a couple of hours ago, dragging herself out the door with a "See ya."

"Ah. Do you like her?"

"Not particularly. How's Cam?"

"Changing the subject?" Peg asked.

"Is this the inquisition?" she snapped. "Sorry. I've got a headache like you wouldn't believe. Feels like my face is going to break into pieces."

"Wish I were there to take care of you."

"Me too. Wish I'd stayed home last night." She leaned her head against the wall. "Look, I have to go lie down. I'll talk to you tomorrow."

She hung up and the front door opened. Her mother, dressed in a pantssuit and jacket, her ashen hair pulled back severely, came through it like a mirage. Her gray eyes met Julie's, and she frowned. Behind her stood Jim, looking pretty sick himself. She must have caught him in a weakened state.

Julie blocked the stairs. She'd dumped the vomit, but the room still smelled. She hadn't the energy to open the windows.

"Aren't you going to invite me in?" her mother asked, and Julie thought how much she and Peg looked like their moms.

"I think I'll go home now," Jim said, turning away. "If you need help, let me know."

Julie's mother dismissed him with a kiss on the cheek and followed Julie up the stairs. "It's a disappointing day when I have to ask your cousin to find you. Were you at the party last night?"

"What party?"

"Come on, Julie. I was at his apartment. It smelled like a den of iniquity."

Julie laughed. She couldn't help it. "Den of iniquity, Mom?"

"Yes. Don't you think I know what marijuana smells like and wine and beer? You apparently partook and now have a massive hangover."

"Can you make it go away?" She lay down gingerly on the messy bed. Her heart beat too fast. It thumped, missing beats. People died from irregular heartbeats. "I think I'm dying."

Now her mother laughed. "Water helps." She poured a cup and gave it to Julie who slurped it down. Her mom refilled it. "Where's your roommate? Peg, is that her name?"

Julie covered her face with her hands and told her mother about Cam's accident.

"That's really terrible. Now listen, I came to take you home. Since you don't have a roommate, it makes things less complicated. I can pack your things and call Jim to carry them down. It doesn't look like there's much."

"What makes you think I want to go home?" Julie rolled on her side and curled in a ball, still clutching her face.

"Look, kiddo." Her mother sat carefully on the side of the bed and placed a cool hand on Julie's face. "It's not a defeat. Consider it a chance for you to regroup."

Her mother's touch took her back to her childhood when her mother had sat by her bed and read to her when she was sick. Those were the times she'd felt loved and wanted, instead of the third and unexpected child.

Against her feeble protestations, her mother began packing her things and cleaning out the fridge. She called Jim for help, and Julie tried to drag herself off the bed, but couldn't. She fell back into the black hole of her misery.

When her mother turned the keys over to Mrs. M., who looked somewhat bewildered, Julie called Hal and left a message on his machine. Then her mother put her in the car and headed south toward Chicago.

Julie was sick for three days. She drew her knees up to her breasts and covered her head so that she wouldn't see her huge bedroom with its private bath, the one she'd missed a few days ago. That way she could pretend it wasn't over between Peg and her, the great experiment that had lasted three months.

The phone rang during the morning of the fourth day. She'd woken up sweaty, smelly and hungry in the night and drifted off again without getting up to wash or eat. She swore she'd never smoke dope again or drink wine. The combination had been deadly. She had spent her waking hours trying to dredge up memories of that night.

"Hey," she said into the receiver.

"Hey," Peg replied. "You didn't wait for me."

"Mom dragged me home. I was so sick after Jim's party, Peg, I couldn't resist. I'll go back when you do."

"Cam woke up. His eyes just sort of fluttered open, and he knew us." Julie sat up and nearly passed out.

"Whoa! That's great," she said weakly.

"I can't leave yet. He won't be able to take care of the horses for weeks, maybe months."

"Can't your mom and dad do that?" She'd get her things together and go back, although the thought of returning to Murray Street depressed the hell out of her.

"No. They have so much catching up at work to do. In the summer, maybe."

"Yeah, sure."

"I love you, Julie."

"Me too," she said dispiritedly.

"You never say you love me." Peg's voice cracked on "love me."

"You should have let me come."

Peg sniffed back a sob. "I couldn't. I'm sorry."

"I love you, Peg, but I don't know what to do about it."

After the phone call, she showered and wandered through the condo to the kitchen where she choked down a bowl of cereal. Tears dripped into the bran flakes.

V
Julie

Julie walked along the Lake Michigan shoreline, weaving her way through the other walkers and runners. The cool breeze off the lake countered the April sun. She liked walking along the lakeshore. She had trouble staying awake these days. Sometimes she nearly fell asleep on the drive to the clinic. It wasn't the clinic for the less fortunate. Her mother thought that area too unsafe for her, although it was no less safe than the walk to and from The Diner.

She'd talked to Hal once. He had no trouble replacing her in the kitchen. He and Lisa had placed third in a dance competition. "You and I would have won," he'd said. He was graduating from UWM next year. The Diner would have to soldier on without him and Lisa, who now had a scholarship. Julie said goodbye to that part of her life. She wouldn't be going back, she knew.

Jim and Pete had split. Jim was graduating in May and had a

new lover and a job in Racine. She had talked to him once, trying to reconstruct that evening. Something was wrong with her body. It wanted to sleep all the time. She dozed off during meals, while watching TV or trying to read or behind the wheel. Had something happened at the party that she'd blocked out?

Daphne had stuck to her like a burr that night. She called the university and talked to Annie who said she now kept in contact with Peg. Annie gave her Chloe's number and through Chloe she managed to connect with Daphne. Daphne told her she remembered nothing. Maybe there wasn't anything to remember.

Peg wanted to see her. Cam was hobbling around in a walking cast, she told Julie, unable to ride yet or handle the horses. He had asked Peg to show his young horse, Hombre.

"Come visit," Peg begged every time they talked.

"It's your turn to come here." She nursed resentment that Peg hadn't let her visit when she could have made a difference. Maybe they'd still be together if she had.

"Give me directions."

"You'll get lost if you drive downtown," she said. "We'll stay in a motel near the toll road. I'll make reservations." They agreed to meet the last weekend in April.

Someone calling her name brought her back to the present. "Julie, Julie. Wait up."

Turning, she blinked in surprise at Charlie. "What are you doing here?" His hair was longer, curlier, his mustache shaven off.

"Chasing you," he panted, hands on knees. "I'm staying in a motel off Michigan Ave. And you?"

"Visiting relatives."

"Yeah? What are you up to these days?" He walked alongside her, kicking up little puffs of sand that blew away.

"Working in a clinic."

"You wanted to be a doctor."

She shrugged. "I talked the talk."

"Are you still living in Milwaukee?"

She paused, not sure she wanted him to know where she lived. He would tell Joe. "No. Are you still at the university?"

"Yeah. Nothing's changed. I'm here for a book expo. I have to go to the exhibition hall in an hour, and I'll be tied up into the evening. Wish we could get together." They sat on a bench a couple vacated and faced the lake. "How's Peg? Annie told me what happened to her brother. What a bummer."

"She's good. Cam is out of the coma, still in a cast. We're going to meet at the end of the month."

"Say hello for me. Okay? We had some good times."

"We did. How's Joe?"

Charlie smiled. She'd forgotten the dimples. "He's good. He's seeing someone. So am I."

"Hey, that's cool." The sunlight glinted on them, giving off heat the lake breeze whipped away.

"Are you still planning to be a doctor?"

"No, but I'm going back to school. I'm going to be something." She laughed.

"You already are, Julie."

She parked in the Holiday Inn's lot near Park Ridge. Planes screamed over the Tri-State Tollway toward O'Hare. Peg had told her what she'd be driving and about what time she'd arrive—four o'clock. They would have two nights and one day and a half. Leaning against the back of her Honda Civic, the sun warm on her head and shoulders, she waited.

She'd have said she wasn't excited except that she was unable to hold a thought. But then she hadn't been able to concentrate for weeks, not even to read a good book. Straining to separate Peg's Taurus from the hundreds of cars on the road, she stood blinking to refocus when Peg drove in. A slow smile stretched across her face as Peg parked and got out.

Grinning, Peg ran her fingers through windblown waves already lightened by the sun. "Hey, you look good."

"Good enough to eat?" Julie took her by the arm and led her inside the hotel to a stairway. Leaving the lush carpet behind, they took the stairs two at a time. Across from the stairwell on the second floor, she slid a card through a slot and the door opened. When the door locked behind them, they looked at each other shyly.

"I have to use the john." Peg slipped inside and shut the door behind her.

Julie sat on the queen size bed, waiting. It had been weeks. What were a few more minutes?

When Peg came out, she plunked herself down so close to Julie that their hips and shoulders touched. "Hey," she said, amusement in her eyes. "How the hell are you?"

Julie gently pushed her onto her back. "Horny as hell. How about you?"

"Just a little bit." Peg laughed.

After kissing Peg's eyes, her cheeks, her ears, her neck, Julie paused to whisper, "I could devour you."

"I know the feeling."

"Let's get out of these clothes."

When naked, there was another moment of awkward shyness before Julie's wicked smile made Peg laugh. Falling together on the sheets, they did what they'd learned to do so well—please each other. Julie ceased to hear the planes passing overheard as they rolled over and over, once falling off the bed. They stretched like cats with toes spread.

"Wow!" Peg said afterward, "I'd almost forgotten."

Julie traced the soft curve of Peg's breasts, the flatness of her belly, the tightness of her butt and thighs—recommitting them to memory. "You must be riding every day." Their ankles crossed.

Nodding, Peg began the same gentle searching touch. "You've lost weight."

"I know." Julie lacked appetite these days. Her mother tempted her with good food, which filled her up after a few bites.

"How much weight?"

"A few pounds. I've been walking a lot."

"Cam got on a horse the other day. He's losing patience with how long the healing takes." Peg looked into Julie's eyes. "We could start over somewhere else. Go back to school."

"Do you know what you want to do for the rest of your life, Peg?"

"Live with you?"

"That's not a vocation. That's a dream."

"I know I need a degree."

"I saw Charlie running along the lakeshore. We talked a little. You keep in touch with Annie, don't you?"

"Her life is incredibly busy. How was Charlie?"

"He looked good. He said to say hello."

They ordered Chinese take-out and Julie went to get it, hungry for the first time in weeks. The lethargy she'd carried had sloughed off, too, as soon as she saw Peg. She needed her roommate back. She told Peg as soon as she returned with the boxes of pot stickers, egg rolls, chicken broccoli stir-fry and sweet and sour pork.

"I applied at UW-Oshkosh for the fall semester," Peg said, looking down at her food. "I have to be near home to help till Cam can take over."

"Can't he hire someone?" She popped a pot sticker in her mouth, disappointment rankling.

"With what, Julie? He doesn't have any money. Where did you want to apply?" Peg asked softly.

"I don't know. UWM, Madison, U of Chicago."

"As if we can get into any of those schools. Remember, we damn near flunked out."

"We could try." They were arguing. Had they ever fought before?

Peg backed down first. "We will but not just yet. Why don't you come visit me?"

"Why didn't you let me come help when Cam was hurt?" She had to settle that first.

"I couldn't. My parents didn't want anyone else around, but now it's fine. Annie comes. She fell for Cam."

Julie's vision blurred. "You let Annie come but not me? When?"

"She didn't come to see me, Julie. She started sending Cam cards, and he invited her about the time I tried to get you to visit and you said for me to come here. They're a mismatched pair if I ever saw one. She's not interested in horses." She smiled at Julie. "Not like you."

"Why didn't you tell me?"

Peg shrugged. They sat cross-legged on the messy bed, the boxes of Chinese food open but barely emptied. "I was afraid you'd be mad."

Julie cleared the food off the bed and lay Peg down. "Don't hide things from me. If you prefer Annie, say so."

"Annie's nuts about Cam." Peg ran her fingers through Julie's hair, separating the gold strands. "Tell me about Daphne? Did she spend the night? Why did you go home?"

Julie rolled onto her back. "Yes, she spent the night. I don't remember that either. I went home with my mother because I was so sick, and I didn't think you were coming back." She met Peg's serious gaze. "You weren't either. You still won't leave home."

Peg said, "I don't care about Daphne. I don't care about Annie. We only have a couple nights together. Let's not ruin it."

Julie took Peg's face in her hands. "Okay." She needed something to remember, something to get her through till the next time.

She drove back to the city barely noticing the speeding traffic. No one drove the speed limit. When a cable van nearly clipped her cutting into her lane, a painful jolt of adrenaline brought her into the present. She'd been reliving her last few minutes with Peg. They'd been holed up since Friday and had blinked in the sunlight when they'd emerged from the hotel.

"Hey, two weeks and we'll be together again."

"At your house." Julie forced a smile.

"We'll have two nights," Peg said. "When it's dark . . ."

"Yeah, we can play. I know. During the day we horse around."

"I thought you liked horsing around."

"I do." She was suddenly tired again.

They had hugged and gone to their separate cars, following each other out of the lot and turning in opposite directions.

She parked her Honda in the underground lot, slung her backpack over her shoulder and took the elevator to the condo. Her parents looked up as she passed the living room where they were reading. "Have a good time?" her mom said as Julie tried to slip unseen past the open door.

"Yeah. It was okay." She'd told them she'd been invited to a freshmen get-together. Kind of early for a reunion, wasn't it? The year wasn't over yet, her mother had said. She'd only shrugged.

Her mother followed her to her room, a piece of paper in one hand. "Somebody named Joe Danforth called. He left his number."

"Thanks." Wasn't he seeing someone? She tossed the paper on the bed with the backpack. "I'm going for a walk on the beach."

"Want some company?" her mother asked as she started to leave.

She hesitated. Her mother seldom asked to accompany her

anywhere. "Sure."

The sun beat down from a flawless sky. They joined the large number of runners and walkers and dogs on the beach. Julie had inherited her mother's high cheekbones, wide mouth and gray eyes. Her mother wore her looks easily, taking them for granted.

"Nice day," her mom said.

"Yeah. Look at all these people."

"Julie, your dad and I thought maybe it would be a good idea for you to see someone. Professionally." Strands kept slipping out from under the band holding her hair and fluttering in her face.

"If you mean a shrink, I'm all right." She hadn't realized anyone noticed the difference in her. What would she say to some stranger? How would it change anything? She pictured Peg in the parking lot, the trembling smile. Two weeks. She'd better tell her mom.

"Didn't you see Peg at the reunion this weekend?" Her mother looked puzzled.

"She has horses, you know," she said. "We'll ride." This was how it was going to be. She'd have to come up with excuses to see Peg. "I'm thinking about applying at UW-Oshkosh." Was she really?

"Oshkosh!" her mother repeated with dismay. "Is that where Peg is going?"

"Yes." She tensed for an argument.

Her mom sighed. "I guess it's a start."

"A re-start," she said.

They fell into a long silence broken only by the water slapping on the beach, the huffing of runners passing, dogs barking, kids yelling and walkers scuffing. After what seemed like a short time, but was actually nearly two hours when Julie looked at her watch, they found a bench and sat. A young guy threw a ball into the waves for a golden retriever to splash after. The dog barked when he returned and dropped the ball at the man's feet, obviously wanting more. Julie thought of Bert and smiled. No longer clear, the sun strained through thin clouds, and the breeze off the lake turned cool.

"Let's go home." Her mother stood and stretched.

They walked quickly in the other direction. Julie's calves ached.

Resisting her mother's suggestion that she see someone, she walked the lakeshore for hours in the lengthening daylight. She and Peg talked twice a week. She had sent a completed registration form to UW-Oshkosh and enclosed her grades from that disastrous first semester at Madison. She told no one, not even Peg.

When the two weeks finally passed, she threw some clothes in her backpack and took off. Joy coursed through her as she drove through the warm May afternoon. She'd left the clinic early, so that she'd get to Peg's around dinnertime.

The northbound lanes were clogged with Illinois citizens escaping to Wisconsin. All those lakes and forests and rivers and streams drew them. Her dad belonged to Trout Unlimited. He took two weeks off every year to pursue this hobby, spending one week in Montana and one week fishing the Mecan River in Wisconsin.

Following Peg's directions, she turned off US Hwy. 41 onto St. Rd. 21 at Oshkosh. The road led her to Waushara County and a combination of roads, which ended on the rustic road where Peg's family lived. Turning in the driveway, she parked near the garage.

Bert came running with Peg behind him. The dog put his feet on Julie's chest, pinning her to the car, licking her face. "Down. Off," Peg ordered. "You know better than that." The dog dropped to all fours. "How was the drive?" Peg gave Julie a quick hug. They grinned at each other.

Dressed in jeans, Peg's mom came out of the house and embraced Julie. "It's good to see you again. We'll have to talk later, though. I'll call you when dinner is ready." The dog tailed her to the door.

"Come." With an irrepressible smile, Peg headed toward the barn. "God, I'm glad to see you. Two weeks seemed like two months."

"I know. What's on the agenda?"

"We're getting ready for a horse show tomorrow." Peg's smile widened. "I'm showing Hombre, the horse Cam was riding at Thanksgiving."

Thanksgiving seemed a lifetime away. She'd been a kid then. "What does that mean?"

"You'll see. Cam and you and I are going." The dog streaked past them as they approached the barn. "And maybe Mom."

She nodded slightly. "A family affair."

"Well, yeah. Is that okay? Cam can't show yet."

Julie almost said, *Is it always about Cam?* But how childish would that sound?

Peg put a comradely arm around Julie's waist. "It'll be fun. I thought you liked horses."

"I like you better."

Refocusing as she left the bright light of May and entered the barn, Julie saw Cam standing in the aisle, a crutch under one arm, brushing a huge horse. "You look terrific. So does the horse. Has he grown?"

"I'm not complaining. Do you remember Hombre? He's filled out some."

Julie helped Peg load the trailer. Hay in the mangers, western saddle and show bridle and halter in the tack compartment. The leather and silver shone on the tack. Peg put her show clothes in the dressing room. "We're just showing Hombre, so after the junior western pleasure class, we'll come home. The show is at the fairgrounds in Oshkosh. It's not far."

81

"Pretty big trailer for one horse." It must have been at least thirty feet long.

"We're taking Cosmo, too, to keep Hombre happy. I put in a saddle and bridle in case you want to ride him around. That way Hombre won't freak out."

"Does he freak out?" She thought of the horse that had fallen on Cam.

"Never has. He gets a little excited sometimes." They were standing in the cramped dressing room. Peg leaned forward and kissed Julie. "Thanks for coming."

"Mmm. Thanks for asking me."

"I can't wait to go to bed."

But there seemed to be an endless number of things to do before that happened. Julie watched while Peg clipped Hombre's muzzle, his bridle path, his ears and fetlocks. Cam put a twitch on the horse's nose while Peg buzzed the inside of his ears. Then Peg and Cam washed him. After Peg vacuumed the excess water off, she threw a light blanket over the horse, wrapped his legs and tail and put him in a clean stall. They'd hose him off again in the morning, she said, and put hoofblack on.

Peg clipped Cosmo next. "I'm embarrassed to take him out in public, he's so hairy. Shedding like crazy. Hold his ear, will you, while I clip the other one?"

Julie nervously reached for an ear. Cosmo stopped shaking his head when she twisted it the way Peg told her to. By the time they went inside, all three of them were covered with horse hair.

She and Peg showered before eating. Peg locked the door and dried Julie off. "You wouldn't have wanted to be here, Julie, after Cam was hurt. It was a zoo. People wherever you turned. I slept on the couch a lot of the time. Mom and Dad came home at all hours of the night and day."

But she had wanted to be here. She couldn't let herself think about Murray Street without Peg. How she'd wondered what the hell she was doing there. Now she wondered what she was doing working at the clinic and living at home. She told herself she was in between phases in her life, that this was normal for someone her age.

After supper, after she and Peg cleaned up the kitchen and checked on the horses, and after waiting a respectable time to go to bed, Julie followed Peg up the stairs to her room. Peg set her clock for six, then turned to Julie with a warm smile.

"I opened the windows so you'd use me to keep warm."

"I was on to you from the beginning."

"Were you?" Peg asked as they climbed into bed.

"I knew by the way you looked at me. Remember how that sofa bed at Jim and Pete's folded us together?"

"Yeah. Nice. How are they anyway?"

"Not together anymore."

They were close enough to exchange breath, to kiss without moving. "Can we take our clothes off?" Julie whispered.

"We can pull up our T-shirts and take off our panties. Is that close enough?"

The touch of skin warmed Julie. They made love quietly, carefully, listening for voices and footsteps in the hallway outside the door.

The horse show was an eye-opener. Julie had gone to shows where she'd taken lessons, small exhibitions put on for the students. How different this was. Horse trailers, some pulled by motor homes but most attached to matching trucks, filled the grounds.

Cam brushed and sprayed Hombre. Peg dressed in the trailer, coming out in pressed jeans, a long-sleeved shirt and western hat. She carried chaps over one arm.

Peg led Hombre to the arena. Julie and Cam and his mom followed. Hombre whinnied and Cosmo answered. Peg clamped a hand over his muzzle, and his nostrils fluttered. With a lovely head, long neck and legs, a streamlined body and a tail that nearly dragged on the ground, Hombre looked to Julie like a Kentucky Derby winner. Peg had explained that he was a quarter horse with some thoroughbred blood, that's where he got his height—seventeen hands—and racehorse body. Julie was wary of his size, his skittish ways, which Peg attributed to being three years old. All horses are officially another year older on January first, Peg had told her.

Peg placed in both classes—third in halter, third in junior western pleasure. Seeing Peg looking so small and self-assured atop Hombre in the make-up and show arenas gave Julie a new perspective on her.

This was Peg's life, not Murray Street, not the university. If Julie were going to fit in, she'd either have to become a part of it or stand in line behind the horses. Peg had dedicated herself to helping Cam.

The two young women walked to the trout stream before Julie left on Sunday. The sun played peek-a-boo between fast moving clouds.

"I wish you didn't have to leave," Peg said, squatting down to feel the water bubbling over rocks.

"What will you do when I go?"

"Cam has a lesson coming in. I help. We're trying to keep his business afloat."

Julie crossed the stream on the log. The woods on the other side closed around her. "Come on." Patting the ground next to her, she sank to the soft needles under an immense white pine. Looking in Peg's eyes, she told her the secret she'd been saving like a gift. "I applied to UW-Oshkosh."

"Great." Peg sat down beside her and crossed her legs.

"Well, will you be my roommate?" she asked. She'd expected

more enthusiasm.

Peg looked away. "I'm going to live at home the first semester. Maybe you can live here too."

Dismayed, Julie said, "But I thought we talked about this."

"I can't leave till Cam can take care of things here."

Julie leaned against the pine, arms crossed, defeated and angry, once more tired. "Well, I haven't been accepted yet. Maybe I'll apply somewhere else."

"Don't, Julie." Peg leaned over to kiss her, but Julie turned her head.

"Don't what? When am I going to count?" It occurred to her that this was Peg's choice, how she wanted to live at least for now. "I should go. It's getting late." She laughed harshly. Who was she to talk? She too was living at home.

Peg chased her across the field, finally catching up with her at the gate, both breathing hard. She said again, "I don't think anyone would mind if you stayed here instead of on campus." Her brown eyes, having lost their glow, were dark and flat.

Julie lashed out. "Now I can, huh? Well, maybe now I don't want to."

"Call me when you get home, okay?" Peg asked.

VI
Julie

She drove the three and a half hours home hardly aware of the traffic that had reversed its flow. It seemed like everyone was now going south. She'd managed to pull herself together to say good-bye to Peg's family, who'd told her to hurry back. Well, Peg's mom had.

She felt a fool, a hanger-on. She knew she couldn't keep returning like a boyfriend. Nor could Peg visit her now that the show season had started. If she was a guy or Peg was, her visiting would make sense to everyone.

Her footsteps echoing in the large underground garage brought home her loneliness. She carried her backpack to her room, poking her head in the living room on the way.

"Dinner's in the fridge," her mother said. "How was your visit?"

"Okay. Horsey."

Her dad looked up and smiled. "I think I smell one."

She faked a laugh. Instead of going to the kitchen, she dumped her backpack in her room, took the stairs down to ground level and crossed to the beach. Walking till dark, till her calves ached, she tried to quell the dull pain that wouldn't leave her alone. Finally, she returned to the condo. As she was passing the living room, her mother called out.

"Did you eat?"

Julie started. "Yes," she lied. "I'm going to bed."

"Peg called."

"Okay."

"It's nice to have you home, Julie."

"Thanks."

She went to her parents' bathroom first. If her mother followed, she'd say she was looking for pain reliever. Picking through their medicine cabinet, she found what she was searching for.

In her bathroom, she stripped off her clothes and showered the weekend off. Sinking into the tub, she pushed the knob with her toe so that the water came out of the faucet. When it was three quarters full and very hot, she took the straight edge razor sitting on the lip of the tub and cut one slit in each wrist. Leaning back, she watched the blood well up and trickle into the surrounding water before closing her eyes.

Somewhere in the house the phone rang. When she realized it was her private line and probably Peg, she stumbled from the tub. The now cool water cascaded off her, and she slipped on the tile. Looking up from a crouch, she saw her mother standing in the open doorway. Too late she reached for a towel to wrap her wrists, but it hung out of reach.

"Are you all right, Julie?" Her mother's gaze fell to the drops of blood staining the cream colored floor and up to meet Julie's eyes. A wounded, questioning look passed over her face before she became all business. Lifting Julie onto the closed toilet seat, she wrapped a towel around her. Turning Julie's wrists over, she swathed the wounds in gauze before drying her off and dressing her in sweats. Only then did she call for Julie's father.

Her parents bustled her to the car and took her to their nearest clinic. Not the one where she worked. She shook uncontrollably. In the backseat, her mother held her as if she were a child. She hadn't lost much blood, her father said, putting strips on the tiny slashes that were already drying up. He gave her a tetanus shot.

Her mother slept in Julie's bed that night. To keep an eye on her, she knew, but it comforted her anyway. She awoke to sun streaming through her windows, blanketing her bed. Her head ached, and she covered it and tried to sleep again, but it was no use. Getting up, she went into the bathroom and opened the medicine cabinet. Empty. She looked under the sink. That was empty, too, except for tampons, pads, toilet paper, soap and shampoo. No razors, no tablets or pills, not even the cough medicine that had been under there for years.

"What are you looking for?" her mother asked, coming into the room in her chenille bathrobe.

"I've got a headache."

"I'll get you something." A few moments later she returned with a couple of tablets. "Take these and then come have breakfast."

She had eaten nothing since lunch at Peg's the previous day. "I'm not hungry," she said, wanting to stave off the conversation she knew was coming.

"Surely you can manage a piece of toast or a bowl of cereal."

Surprisingly, her dad was still home. The three of them sat at the kitchen table. The only sounds were her parents drinking coffee and her crunching and swallowing cereal. When her dad cleared his throat, she jumped.

"Wait, Bill, let her finish eating."

Julie imagined her father anxious to get to the clinic. She was wasting his day. She acknowledged the cup of coffee her mother set in front of her. "Thanks." Her voice sounded unused, croaky.

Instead of asking why, which was what she expected, her dad told her he and her mother had set up an appointment that day with a therapist they knew. "You'll like her. If you don't, we'll find another, but give her a chance."

Humbled by their attempts to help and relieved they hadn't pried, she nodded.

The therapist was somewhere between her parents' and her own age. She had flyaway brown hair and too short slacks that were probably in fashion ten years ago. Her eyes reminded Julie of Peg's—a chocolate brown. Kind. Keen. She had come out to the waiting room to get her, had exchanged greetings with Julie's mom who had cancelled her morning appointments to bring Julie there.

"Mom, I'm all right," she'd said as she dressed. "I won't do it again." "It" was the elephant in the room that no one had put into words yet.

"That's okay. I want to go with you."

"You can't spend every minute with me."

Now she sat in a corner chair in the small room that was the therapist's office. A spider plant hung in the only window, which looked out at a grassy lawn. Children's drawings were tacked on the walls. Crude houses, bright suns, brown tree trunks, stick people.

"I'm Jan Dickensen, Julie. Call me Jan. I know your parents on a professional level."

Julie nodded. She wore dark green Lee jeans and a long sleeved blouse that covered her taped wrists.

"How are you feeling?" The woman's lightly clasped hands lay in her lap.

Julie met her warm gaze. "Tired. How are you feeling?"

"Okay. What's happening?"

"Are those your kids' drawings?" She nodded at the wall.

"Yes. There are too many to put up at home, so I bring some here." She smiled. Nice teeth.

Julie looked down at her clenched hands. "What do you want me to say?"

"Whatever comes to mind."

"Like why did I do it? I don't know. It just sort of seemed a way out." She flushed, something she rarely did.

"A way out of what?"

"I can't even answer that. I don't think I was serious or I'd have done a better job."

Jan nodded. "What happened Sunday?"

Yesterday. It seemed days ago. "I came home from visiting a friend and went for a long walk along the lake." She hadn't talked to Peg since she left her standing in the driveway. "Look. It didn't solve anything. I won't do it again."

"Who were you visiting?"

"Peg. We were roommates at the university."

"You're good friends?"

She decided to shock the woman. Whatever she said was confidential, after all. "We're lovers."

It didn't work, though. Jan's expression softened. "I see."

"Do you?"

"Why don't you tell me about Peg?"

"I didn't even know this about myself till I met Peg. I dated boys in high school. They called all the time. Drove me nuts. It was the same way in college." Joe had latched onto her. "It was like Peg rescued me."

"From what?"

"From being taken over, and then I let her take over me."

"What do you mean by 'taken over'?"

She picked her words carefully. "I thought she cared about me more than I cared for her. That's the way it's always been

90

with guys." Did she need someone to define her? She sighed. "This is stupid. It's not about Peg, is it?"

"It's about you."

"Yeah. I feel like a fool." She looked at the therapist through a blur of tears.

Jan handed her a box of tissues. "Want to talk about that?"

"What's there to say? I blew everything." Peg had the horses and Cam to look after. She had her old bedroom back and a job at one of her parents' clinics.

"What do you mean by blowing everything?"

She told the therapist about leaving school, about Peg leaving her.

After the appointment, her mom took her to her job. At the end of the day, she was exhausted. She fell asleep after eating. The ringing phone woke her.

"You didn't call last night, and you didn't answer when I called. Where were you?"

On the bathroom floor, bleeding. "I went for a long walk on the beach."

"Come back in a couple weeks. Please?"

"Tell your mom and dad we're lovers and I'll come next weekend."

"What?" A pause. "Did you tell yours?"

"No. I told my therapist." She had started taking antidepressants that afternoon, but they wouldn't kick in for a few weeks.

Another pause. "When did you start seeing a therapist?"

"Today."

"I probably should too."

"Did you slit your wrists?"

"No! You? Why?"

"I don't know."

"I want to see you."

"Don't you have a horse show this weekend?"

"Now. I want to see you now."

"I work during the week. You have to clean stalls or something, don't you?"

"I'll come on the weekend then."

"You'll have to come here. No motel. Mom won't hardly let me out of her sight."

She walked the lakeshore before and after work. It seemed like everyone was out strolling and/or running, even early in the morning, especially in the evenings. She'd always loved spring— the lengthening days, the heat of the sun, the soft carpet of grass, the new leaves unfolding, the flowers bringing color back into the world.

Her mother doled out Lorazapam every night and Prozac in the mornings. She slept like the dead that first week, going to bed shortly after dark and waking long before seven. At work she was efficient and polite. Guys hit on her as they always had. She never encouraged anyone, responding with polite smiles and noncommittal statements.

On Thursday, a girl stopped at the desk. Julie looked at her short blondish hair, slender body and dark eyeliner and recognized her, just as the girl said, "Julie? What are you doing here?"

"Working." Obviously. "Do you have an appointment, Tammy?" She glanced at the computer. "Of course. Here you are. Tamarinda Jones. Is the university out?"

"Thank God. Are you coming back in the fall?"

"I think I'm going to another UW campus. Oshkosh."

Tammy tried to hide her surprise. "How's Peg? I heard about her brother."

"She's coming this weekend to visit. She's going to Oshkosh, too."

"That explains it. Hey, you want to hang out after work?"

"Sure. You can always find me on the lakefront."

"Sweet. I'll take a bus."

They walked till dark, catching up on things. "Do you ever see Joe and Charlie?" Julie asked.

"Sure. They're dating a couple of sorority sisters. Hey, what was it with you guys? We thought you were seeing them, and then you ran off together."

"Yeah, we nearly flunked out. I met Chloe's sister, Daphne, at a party in Milwaukee."

"Daphne and Chloe. Isn't that a hoot? Chloe and I are like a light switch. Right now we're off. Let's go out some night. I mean just for fun. Have you ever been to Clark Street?"

"I'll go with you sometime, but not this weekend. Call me at the clinic." One more night and Peg would be here with her, watching the dark green waves turn white as they rolled over. Excitement stirred, and she walked faster as if she could make the hours pass quicker.

On Friday she drove to the Holiday Inn in Park Ridge where she and Peg had spent a weekend. Peg would park her car there and drive into the city with Julie. No getting lost that way. She went inside to reserve a room and came back out with the key card as Peg drove in.

"I thought we were going to your house," Peg said, searching Julie's face.

"We are. I just thought we needed a little time alone."

"You are so smart."

Peg was tanner and fitter from hours of riding outside. But so was Julie, who spent all that time walking on the sand. After a separation, they always came together shyly as if it were the first time. Foreheads touching, they stood close for a few moments breathing in each other's scent. Then began the slow removal of scant clothing. Shorts and panties fell to the floor beside tops and bras. Their hands remembered the warm skin, the soft curves and taut muscles. Julie pulled back the covers, and they lowered themselves onto the pilled sheets. The pleasure that followed was sometimes so exquisite it edged on pain.

After, Peg looked Julie in the eyes and asked, "Why did you go home and do that to yourself?"

"I told you, I don't know. I guess I wanted something to change."

"How can anything change if you're dead?" Peg gave her a hurt look, her eyes nearly black.

"Well, I'm not dead, am I? Don't you get tired of pretending? If I'd been your boyfriend, I could have come and helped when Cam was hurt."

"That again?" Peg sounded exasperated.

"Yes, that again. I'm tired of living a lie."

"I'm not a lie." Peg threw an arm over Julie and pulled her close.

"Well, it wasn't a serious attempt. They were just little cuts. Want to see?" She pulled back the bandages. Pink scars had formed.

"Don't do it again, Julie. Promise me. I'd want to die if you did."

"I promise, but I've been thinking that maybe we should tell our parents about us." Was it foolish to expect Peg's family to make room for her? Would her parents? Would they instead shut them out?

"I think my mom knows anyway, but it could backfire, you know. They might try to stop us from seeing each other. What then?"

Right now her mom was so worried she'd probably be glad to know there was a reason for her half-hearted suicide attempt. "We can run away again," she said with a wry smile.

Peg shook her head. "We can't. Not yet."

Julie looked at her watch. "We better go. Time for you to meet the folks."

She wondered if Peg was as anxious as she was when she pulled into the underground garage and walked with her to the elevator. Would her mother guess?

Peg looked around. "It's spooky down here."

"No one can get in who doesn't belong here," Julie said.

She found her parents in the kitchen. Her mom tried to hide her annoyance, but Julie could tell. "I thought something happened to you."

"It's only seven." She introduced Peg.

Her dad stood up and smiled. "Nice to finally meet you." He was a good-looking man with eyes that matched in color his thick sandy hair. Still trim, he found time to exercise at the gym next to one of the clinics. However, Julie was more comfortable with her mother. Although she'd always felt her father's love, neither knew how to express it, especially after she began to develop sexually. It left her confused. "Are you hungry? Julie's mother has fixed a feast in your honor."

Peg flushed, and Julie laughed nervously. "I'm starving, actually."

"We were horrified by your brother's accident, Peg. How is he?" Julie's mom asked.

"Sit, sit." Her dad pulled out a chair and Peg sat.

"He's doing well. He's still on crutches. He remembers nothing about the accident."

"He was in a coma, wasn't he?" Julie's dad asked.

"For weeks. He doesn't remember that either."

"The mind remains a mystery even to us doctors. Right, Viv?"

"Yes." Julie's mom set a bowl of blue chips and bean dip on the table. "I've had a craving for Mexican. Don't fill up on these, though. We're having carnitas for dinner. Pork."

Peg ate. "This dip is wonderful. Can I help with anything?"

"I'll set the table," Julie said. "Mom's a terrific cook."

"You were a cook, weren't you? At that restaurant?" her dad asked.

"You wouldn't have liked the cuisine, Dad. I was a sous-chef for fried foods."

Dinner was every bit as good as Julie knew it would be. She actually ate till she was stuffed, laughing and talking instead of glumly playing with her food. She felt her parents watching her and guessed they were thinking that a person who wants to die doesn't act like this.

"We'll clean up," Julie said. "Then we're going for a walk on the lakeshore."

"And we're going to Will and Jean's for a while." Will was a radiologist. His wife, Jean, was an X-ray technician. They worked with Julie's parents and occasionally played bridge with them. Her parents hadn't left her alone at home since her suicide attempt, which they'd taken a lot more seriously than she had.

A slight cooling breeze blew off the lake. Gulls screamed overhead, bobbed on the waves, and strutted on the ground where they pecked the earth.

"There are a lot of people out," Peg said. "I wouldn't mind living here. This is great. So close to the water and all."

"Yeah, well you have to be rich to live here, Peg." Julie picked up a broken shell and threw it into the lake. "Want to go out? Maybe we can find a gay bar."

"I'm happy just to be with you." Peg looped an arm through Julie's. Runners passed them going in both directions. Walkers strode with purpose, also overtaking them. Sailboats plied the waves in the wind offshore.

Julie felt a temporary peace. "Maybe we should go inside and make the most of my parents' absence. What do you say?"

"Kind of early to go to bed."

"Another half hour. By then the sun will be gone." It hung, a huge orange orb, over the far edge of the lake.

Monday rolled around and Julie found herself in Jan's office, thinking about the weekend. She and Peg had spent two final hours Sunday afternoon in the motel room Julie had reserved.

When Peg drove away, Julie stood under glowering clouds hugging her midriff in a futile attempt to ease the ache.

Later, when her mother said Peg was a lovely girl and a good friend, Julie replied, "She's more than a friend."

"How was the weekend?" Jan asked, bringing her back to the present.

Julie shrugged and slid further down in her chair, which was not terribly cushy.

"What does that mean?" Jan imitated the shrug. "Peg visited, right?"

Nodding, she straightened a little. "Yes. We had an awesome time, but it always ends, and one of us leaves."

"That must be difficult. Will you be seeing her soon?"

"Probably in a couple weeks. I told my mom we were more than friends."

"And how did that go?"

"She said I was like a different person around Peg—happy and vibrant instead of gloomy and introspective. Her words, not mine. I could tell she was disappointed, though, and she's a staunch supporter of women's rights."

"Give her time to digest. How did you feel after you told her?"

"I nearly collapsed in a puddle of sweat."

Jan laughed. "I suppose. Some people never talk about their sexual orientation with their parents, and some parents don't want to talk about it."

"Well, we didn't really discuss it, but yeah, that's the way it is with my cousin Jim and my friend Hal. But now I'm going to feel awkward around Mom. I almost wish I hadn't said anything. I look at girls with guys and think that's how it's supposed to be. I dreamed last night that I married Joe. He did ask me to marry him once. In the dream Peg wouldn't quit crying. I felt so sad."

Before she left, Jan asked, "How are feeling? Are you sleeping all right?"

"I sleep fine. I'm okay." She didn't want the therapist to think she might try to do herself in again.

This time she'd taken her own car to the appointment. After work, she drove through pouring rain to meet Tammy. She was the one who had called Tammy, not the other way around. The last thing she wanted to do was confront her mom without some false courage. Tammy said they'd be able to get beer at a gay bar.

Julie really didn't like beer much. She drank it for the high, for the feeling of well-being it gave her. She liked the buzz so much that she began doing this night after night. One night she took her clothes for work and slept at Tammy's. Her mom left messages that Peg had called.

The days turned into a week, and she thought her mom had forgotten that she'd said Peg was more than a friend. One morning, though, when Julie staggered into the kitchen still feeling the effects of a night of drinking, her mom asked, "Who is this person you're seeing now?"

"Tammy. I met her at the university. She's fun."

"I see. Julie, you can't keep drinking and driving. I don't have to tell you why."

Her dad sat at the table, a magazine spread out before him, while her mom fried eggs. "Your mother's right. We'll have to take the car away."

"It's my car," she said indignantly.

"No, it's not. It's registered to your mother."

She shrugged a shoulder as if indifferent, saying "Take it. I don't care," and caught the wary glance that passed between them.

"Are you going to see Peg next weekend?"

"Not if I don't have a car."

"You can take the car to work, and you can go see Peg, but no more drinking and driving." Her dad met her eyes, and she looked away. She wondered if her mom had told him about Peg.

She planned to pick Tammy up that night. Feeling trapped

made her snarl. "Okay. You own the car, you own the house, and you own me." She started out of the room.

"These two envelopes came in the mail yesterday." Her dad pushed them toward her, drawing her back to the table.

One was from UW-Oshkosh, the other Madison, where she'd re-registered as if she hadn't missed a semester. Tammy had said they'd take her since she hadn't been kicked out. Both accepted her on probation.

"I thought you were going to Oshkosh," Peg said accusingly on Julie's next visit.

She would if Peg would room with her and said so.

"Why not live here with me?" Peg begged. "Don't be so stubborn."

"I'm not and I can't. When you come back to Madison, we'll room together." Shading her eyes from the sun with one hand, she held Red's lead rope in the other. The horse chomped grass at her feet. It was a Friday evening in June, and Ginny was riding Cosmo in the outdoor arena. Cam sat on Hombre. One leg stuck straight out as he called instructions and encouragement to the girl.

Peg took the lead rope from her. Emotions chased across her face like shadows. Dismay, disappointment and hurt were all there for Julie to see. She felt them too. They would be going in different directions in the fall.

"My therapist says an experience is never the same the second time. We change or the circumstances change." Jan had been talking about going to an art museum or a play or movie. Idle talk at the end of a session that wasn't so idle when Julie thought about it later. "Did you tell your mom?"

Peg shook her head and started toward the barn to saddle Red up for Julie to ride. "Not yet but she knows."

"Mom prefers you to Tammy." Julie recalled her mother's

reaction to Tammy, to the kohl around her eyes and skintight clothes.

"I suppose you and Tammy are doing it," Peg said angrily.

She walked faster to keep up with Peg and the horse. "Hey, that's not fair. You're the one who left, not me. Tammy and I have fun. That's all."

"Where are your old friends?"

"Scattered. Where are yours?" she shot back.

"Married or working," Peg said. They stepped into the barn out of the heat and light. It smelled of hay and grain and horses. At least, that never changed.

"That's the difference between us. I don't have a bunch of animals to take care of after work and show on the weekends." She was mad now too.

Peg tied Red and went for a brush and currycomb. "How do you know your mom prefers me to Tammy?" She handed Julie the brush and after looking both ways, kissed her hard.

Disarmed, Julie smiled. "She said you were more my type." Her mother blamed Julie's drinking on Tammy's influence.

"That's no compliment."

"I didn't say it was."

When Julie rode Red into the arena, Peg took Hombre from Cam and worked him for a while. Cosmo and Hombre were already clipped. Tomorrow morning Peg would give them baths and they'd leave for the horse show. There were always shows on the weekends. This one was open to all horses, not just one breed.

Julie liked her new routine—talking to Jan on Mondays, seeing Tammy during the week, and driving to Peg's on weekends. She was the gofer and groom at the shows. Spraying the horses before they went into the show ring, pinning on numbers, running for a necessary item left in the truck or trailer. It made her feel needed.

❧

100

Summer ended for Julie when she packed to return to Madison in late August. At what she thought was her last session with Jan, she felt both mournful and a little desperate.

"What if I need to talk to you?"

"Well, I guess we'll have to schedule a Saturday morning session."

"You'd do that?"

"Sure." Jan smiled. "You okay?"

"Yeah. I'm a little worried about going back. Peg's mad as hell because I'm going to room with Tammy."

"Should she be?"

"I'd be. I keep telling her Tammy and I are just friends. We tried it once, and the connection wasn't there." That had happened the first night she'd spent at Tammy's house when they were both shit-faced.

"Did you tell Peg?"

Julie looked out the window. A rainbow cut through the sprinkler water. "No. She's a little like a volcano now, you know, ready to explode. That's the thing about women. They're so emotional."

Jan looked amused. Her eyes glittered in the sunlight. "It's true that women talk more about emotions and guys talk more about things. You said you were worried about going back to school. What are your concerns?"

"That I'll blow it again. That people will think I'm gay." Would that keep guys from hitting on her?

"Wait. Stop there. I thought we'd made some progress. You don't think of yourself as a lesbian? Or you don't want others to think you're a lesbian?"

"I don't want to be publicly pegged. No one goes around saying so-and-so's heterosexual. Anyway, I could be bisexual."

Jan looked puzzled. "You could. I guess I didn't realize this was a real problem for you."

"It's different at school. I don't want to be stuck in some lesbian clique."

"Well, surely you have control over that."

"Yeah, especially with Tammy as a roommate. I should have said no when she asked." She looked directly into Jan's eyes. "I'm going to miss these Monday talks."

"Me too." Jan smiled. "Call me some Saturday when you're home and we'll set up an appointment." Jan handed over her business card.

This came as a huge relief. She wasn't ready to cut the cord with Jan. When Jan hugged her at the door, she felt weepy.

VII

Annie arrived at Peg's house alone. "Man, that's a long drive every Friday night. Julie sends her love. She's got too much studying to do. Exams coming up, you know." She and Cam swayed together, arms crossed behind their backs.

Peg kicked the bale of hay she'd tossed down from the loft. She had exams, too, yet they were going to a show on Saturday. Annie came more weekends than Julie these days. Maybe Julie was tired not only of the shows, but of her. Peg was tired too. She kept a wicked pace, and even though Cam was taking care of the horses, she still worked Hombre and showed him. She felt trapped by the horses, by the shows, by Cam's need for her. He was trying to qualify Hombre for the World Show. They'd have to go without her, but in a couple of weeks Cam should be able to do it all alone. She looked forward to that day when the doctor gave him the go ahead.

Annie tossed her hair back, and Cam gathered it in one hand.

Peg felt a stab of envy. The silken feel of Julie's hair between her fingers was almost tangible. Already she was tired of the drive to Oshkosh, of not feeling a part of campus life because she had to go home at the end of the day. It was totally different from Madison anyway. A small conservative campus in a small conservative city where she failed to fit in. How could anyone be a gay conservative? She went to a few meetings of the GLBT group. One guy was gung ho on making changes, one girl fascinated her, but everyone else was still in the closet. Mostly, she went to classes and came home.

She had been relieved when Julie switched rooms with Tammy and moved in with Annie. Tammy and Chloe were now roommates and lovers again. She remembered her fascination with them and kicked the bale of hay again.

"I'm going inside. I have to study too." She and Cam had already clipped Hombre and loaded the trailer.

She went to her room and stared out the window at the horses on pasture—Cosmo and Red and Buck. She thought of the girl in the GLBT group. Black hair and eyes, full breasted and fiery, Sophie Biancelli fascinated her. She'd talked to her last time she'd been there.

"Where do you live?" Sophie had asked.

"At home." She avoided telling anyone the whole story. Their eyes glazed over before she finished.

"Me too. Are you a sophomore?"

"Second semester freshman." That also was complicated.

"Would you like to get a cup of coffee or something?"

"Sure. Now?"

They went to the union. Sophie wanted to transfer to Madison for her last two years if she couldn't go to Juilliard. She sang in the university choir and the women's choir and invited Peg to attend a concert Saturday night. Peg said sure. It started at seven. She should be home from the show in time.

When Sophie asked about her, Peg told her she'd come home

when her brother got hurt and that she hoped to go back to Madison next semester. She'd said nothing about Julie.

The phone rang in the distance. A few moments later, her mother knocked on the door and handed her the portable receiver. "It's Julie."

"Thanks." She waited till the door clicked shut. "Hey. I was hoping you'd come with Annie."

"Me too, but I've got a paper to write and an exam on Monday."

She fiddled with a pencil. "So, you're hitting the books all weekend?"

"Yeah. You're going to a show on Saturday anyway."

"Cam will be showing all by himself in a couple of weeks." Would she miss the thrill when Hombre placed or won? She had put the points on the gelding, but Cam would take him to the Quarter Horse Congress and World Show.

"Great. You can come here for a change. I wish you were my roommate."

"We didn't study much when I was, did we?"

"We would now. You have to trust me, Peg. I trust you."

"Do you?" An undercurrent of anger rippled through her. Since they'd started school, they always seemed to be on the edge of a fight.

"Shouldn't I?"

"Annie said Joe comes over to study." She'd been carrying this around for a week now, wondering if it meant anything. Annie had let this slip and then tried to minimize it, saying he and Julie had a class together, that they were just friends.

"Sometimes. What are you doing this weekend?"

"I'm going to a horse show." She considered telling Julie about Sophie, but there was nothing to tell, and suddenly the anger drained away. "Hey, good luck on the paper and test. I've got a couple of tests on Monday too. It's just as well you're not here. Say hello to Charlie if you see him."

Peg went to Sophie's concert Saturday evening. They'd gotten home late from the horse show, and she'd only had time to take a shower, dress and go. Sitting alone in the fourth row of the auditorium, she was totally surprised when Sophie stepped off the risers for one of the solos. Her lovely soprano voice, sweet and pure, sent chills racing across Peg's skin. After the concert, Peg waited in the hall.

"You were awesome," she said when Sophie appeared, dressed in a white blouse and black skirt.

"Yeah? Think so? Want to come to our party?" Sophie smiled, showing off white teeth. She was no beauty like Julie, but she had an interesting face, dominated by a slightly hooked nose. Handsome, Peg thought.

The party was in one of the rooms in Music Hall where the concert had taken place. Plates of crackers and cheeses and fruit rested on one banquet table. On another were different types of cakes and cookies and a huge bowl of punch. Peg filled her small plate to overflowing.

"You must be starving, woman." Sophie held a plastic glass of punch.

"I didn't have time to eat." But she backed off on the food.

Peg recognized a few of the students. Sophie, of course, knew all of them. They made the rounds, chatting with everyone. Peg had never been good at small talk, but Sophie stayed by her side and included her in every conversation. She reminded Peg of Julie that way. Julie had charmed everyone and had chosen Peg. Her heart twisted.

Sophie walked her to her car. The cool, clear night smelled of fallen leaves. They stood talking a while before Sophie said, "I wish there was somewhere we could go. You live at home. I live at home." She shrugged as if it were impossible.

"Why don't we get in my car?" Peg unlocked the doors and

threw the books that lay on the front seat into the back. She pretty much lived out of the car during the week, and it looked like it. A single streetlight lit the parking lot, but she had parked near the end where it was fairly dark.

"Hey, I thought you'd never ask."

When Sophie kissed her, Peg recalled the night in Milwaukee when Joe and Julie had reached across the front seat for each other and she'd done the same with Charlie. The betrayal.

"Sweet," Sophie said, her face in shadows. "Do you mind?"

Peg shook her head. "Not at all." Did she?

She called Julie's room as soon as she got home that night. When the ringing rolled over to the answering machine, she hung up.

Julie was out with Joe and Charlie and Andrea when Peg called. They were at the Roadhouse, drinking beer, the pounding music making talk impossible. She smiled at Charlie across the table, wishing it were Peg who was with him. She knew he wished the same. He'd told her so.

"Want to get out of here?" Joe yelled in her ear.

"Let's go get something to eat." She'd skipped supper.

He looked annoyed as he stood up and waited for her to slide out of the booth. "We'll get take-out and go look at the lake. Have you got some good weed, Charlie?" He'd found this secluded dead end where fishermen put their boats into the lake.

"Not tonight," Charlie shouted back.

She should have stayed in her room, but she was tired of studying. Chloe had mentioned a gay bash at one of the dorms. She and Tammy were going. Next time she'd go with them.

Joe swung by a MacDonald's, and they all ordered fries and cheeseburgers. Julie said, "I think I should go back to the dorm, Joe. I've got a lot of studying to do."

Joe looked at her in disbelief. "Why didn't you just stay

there?"

"Because you asked if I wanted to go to the Roadside for a while. I don't want to park somewhere."

"Come on," he said. She could hear his disappointment and wanted only to escape it. He'd been trying to screw her since they'd reconnected the first week of the semester.

"Hey, I've got to study too," Charlie said, coming to her rescue, "and so does Andrea and so do you, Joe."

"Who asked for your opinion?" Joe said in a surly voice. "I'll take you all back and go out by myself."

"I don't have to study," Andrea put in.

"Okay. You can stay."

No one said anything on the way to campus. When Joe dropped Julie off in front of her dorm, he told Charlie to get out with her. The doors barely slammed shut before he squealed off.

"Sorry," Charlie said, standing by the curb.

"We both lost our dates. Want to go to the union and hang out by the water? We can eat our burgers and fries and listen to the music." There was usually some musical combo with a singer.

"Thought we were going to study." His newly grown mustache twitched.

"That was just a ruse. I didn't want to spend the night fending Joe off." She should never have let him get his hand in her pants in the first place.

They found an empty bench by the lake and sat down. Ducks swam in little groups around the pier. Gulls strutted near their feet. She opened her bag and pulled out a french fry. "I have to fight off the gulls now. Thank God, they only want my food."

He laughed. "Don't give them any. We'll never get rid of them."

"That was my mistake with Joe. He wants more."

"Give an inch and you lose your credibility. He does care about you, Julie. Really care. He no more wants to be with

Andrea than I did."

"Why did you ask her out?"

"Joe asked her if she wanted to come along. For me."

"I wish Peg were here too." Just saying it opened up the loneliness. "Maybe next semester. She applied."

"That'd be great."

When Charlie walked her back to her dorm, he bent to kiss her cheek. "Say hello to Peg for me."

She glanced at her watch. It was after ten, too late to phone Peg. The message machine flashed and she pushed the button. Nothing. Someone had called and hung up. Probably Peg.

The ringing woke her from a deep sleep. She fumbled for the phone. "Hey."

"Hey, it's me. I called earlier," Peg whispered.

"I was out for a while. Charlie says hello." She related the evening. "I don't think I can go out with Joe anymore."

"Go ahead. Say hello to both of them for me."

"What does that mean? Go ahead? You don't care if he gets into my underwear?"

"Well, sure I do, but you can take care of yourself."

"What's going on, Peg? Did you meet someone?"

"There's this girl in the GLBT group. She's a singer."

"And?" Julie felt a little sick.

"Well, she likes me."

"What does she look like?" Wide-awake now, she sat up. Of course this was going to happen.

"She's Italian. Her voice is beautiful."

"Is she?"

"Not like you. She's got a noble nose." Peg laughed a little, but Julie wasn't laughing.

"What's her name?"

"Sophie. Why?"

"Just wanted to know."

"We're friends. I don't expect you not to see people."

Julie felt the french fries and burger backing up in her throat. "Okay, Peg, if that's the way you want it. I just told Charlie you might be coming to Madison next semester."

"She might be too."

"Great." She wanted to hang up, but she found she couldn't break the connection, couldn't say good-bye. "Is this it then?" The words sounded so corny.

"No, Julie. I love you. I'll tell her that. I want to come down next weekend."

She lay back on the bed. "I can't wait to see you."

"I've got to go. Mom is coming down the stairs. She has trouble sleeping sometimes. I'll call tomorrow."

"I love you, Peg." Had she ever said it first? Had she waited for Peg to blow her off before she admitted how she felt?

Peg hung the phone up carefully and switched on the kitchen light. Her mother walked through the dining room and blinked in the glare. "Were you talking to Julie?"

Peg felt a twinge of annoyance at her mother's intuition. "Yes. The only time I have any privacy is when everyone's in bed."

"Sorry, honey." Her mom plopped down at the table. "When are you going to Madison?"

"Next weekend."

"Good. Cam can do his own showing. It's time you got on with your life." Her mother's level gaze caught and held hers.

"Yeah. Thanks, Mom." She gave her mother a kiss and escaped.

Sophie called her the next evening, catching her as she came in the door. Next weekend Cam was showing alone, and she was heading to Madison to see Julie.

"What's happening?" Sophie asked in a low, sexy voice.

"I just got back from a horse show, my last one this year. Thank God," she said, although she knew she'd miss showing.

"What's a horse show?"

"It's like a dog show, except mostly you ride the horse."

"You have horses?"

"A few. My brother trains."

"Yeah? What does that mean?"

So she had to go into a long explanation and answer Sophie's questions.

"I remember seeing horses at the county fairgrounds. Is that what they were doing there? Showing them? Is there money in that?"

"Some, if you win or place." The real money lay in putting quarter horse points on the horse, making it more valuable. "What's up?"

"I wanted to see you again. Could I come out and look at the horses?"

"Tonight?" She was beat, having gone to bed late and gotten up at five thirty.

"Well, how about tomorrow after classes? I have no rehearsals."

"Sure. You can follow me then. I'm out at three. How about you?"

"Three thirty."

"Wear jeans and tennis shoes. No flip-flops or sandals."

The next afternoon Peg leaned against her car, waiting for Sophie to show up. The heat of the sun caused her to zone out, and she jumped when Sophie walked up behind her.

"Scared you, huh?" Sophie laughed, transforming her sort of haughty face to impish. She went to her car, parked two vehicles over in the Music Hall parking lot, and threw her backpack inside. "I'm ready, woman."

Peg drove out of town on Hwy. 21, keeping an eye on Sophie's Volkswagen Rabbit in the rearview mirror. At home, she parked next to the garage and looked in the window. Empty. Nor was Cam's truck out by the barn.

Sophie parked the Rabbit next to Peg's secondhand Escort, bought to get her back and forth from school, and got out. A soft breeze lifted Sophie's black hair away from her neck, and a smile stretched across her face and lit her eyes.

It was impossible not to smile back. "Come on," Peg said, heading for the barn. She wore jeans and changed into a pair of old cowboy boots in the tack room. Slipping them on, she watched as Sophie peered into Hombre's and Cosmo's stalls. The horses wanted out, and Hombre pawed through the saw-dust to the hard earth beneath him. Cosmo hung his head over the half-door. Sophie tentatively touched his muzzle. He blew the dust out of his nostrils, a soft, fluttering sound, accompanied by a spray of snot. She jumped back, and Peg laughed.

"He's so big," Sophie said.

Peg remembered Julie saying the same thing. "He won't hurt you. I think I'll put Hombre out in the arena and Cosmo on pasture. He's in here to keep Hombre company."

"I'll put Cosmo out," Ginny said, seeming to appear out of nowhere, "and I'll clean stalls."

"Hey, good girl. Cam can do the rest when he gets home." She introduced Ginny to Sophie. Putting a halter on Hombre, she took his blanket off and turned him loose in the outdoor arena. He galloped off, kicking, bucking and farting before drop-ping to his knees and rolling over.

"My god!" Sophie said, one hand on her chest.

Peg laughed. "He just needs exercise." The horse got to his feet, shook and began running along the wooden fence, whinny-ing to the horses in the pasture.

Out of the corner of her eye, she saw Ginny being dragged by Cosmo toward the pasture gate and went to open it for her. Red and Buck were hanging around the opening. "Make him walk, Ginny. Don't let him pull like that."

The three of them stood at the gate as Cosmo raced off much like Hombre had done. The other two horses followed him. "They scare the shit out of me," Sophie said and apologized to Ginny.

"Don't worry," the girl said. "Cam says worse than that."

"Let's go for a walk." Peg slipped inside the gate and held it open for Sophie, but Sophie balked. "They won't come anywhere near us. They don't want to go back in the barn. Come on."

Peg watched the uneven ground, while Sophie eyed the horses warily and tripped. The only trees grew near the fence line, and it was breezy in the pasture. Peg smelled fallen acorns and hickory nuts and dry leaves, the odors of fall.

"Hey, trust me. The horses won't hurt you."

Sophie's big, dark eyes were fixated on the animals grazing in a group. "I'm not used to horses."

At the end of the field, Peg opened the gate and let Sophie out before she followed. A path led down to the trout stream, which they crossed on a fallen tree. The woods on the other side hid them from sight. There the odor of pines hung almost palpable in the sunlight.

Sophie turned to Peg. Her eyes shone. "You are fearless."

Peg laughed and eyed Bert, bounding across the field toward them. "I was raised with horses. They're like big dogs to me." She had forgotten to let him out of the house. Her mom must be home. "Here comes Bert."

Sophie watched as the dog crawled under the gate and wiggled up to them. She still looked scared. Was she afraid of dogs, too?

"Is he friendly?"

"Doesn't he look friendly?" Peg asked as Bert leaped around them, trying to lick her on the face. "Sit," she ordered, and when she looked at Sophie again, she was only about a half a foot away.

"You're awesome," Sophie said.

She opened her mouth to tell Sophie about Julie, and Sophie kissed her. Excitement strummed through her as Sophie's large breasts and soft pelvis pressed her against a big white pine.

"Yes?" Sophie asked.

Peg shook her head, but instead of telling Sophie about Julie, she said, "Not here, not yet."

"What better place?" Sophie gestured at the ground. "There's a bed of pine needles." She took Peg's hand and led her deeper into the woods.

"We need to talk," Peg said when Sophie sank to the ground and tugged on her hand.

"There's someone else?" Sophie was smiling.

Peg nodded. "Julie," she whispered, the word barely audible.

"Come on. Julie will never know unless you tell her."

Peg dropped to her knees, and Bert danced around her play-fully. He would save her from this, she thought, but his ears perked and he wriggled under the gate and ran off. She figured Cam had driven in, and looking through the trees, she saw him getting out of his truck.

"My brother's home and probably my mother. We better not."

"Come on." Sophie wrapped strong arms around Peg and pulled her down next to her.

This was the exact place where she and Julie had performed what they called a quickie, and now she was about to do the same with Sophie. She resisted, getting to her feet with difficulty. "I can't. I'm sorry."

Sophie shrugged. "No reason to be sorry." She too rose to her feet and brushed the pine needles off.

They walked back across the field, and she introduced Sophie to Cam, who was riding Hombre. She took her in the house to meet her mother, who was working on dinner. Her mom invited Sophie to stay, and Sophie said, "I'd love to. Thanks."

Lively throughout the meal, Sophie talked about her music,

inviting all of them to a concert in two weeks. The sun had dropped behind the trees when she and Peg went back outside. It was still warm and Sophie seemed in no hurry to leave.

"So can we do something this weekend?" Sophie asked.

Peg shook her head. "I'm going to Madison."

"To see Julie? What will you tell her?"

"What is there to tell?"

Sophie changed tack. "Want to meet for lunch tomorrow? At the union?"

Peg always carried her lunch. "Sure. I'd like to be friends, Sophie."

"We can try." Sophie smiled and got into her Rabbit. She waved out the window as she drove away.

Julie waited in her room for Peg's arrival. She thought she'd get some studying done, but concentration eluded her. A knock on the door brought a rush of blood to her face, but it was only Joe and Charlie.

"What are you guys doing here?" she asked, trying not to sound aggrieved.

"Isn't Peg coming? We thought we'd all go out like old times," Joe said.

"I don't know if she wants to go out. Why don't I call you when she gets here?" Joe had a cell phone now. "Give me a little time to talk to her first."

"Come on, Joe," Charlie said.

"Why can't we just wait here?" Joe asked.

"Because I'm studying." Julie pointed to the open book on her desk. "This is all the time I have."

Peg arrived a half hour later, after Julie went down to the street to watch for her. She pulled into the parking lot, got out of her Escort, and reached into the backseat for her backpack. Julie was right behind her when she turned around.

"Hey, I've been waiting forever."

Peg shouldered her backpack. "I got here as soon as I could. I had to put on cruise to keep from going eighty. There were cops all over." She smiled, and Julie grinned back.

Between them lay that inexplicable tug, like a rubber band. Taking the stairs two at a time, Julie locked the door and put a chair under it. "God, I wish we were roommates again," she said.

"Me too." Peg dropped her backpack on the floor and gave Julie an indecipherable look.

She's hiding something, Julie thought as Peg sat on the bed next to her. "So tell me everything. You're seeing this Sophie?"

"I had lunch with her this week. She came out to the house to see the horses one day."

"Is she into horses?"

"She's afraid of them. Cam is doing his own showing now. I'm off the hook."

"Were you ever really on it?"

"Mom said I should get on with my life."

"She should have said that last spring." Julie lay down and tugged at Peg's shirt. All she wanted to do was hold her, feel her heart beating, taste her mouth, but she knew Joe would be knocking on the door if she didn't call him. She sighed and told Peg that Joe and Charlie wanted to see them.

"Joe wants to see you, not me. Can't we get together with them tomorrow night?"

Julie phoned Joe and told him that they'd meet them at the union around seven on Saturday. That gave Peg and Julie the rest of Friday night and all day Saturday. They could lock the door and only go out for food, since Annie was visiting Cam.

There was catching up to do, things they hadn't talked about on the phone. "Have you done it with Sophie?" Julie asked in the middle of an embrace, her mouth inches from Peg's. Did she really want to know?

Peg looked startled. "No way."

Julie didn't believe her. Suddenly furious, she rolled away. "Let's go get something to eat. I'm starving," she said, although she felt nauseated.

"Come on, Julie. Don't spoil the weekend."

"Let's go." She sprang to her feet and began dressing.

"Do you want me to leave?" Peg asked, looking up at her.

"No. I just don't want you fucking someone else," she spat.

"I don't want you to either, but you have, haven't you? Joe or maybe Tammy?"

Julie stared at Peg with surprise, which must have changed Peg's mind.

"I guess not. Sorry. I don't like being accused of something I didn't do either."

Searching Peg's face, Julie knew if they weren't guilty now, they would be. Peg seemed to be measuring her, making a decision.

"Remember the night in Milwaukee when we cheated on each other with Joe and Charlie, how it just sort of happened? Well, this time I said no. Sophie kissed me, nothing else."

Lying down again, Julie tried to take them both back to where they'd been before they separated. They were really getting into it when someone knocked on the door and shook the knob.

"Come on out and play." It was Joe.

Julie looked at Peg. "Goddamn it. Caught again." And they laughed.

When Peg left on Sunday, Julie thought they'd gone a long way toward mending their relationship in spite of spending a lot of time with Joe and Charlie. Chloe and Tammy had camped out in Julie's room for two hours on Saturday. At night, though, they had curled up in Julie's bed together with the chair again propped under the knob.

Still, Julie knew Peg would keep seeing Sophie and that odds were Peg and Sophie would end up intimate. There was nothing she could do about it but worry. When Peg left on Sunday, Julie hugged the ache in her chest and blinked back tears.

"Hey, you all right?" Annie asked, getting out of her car.

"You're back early." Julie wiped her face with her shirtsleeve. "You and Cam have a fight?"

"I've got studying to do. Let's drive there together next time. Save on gas." She put an arm around Julie's shoulders. "Long distance relationships are a bitch."

Julie forced a smile. "Aren't they?"

Part II
2004

VIII

There was nothing Peg hated more than a ringing phone in the middle of the night. It always made her sure the worst had happened. An accident. Someone she loved dead or maimed. Peg fumbled for the receiver and fell back on the bed. "What?"

"Hey, it's me, your sister-in-law."

She raised her head to look at the glowing digits. Ten fifteen. Mouth open, Sophie slept on beside her. "What's up, Annie?" She yawned.

"Did I wake you? God, you're asleep already?" Annie sounded disbelieving. "It's Friday."

"I went to a cycling class at the Y after work." Fridays in spring drained her. The kids stared out the windows, hoping she wouldn't call on them because they hadn't done their homework. At spinning the instructor had made them stand most of the time, adding in a few jumps and sprints. To top it off she'd had another fight with Sophie.

"Charlie is coming to town to sign his book."

"Charlie Schmidt?" she whispered excitedly into the receiver. She'd lost touch with Charlie years ago, about the time she stopped traveling to Madison to see Julie, but she was reading his first novel. It lay on her nightstand.

"None other. Didn't you read the paper?"

"I was too beat tonight. I'll go do that right now."

Sophie stirred and growled. "Who is it?"

"Annie, I'm going in the other room. I'll talk to you later," she said to both.

"Hey, what's going on?" Sophie struggled up on her elbows.

"Charlie is coming to town to sign his new book. I have to go read the paper." She grabbed Charlie's book.

"Don't wake me up again. I'm singing tomorrow night. Remember?"

What if Charlie was signing at the same time as Sophie's concert? Sophie might not forgive her if she went to see Charlie instead. Would that be a bad thing? She closed the door quietly and padded down the hall to the living room. Turning on a light, she picked up the newspaper and read the review in the entertainment section.

"Charles Madison Schmidt in *The Closing of the Day* tells the story of an idealistic attorney turned politician whose principles are compromised by the need for funding. John Harrison, third in his graduating class at law school, and a member of the editorial board of the university's *Law Review*, goes on to win election to Congress. As his career advances, the fragility of his marriage to beautiful, brilliant Caitlyn becomes apparent. His old friends and grassroots supporters fall away. This is a book about how money corrupts even those with the best intentions. It is an excellent read, well written and timely."

Joe was the lawyer turned politician, Julie the beautiful Caitlyn. She'd seen herself and Charlie in the minor characters.

Leaning back on the couch, she wondered if Charlie knew she lived here. She would go to the book signing tomorrow afternoon, and if she missed Sophie's concert, so be it. She wondered if Charlie still had that little mustache. Smiling to herself, she opened her copy of Charlie's book and read until she fell asleep on the couch with the cat on top of her.

Sometime during the night Gato jumped down, and she reached for a lap blanket to cover the spot he'd warmed. When she smelled coffee, she opened her eyes and squinted against the sunlight pouring through the windows. El Gato sat on a windowsill, his tail twitching. She got up and wandered into the kitchen where Sophie stood looking out the window, drinking coffee and singing softly.

"Hey, girlfriend," Peg said in a friendly voice.

Sophie turned toward her and smiled. Sophie didn't go to cycling or do water aerobics or even walk. Physically soft but emotionally ferocious, she still had luxurious black hair, snapping black eyes and the full figure that used to excite Peg.

Trouble's brewing, Peg thought, as she poured herself a cup. The cat curled around her legs, purring, making it nearly impossible to walk. "Okay, okay." She poured food into the animal's small bowl, and he crouched over it.

"What should I wear?" Sophie asked. "My Nicole Miller?" Sophie had thousands of dollars of dresses hanging in her closet with designer names like Oscar de la Renta and Gianni Versace. She wore them for singing engagements.

Peg knew that Sophie would have already made that decision, that she would have had the dress cleaned, her shoes polished and her jewelry chosen.

"I'm going to Charlie's book signing this afternoon," she said. "Do you want to come?"

"I have rehearsal. You know that." A quick frown drew the black brows together.

"I'd like to spend some time with Charlie. I haven't seen him in years." This took some courage to say.

"Why don't you give him a ticket to the concert? I have extras."

"I want to talk to him, maybe go out to dinner with him. We can't do that there." The quiet before the storm, she thought nervously as Sophie silently assessed her.

"Okay. Miss my concert. You've missed them before. Go see your old boyfriend. There are other mermaids in the ocean." Sophie tended toward drama.

Peg smiled and took a deep breath. "Thanks." She leaned forward to kiss Sophie's cheek, but Sophie turned away. Were all small town divas as difficult as Sophie? She tried to remember what had triggered last night's fight. If anything, not going to tonight's concert should have set Sophie off, and it hadn't. Peg had gone to a few of the out of town concerts but had never missed a local performance, until now.

Then she remembered. They'd fought over all the hours she spent at the barn, working with the horses and enjoying Cam and Annie's two kids. Sophie hadn't lost her fear of the horses. She thought they were smelly and dangerous. Look at what happened to Cam, she'd point out.

And look at him now, Peg would retort. Cam was a well-known trainer and horse show judge. Annie taught math at a local university. Their two kids, Katie and Brian, were already riding at four and six years of age. Peg admitted that she doted on her niece and nephew but saw no harm in it. Sophie, who had never held them as babies, who cringed from their grubby little hands, sang them to sleep whenever they stayed overnight. She'd pace the room, hands behind her back, singing Puccini arias or Brahms lullabies.

Sophie's only real interest was choral music. On the faculty at the same university as Annie, she made herself available as a paid soloist for concerts around and outside the state. Peg liked music, but she spent the week cooped up in a classroom and longed to be outside after school and on weekends.

"You'll be a star," she said. "What do you want for breakfast?"

"An orange and a piece of toast. You know I eat lightly the day of a concert."

"You'll faint from hunger," she said, even though she knew Sophie would probably skip lunch and eat only after the concert. Adrenaline would keep her on her feet.

"At least I won't have gas like that tenor I sang with two weeks ago. I thought I'd pass out. He farted every time he hit a high note."

Peg smiled. She'd heard the complaint before. "So, what are you going to do till rehearsal?" Leave early, she hoped. She wanted to go to the barn.

"I have a hair appointment at ten. From there I'll go to the university." Sophie peeled an orange and cursed when it squirted juice.

Good, Peg thought, filling a bowl with cereal and milk. Sitting at the table, she wished she could read, but Sophie wanted to talk.

"You used to go out with this Charlie, didn't you?" Sophie fingered Peg's book, flipping the pages.

Peg watched, knowing better than to snatch the novel away from Sophie's sticky touch. "We hung out. We didn't go together."

"Yeah. You were in love with Julie."

She still loved Julie. She woke in the night, aching for her. Julie had married Joe in a surprise civil ceremony. She had been invited, not that she would have gone. Joe became the congressman that Charlie had written about, and Julie got her degree as a psychologist. Was their marriage in jeopardy? Was it ever not?

Peg came home from the barn, where she'd let the kids ride in the outdoor arena, and made herself a sandwich. El Gato followed her around, rubbing against her, until she gave him a treat. She had found the cat hissing at Bert from atop several bales of hay. He was young and skinny, and she'd taken him home after having him vaccinated and neutered. There was no place for him in nature. Cats killed birds and small animals that fed owls and hawks. If Gato cared that he was housebound, it didn't show. Instead of stalking his prey outside, he crouched inside the windows, his behind wagging, eyeing the birds beyond his reach.

Peg showered and pulled on a nice pair of slacks and a short-sleeved pullover and set out for Book Ends, where Charlie was signing from two to five. Finding a parking spot out back, she went through the rear door. "Is Charles Schmidt signing this afternoon?" she asked the girl behind the counter, and then she saw him.

For a moment she paused. It had been how many years? Eight? The last time she saw Julie, he was just starting a job as a journalist. He might not recognize her. He stood at the front register, talking to someone whose back was turned to her. He clapped the man on the shoulder and walked past him toward her.

She noticed the changes. The little mustache was gone. Without it, his face looked bare, somehow more vulnerable and young. His hair was shorter and curlier. "I hoped you'd come," he said, gathering her up in a hug.

"You're famous," she said into his blazer, unexpectedly on the verge of tears.

"Don't I wish," he replied into her hair. "How I've missed you."

They moved apart, and she smiled shakily. "Me, too. I didn't know how much till now, but I don't want to keep you from signing books."

"You're not. I've signed maybe three."

She handed him hers, which she'd put into a plastic sack. "This makes number four. I'm so impressed, Charlie. It's a really good book."

Grinning, he took it from her without breaking eye contact. "Will you stay so that we can talk later?"

"I hoped you'd say that. Are you going to be here overnight?"

"I am now. Come sit with me. I'll get a chair." He took her hand.

There were so many questions she wanted to ask. Why hadn't he married? Why had he written this particular book, and was he working on another? How were Joe and Julie? Had he seen them? She would wait till they were alone.

Wandering through the stacks of books while he signed and talked to the customers who came in, she found a couple of books and a puzzle for Kate and Brian. She sat next to Charlie the last hour, making small talk, mostly about books they'd both read. That had always been a big part of their conversations.

When they walked out of the bookstore into the sunshine of the late afternoon, she hooked her arm through his, content to just be with him. He smiled down at her.

"You look great, Peg, just like you did at the university."

She laughed. "I've got a few wrinkles here and there. Too much sun."

They wandered down the avenue, looking in windows, reading menus posted outside restaurants, and finally they went into one. Sitting at a window table, Charlie rested his chin on his fists and smiled. "Now we can talk. I've noticed that when I don't see someone for a long time, I often have trouble finding any mutual ground. Whatever we had in common is gone. It's not that way with you, though. I've had a running conversation with you since I first saw you."

She understood. She always had Julie on her mind. "Do you ever see Julie?"

"Joe told me they were getting a divorce. They have a child, you know. A little girl named Peggy."

Peg bit her lip and looked down at her glass. She knew this, of course. Whether she'd heard it from Julie or Annie she wasn't sure. She'd thought the baby's birth cemented Julie's marriage to Joe.

"Julie told me to tell you she misses you, that is if I saw you."

She nodded, unable to speak. Finally she managed to say, "Tell her I miss her too. I just can't talk to her. Was she pregnant when she married Joe?"

"No. I think she thought it was what she should do, and you weren't around." He raised his glass. "Toast to old times?"

She lifted hers in response. "To your book."

He pulled a business card from the inner pocket of his jacket and wrote on it. "Here. Why don't you e-mail her or call her? She's a therapist, you know."

"Yes." She pocketed the card.

She changed the subject. Just being around Charlie comforted her. After dinner, he bought a bottle of wine in the liquor store attached to the restaurant. Then they walked along the avenue again, occasionally sitting on benches.

"Come up with me to my room," Charlie said when they reached his hotel. "We can share this bottle. There's something I want to tell you."

He popped the cork in the bedroom and poured two glasses. Sitting in one of the chairs at a round table, Peg sipped the Shiraz. "Good choice. Tell me why you haven't married, Charlie."

He sat on the bed near the table. "Because I haven't met anyone who's available that I want to marry. And you? Are you with someone?"

She looked away. "Yes. Someone I don't love. Sometimes I don't even like her. How do so many people make these mistakes? You're one of the smart ones."

He looked down at his glass. "One of the lonely ones."

"I'm sorry."

"Hey, it's okay. I'm going to Iraq in a couple weeks. I'll be embedded. So it's better I'm not involved with someone."

Shocked, she stared at him. "You're kidding. Surely you don't support this war."

"I'm a journalist." He shrugged. "Better I go than someone with a family."

"It's like standing in front of a firing squad," she said angrily. "All those people dying for no reason."

"Come here." He patted the bed. "I oppose the war too."

"Don't go. Please." She was pleading now.

"Hey," he said quietly, "I want to write about what it's like to be in combat when you know the war should never have happened." Putting his arms around her, he lay down.

"I love you, Peg. I always have." He kissed the wetness on her face.

Later, she would wonder if those words kindled what followed. She'd had no thought of going to bed with him, yet that's what happened. When she woke up the next morning, he was leaning on his elbow looking down at her.

"Will you take me to see your horses and meet your family?" Then he added before she could respond, "I know that last night was a gift, a fluke. I won't make the same mistake Julie and Joe did. Just give me one day."

She felt like crying again. What was it about this that made her so sad? She wished she loved him because she liked him so much? Was that it? She told him so when she was able to speak.

"I know. Come on. Let's get out of here."

Sophie, she thought. She'd left a message on the answering machine last night, saying not to wait up. She considered calling when Charlie turned on the shower but was afraid to wake her up. Sophie slept late after concerts. She washed in the separate sink outside the bathroom and was ready to go when Charlie stepped out of the bathroom.

They grabbed coffee and a bagel before leaving the hotel. Charlie followed her in his Prius. She had a Focus wagon, nothing fancy, but with lots of room for picking up grain from the feed mill or carrying tack or kids.

Meadowlarks called from the fields she passed. She caught bits of their songs through the open window. Glancing in the rearview mirror, she eyed Charlie's car and wondered how she was going to explain last night and today to Sophie. Maybe this would be the breaking point, the hump they couldn't quite cross. Oh well, it was too late now.

They found Cam behind the barn, washing his latest two-year-old, which he'd nicknamed Dom for Domingo, because he'd bought him on a Sunday. Dom was a stallion. Cam planned to use him for stud once he put enough points on him.

She introduced the two men. Cam set down the hose and dried his hand on his jeans before offering it. "Good to meet you." Dom twisted his head and snapped at a biting fly.

"I've been wanting to see this place for more than ten years. Nice setup you've got here."

"Thanks. We've added on since then. Peg can show you around. She's my right hand." He glanced at her, and she guessed the unspoken question. *Who is this guy?*

Praise from Cam still caused her to swell. "I've known Charlie since I was at the university. He's an author. He was signing his novel at Book Ends."

"Congratulations," Cam said. "I'll have to read it. Do you have the book, Peg?"

"Yep, but you have to buy your own copy. Royalties, you know."

"Annie bought a book yesterday. She was one of my first customers," Charlie said.

Peg took Charlie into the barn and introduced him to the horses. Most were boarders. Hombre had been sold years ago. Cosmo and Red were out in the field. They were the old men. Buck had died three years ago. Cam had bought a small palomino gelding, Barney, for Brian to show in walk-trot. Peg

130

sometimes showed him in the regular and amateur classes.

"I don't know anything about horses." Charlie stroked Barney's muzzle, marveling at its softness, then placed a hand on the rippling muscles in the animal's neck. Barney hung his head over the stall door, eyes half shut. "Such power."

Peg smiled. "Don't tell him. He doesn't know. Want to meet the rest of the family?"

They found Peg's mom and dad sipping coffee and reading the paper in the kitchen. She introduced Charlie, and her mom invited him to stay for breakfast. Peg showed them his book.

"Annie showed me her copy. I can't wait to read it," her mother said. "Peg told me about you, Charlie, how you always wanted to write a book and now you have."

Charlie's face reddened.

Her dad poured him a cup of coffee and lifted his in a toast. "Congratulations, son."

"Thanks." A wide smile lit Charlie's face, and Peg felt that urge to cry again.

"He's going to Iraq." Her voice quivered slightly. When Charlie gave her a look of surprised disappointment, she ignored it. She was again furious to think he would risk his life in a stupid war. "He'll be embedded over there."

The silence that followed her announcement dragged until the door opened and Brian and Kate rushed into the room, their mother behind them. "Sorry," Annie said. "They wanted to see who was here. Charlie! I should have known."

"Breakfast for everyone?" Mom asked.

"No, thanks. We already ate," Annie said.

"Who's the man?" Brian asked, and everyone laughed.

"Charlie Schmidt. He writes books."

"Like *Mother Moon*?" Katie piped.

"Yes," Charlie said.

"I'm going to a show with Dad," Brian announced importantly.

"I want to go too." Tears teetered on Katie's eyelids.

"We have to go to the barn now," Annie said, ushering the kids toward the door. "Don't leave yet, Charlie."

After breakfast, Peg and Charlie cleaned up the dishes. "I see why you still hang around here," he said.

Annie returned to the kitchen with Kate, who was crying. "Her dad and Brian left for the horse show." She picked her up. "Next time we'll go too, Katie."

"You can ride later. I'll saddle up Cosmo," Peg promised her.

"You're a life saver," Annie said. "Now what was all that silence when I walked into the kitchen earlier, or shouldn't I ask?"

When told, Annie looked horrified. "You're going over there voluntarily?"

Charlie nodded.

"I suppose you'll write a book about it."

He nodded again. "I can't do that if I don't know what it's like."

When Charlie left late in the afternoon on his way to Madison, Peg hugged and kissed him. "Write to me. I'll answer." She felt teary again.

"Of course. Shall I tell Julie hello?"

"Sure."

The Prius disappeared down the road as she watched. Annie put an arm around her. "He'll be all right."

She leaned into Annie for comfort. "God, I hope so. It's been years since I talked to him, and it was like we'd just seen each other yesterday. You can't do that with many people."

"He loves you, you know."

"I love him, too, but as a friend."

Annie linked arms with her, and they walked back toward the house. "Annie, I didn't go home last night. I don't know what to tell Sophie."

"How about the truth?"

"Oh yeah, sure, that I spent the night with Charlie."

Annie stopped and smiled at her. She didn't like Sophie much. "Did you?"

"I thought maybe you would back me up if I said I was babysitting the kids and fell asleep."

"If that's what you want, I will."

She and Sophie lived in a twelve-unit apartment building near the edge of town. Sophie's car was in her designated spot, and Peg parked next to it. Sweating, her heart beating faster than normal, she climbed the stairs to the second floor. When she put her key in the lock, the door opened from the inside.

Sophie held the doorknob. "Did you come for your things?" They lay in a heap in the middle of the living room floor, dishes included.

She stared at the pile and looked up to meet Sophie's angry black eyes. "I'll need boxes."

"No, you won't." Sophie picked up a stack of plates and thrust them at her.

Afraid that Sophie would drop them, she took them and set them down again. "I'll get boxes and come back."

"I want you out of here now," Sophie spat.

"But you don't even know where I was." Was she not going to be able to test her alibi? Somehow she thought maybe the truth would be more palatable.

"Yes, I do. You were at the Maple Leaf Hotel downtown with Charlie Schmidt."

"How do you know that?" she asked in surprise.

"Hah. You spent the night with him. I saw you going into the hotel with a man." She'd never met Charlie.

"You were spying on me?"

"Not really. I happened to be across the street at a bar with the other singers. Now take your things and get out."

"I have to get boxes," she repeated.

"Fine. I'll be back when you're done." Sophie grabbed her purse and swept out the door. "Two hours, tops. And take the cat with you."

Of course she'd take the cat. He was hers. She picked him up and buried her face in his fur. "We're out of here," she whispered.

Calling Annie's cell, she told her she needed boxes and help. Then she began loading clothes into her car. It was over, just like that. Six years down the drain. She'd gotten together with Sophie after she came back from that year in Costa Rica, around the time Julie married Joe. She felt only an odd relief as if she'd always known she and Sophie weren't meant to be together.

Cam and her dad moved her stuff above the garage, which she and Annie cleaned while her mom kept the kids out of the way. It was a family affair, yet it left her feeling as if she were going backward. At the end of the day, she was ensconced in the apartment that had been Cam's until he and Annie built a house. She needed to shop for groceries, but she had no energy. Monday she'd have to find time to change her phone number, her mailing address. Thank god, she had her own e-mail address. Sophie did all her e-mailing and faxing from the university.

Several knocks on the door got her out of her chair. Katie and Brian stood at the top of the stairs, thrusting a food tray at her. "Grandma fixed you some meatloaf and potatoes and broccoli." They made a face at the "broccoli."

"Hey, thanks. Come on in." She took the tray, and the kids slid past her.

"This used to be Daddy's place," Brian said, sitting on the computer chair and spinning.

Peg picked up Kate and sat down with her. "You are getting so big, Katie."

"Read me a story," the girl said, curling into Peg's lap. Peg had a stack of kids' books for when Brian and Kate visited.

"They're in one of those boxes. If you can find one, I'll read it."

"Can I use the computer?" Brian asked, fingers poised over the keyboard.

"Wash your hands first, but there are no games on my computer except solitaire. You can play that." He tapped away while she read to Kate. After, she ate. The food warmed the empty spot inside. She hadn't known how hungry she was.

She called her mother when the kids left with the tray. "That was so good, Mom. Thanks."

"I didn't think you'd have anything to eat. Look, if you don't get a chance to shop tomorrow, you can eat with us or I can pick up a few things for you."

"Don't make it so easy, Mom. I'll go to the store after school."

Before she unpacked boxes that night, she e-mailed Charlie her new address and included her cell phone number. A warm breeze flooded through the screens, bringing with it the smell of lilacs. She had forgotten the dark and the quiet. The only sounds were a couple of barred owls, hooting back and forth. She fell asleep with the Spanish text open to Monday's lesson.

That night Charlie ate dinner with Joe and Julie. After, Julie put Peggy to bed and joined the men on the porch. She wondered if she'd forever associate the smell of lilacs with the sadness of this day. No one said anything until the setting sun bathed the houses across the street in hues of pink.

"Do either of you need help moving?" Charlie asked.

"I should be going to Iraq instead of Congress," Joe said in a low voice.

Angrily, Julie lashed out. "Why don't you both go get killed? If a woman were in charge, there wouldn't be any more idiotic wars."

"Answer my question," Charlie said mildly.

"I have to stay here and sell the house," she told him. "Joe gets to move."

"Hey, that's not fair. I'll be in Washington."

"Then be sure you vote to end this war before Charlie gets his head blown off," she snapped, unable to get a handle on her rage.

Into the following silence, Charlie said, "I saw Peg on my book tour."

Julie's pulse jumped. She'd been unwilling to ask.

"Julie wishes I were Peg," Joe said without anger.

He spoke the truth, of course. She never should have married him. She knew it then. But she'd wanted a child, and he'd wanted her, and Peg had seemed out of the picture. Actually, Peg had never gone back to UW-Madison. She'd gotten her degree from UWO.

"She said hello. We spent a memorable afternoon and evening together."

"Hello back," Joe said.

Julie took a sip of wine. She thought by now she'd have let Peg go, but a champagne-sized bubble of excitement burst in her chest. When had they given up on each other? Julie had entered graduate school, and Peg had joined the Peace Corps and gone to Costa Rica to teach English. When she came back, Peg took a high school job near her home, teaching Spanish and English. Peg moved in with someone, and Julie married Joe. Or was it the other way? After that, Peg refused to talk to her and told Charlie it hurt too much to see her.

"I should go," Charlie said, standing up. "Thanks for dinner. You're a good cook, Julie."

She thought of Murray Street in Milwaukee and the job at The Diner. "I wish I could say something to make you change your mind about Iraq." She gave him a hug and a kiss on the cheek.

"Hey, I'll see you before I go, and I'll be fine."

When his taillights flickered as he turned the corner, she said,

"I'm going to bed and read."

"Look, Julie, I'm sorry about all this."

"Is she going to Washington with you?"

"You know I'm sharing an apartment with Dan." It wasn't unusual for less established Congressmen to share an apartment. Housing was expensive and hard to find in Washington.

What a fool she'd been. She could have had a child without marrying. She'd told herself that she wanted to know the father when in fact she'd taken the easy route. "Are you staying here tonight?"

"Yes. I'll take Peggy to daycare."

She nodded and went inside the too large house they'd bought when he started working as an attorney and she as a therapist. She had no wish to stay here. It was meant to entertain, not to live in. She thought she would buy a condo with her share of the sale proceeds.

They'd stopped sleeping together after he admitted he loved another woman, someone who'd gone to the university with them. Andrea Smith, the girl Joe once fixed up with Charlie. She'd seen them one night on State Street, had almost crossed over to say hello when Andrea stretched and kissed him, stopping Julie at the curb. She began to question his late night meetings, and finally she asked, and he told her.

"You don't love me that way," he'd said.

She didn't ask what way was "that way" because she knew. It was how she loved Peg. "We can't stay together then."

"I'll move out," he'd said, but he hadn't—yet. He'd go away for days at a time, which made Julie angry because it forced her to lie to Peggy. She sensed he was trying to minimize the damage to his reputation, but it was time to go their separate ways. However, she had no energy for any more words tonight.

In bed, she picked up the book she was reading. She'd found it at the library while browsing—*Losing Julia*—a wonderful story, poignant and funny. She laughed and cried and knew she would hate finishing it. That's how it was with a good book. You wanted it to go on and on.

The radio clock went off at six fifteen, and she lay in bed listening to the news on Iraq. She knew she'd have to get a mouth guard because she had a headache from gritting her teeth. After a quick shower, she went to Peggy's room.

Joe was already there, looking at their daughter. Peggy slept arms flung wide, pink mouth slightly open, temporarily oblivious to the two of them. Her eyes blinked open, gray like her mother's, and she looked solemnly at Joe and Julie. Peggy's actions reflected the angst she felt about her parents. Clingy and easily upset, she had glommed onto another child at daycare—Daisy Theobald, a cheerful little black girl. She cried when she had to leave Daisy.

Joe spoke first. "Come on, sweetie. Let's get dressed."

"I'll make breakfast," Julie said.

"Don't leave, Mama." Peggy grabbed her hand.

"I'll do it then." Joe turned toward the door and was stopped by his daughter's voice.

"You stay too, Daddy."

If Peggy had put their hands together, she couldn't have made it clearer. She wanted her parents together. Didn't all kids? Julie sighed. "I'll see you two downstairs. You don't want to be late for school, honey."

Over oatmeal and toast, Joe told Peggy he was flying to Washington that day and he'd call her in the evening. Peggy leaned on her elbow, playing with her cereal. Joe stopped her hand. "Eat," he said gently. "When I come back, we'll spend lots of time together."

"Mama, can I have Daisy over?" Peggy asked.

"Saturday maybe. I'll ask her mama."

"Did you hear me, Peggy?" Joe asked.

The little girl nodded, stirring her oatmeal as soon as he removed his hand. "You're going away again."

Julie liked her work. She felt she made a difference in her clients' lives. Jan Dickenson had inspired her choice of profession. When they saw each other at a conference, they fell into easy conversation. Fraternizing with your ex-clients was a no-no, but she considered herself an exception since she was on the same footing.

She poured a cup of coffee and looked at her e-mail before staffing with the others in the phone room. Dennis Jennings came in last with a cup in one hand, papers in another and a donut between his teeth. He sat down on the couch next to her.

"Need another hand?" Sharon Arnold asked. She was fresh out of grad school and had a crush on Dennis, who Julie considered a horse's ass.

Dennis handed Julie his coffee cup. "Hold this for me, will you?"

She set it on the floor between them. She too had a sheaf of papers. Staff secrets spread like the flu. How everyone kept mum in public about his or her clients was a wonder to her.

After staffing, the receptionist buzzed her to tell her that Sammy Thompson was waiting. She walked to the waiting room to get her. As always, the girl looked sullen. Sammy had been forced into counseling after making the same inept suicide attempt that Julie had made at about the same age. She agreed to therapy rather than be sent home from the university. Sometimes they went entire sessions exchanging only a few comments. Julie hoped this wasn't going to be one of them. She decided to push.

"So, what's happening?" she asked.

The girl looked at her hands and mumbled, "Not much."

"Same old, same old, huh? Well, I've been thinking that maybe you might do better with another therapist. What do you think?" Actually, she had someone in mind. Maybe Sammy would relate better with someone younger, like Sharon.

Sammy's head snapped up. She glared at Julie. "You don't like me, do you?"

Julie studied her a moment. The kid was nice enough looking if you could get past the jewelry. She had rings everywhere—in her nose, up and down her ears, through her eyebrows. Her hair looked like she cut it herself, a deep unnatural red shaggy mop. The girl's smoldering blue eyes bore into Julie. "That's not true. Therapy is not a one-way street. I can't help you if you won't talk to me."

The girl looked down at her hands again and said angrily, "Okay. I hate my life. I'm a freak."

"Why do you think that?" she asked, squelching the urge to suggest that Sammy take out a few earrings, brush her hair, put on a clean shirt.

"I don't fit in. I never have," she spat.

"Tell me about yourself."

No answer.

"Do you have a roommate?"

"She hates me."

"There must be someone or something you like."

"My dog," Sammy said, glancing up, her mouth and eyes softening.

"What's your dog's name?" Julie smiled.

"Buddy. I'm his favorite person. He goes nuts when I go home."

"Does he? What is home like?"

The girl's face closed. She shrugged. "It's a place to sleep."

"What do you do when you're not studying?" She knew Sammy came from an upper middle class family with three kids. Her parents seemed genuinely concerned about her.

"I walk around or sleep or read."

"Do you like to be outside?"

"Yes."

"What's your favorite book?"

"*Rubyfruit Jungle*," she whispered.

Bingo, Julie thought. "That's a good one. How about *The Catcher in the Rye*?" Holden Caulfield didn't fit in either.

"And *Other Women, Bastard Out Of Carolina, Marley and Me, Running With Scissors*."

Wow, Julie thought. Sammy was hammering her over the head after all these sessions. "I never read *Running With Scissors*, but I've read the rest. Does your dog look like Marley?"

"Sort of. He's not as big or as bad."

Julie laughed.

"Those are just a few books, by the way." Sammy twisted her fingers.

"Do you know that there is a gay and lesbian group on campus?"

"Of course I know. I can't go anymore."

"Why is that?" She found herself looking for that flash of blue eyes.

Sammy slid down further in the chair. "Nicole and I sort of hung out, and now she's hanging with Patsy. I don't want to see them."

She glanced at the clock. "Will you do something for me and you?"

"What?" Sammy gave her a wary look.

"Go to a meeting anyway. Take out a few rings before you do and dress up a little." Sammy's ragged jeans dragged the ground. "You're an attractive girl. Don't hide it."

"I knew it," the girl lashed back. "You hate the way I look."

"Does Nicole have a lot of piercings?"

Sammy dipped her head. "No."

"Think about it. You can always put them back in."

Only ten fifteen. She dictated her comments before going for another cup of coffee and meeting with another client. At noon she drove to the Y and dropped in on a cycling class. The instructor barked commands—push, push, up, up, sit, sit, faster, faster. His head was shaved, his arms laced with tattoos. There were mostly guys in this class. Their sweat lay in little puddles around their bikes. Hers clung to her shirt. She showered afterward and ate a sandwich on the way back to work.

The afternoon sped by, and at five she picked up Peggy at daycare. Peggy reached for Daisy's hand after Julie helped her on with her jacket. "I asked Daisy to come over Saturday."

Daisy looked at Julie out of thickly shaded brown eyes and smiled shyly. The little girl was a beauty, but so was her mother who was helping her into her coat. Peggy had to release her hand but quickly grabbed it again as if it were a lifeline.

"Let's ask Mrs. Theobald," Julie said.

"Can Daisy come over Saturday?" Peggy asked.

"Can I, Mama?"

Diana Theobald straightened and pushed her luxurious black hair back with one hand. She looked frazzled. "Sure." There was no need to exchange addresses. The girls had been at each other's houses before. "What time?"

"I'll be glad to pick her up," Julie said. "Say nine o'clock?"

"That'll be a big help. I have to work Saturday. Catch up on a few things." Diana was a CPA.

On the way home, Julie asked, "How was school?"

Strapped in her booster seat in the back, Peggy stared out the window. "Okay. Is Daddy coming back?"

She glanced in the rearview mirror but she couldn't see her daughter's face. "Of course, he's coming back." She'd delve into this later when she could see Peggy's expression.

When they sat down to eat, the phone rang. "Why don't you get that, Peggy?" she said, sure it was Joe calling.

She heard the girl talking. When her daughter hung up but didn't return to the table, she went looking for her. Peggy lay face down on her bed. Sitting next to her, she rubbed her back lightly.

"What's wrong, honey?"

"Daddy's not going to live with us. He's getting a partment. Can Daisy go with me when I visit?"

More likely he was moving in with Andrea. She wondered how he would explain that to Peggy.

She ignored the phone ringing in the distance. "We'll see, sweetie." She gathered her daughter in her arms, but Peggy resisted.

"Why can't we all live together?"

When she finally coaxed Peggy back to the table and then to bed, she checked the answering machine. It was Joe apologizing. He said Peggy had asked and he thought he should tell her. By then, she didn't want to talk to anyone and went to bed with her book.

Peg exchanged e-mails with Charlie every day. His were long and detailed, hers short and encouraging. She'd begun writing Julie a letter the day after she moved back home, musings that she added to every day, never intending to attach and send it.

Dear Julie: Charlie gave me your e-mail address. I had no luck trying to talk him out of going to Iraq. What a misbegotten war!

I remember you once saying this was a cool place. Well, I moved above the garage where Cam once lived after Sophie threw me out. I'd forgotten how dark it is here at night. The cicadas fill the air with sound. They drown out the occasional passing car.

Cosmo and Red are old now. I have a niece and nephew, Katie and Brian, Cam and Annie's kids. They (Cam and Annie) built a house next to my parents. The kids have their own horse, Barney, which they share with me. I know it sounds like I never grew up. Sometimes I feel that way. It was pathetic, but she couldn't stop. Every evening, she added a few sentences.

God, she was tired. Falling asleep over students' papers wasn't hard to do, but until now she'd managed to keep her eyes open.

A warm wind crossed the table and blew a few papers onto the floor. As she leaned over, her head spun. She couldn't afford to get sick at the end of the school year. Exams began next week. Always hungry now, she made herself a peanut butter sandwich before going to bed.

Swimming out of sleep to the sound of public radio, hardly believing it was morning already, she felt as tired as when she lay down. Maybe she should see a doctor, but that would have to wait till school was out.

The newscaster spewed out the news from Iraq. More Americans killed, more British, only God knew how many Iraqis. It made her burn with anger to think of how the country had been tricked into this war and how so many of the misled still thought the troops should stay till the area was stable. As if that would ever happen. She recalled sitting in The Diner watching the Gulf War on the small TV high in the corner. Papa George at least had the sense not to stay.

In contrast, the birds sang from dawn to dark, marking their territories, oblivious to the dangerous world they lived in. They trumped nature's hazards with reproduction, only to be put in peril by declining habitat and chemicals. Oh, to be a bird and just worry about carrying on the species.

At school she wrote sentences on the board and told her Spanish students to turn their translations in at the end of class. Then she sat at her desk and paged through stacks of homework, trying to look busy.

The kids hefted their backpacks and called "Adios" or "Hasta luego," as they jostled out of the room. She had a few minutes until her next class, English Comp, and her head nodded over the paperwork on her desk till her forehead touched the papers and she closed her eyes. Only for a minute, she told herself, and startled awake when the first kid clunked into the room. She pretended she'd dropped something on the floor beneath her desk.

On the drive home with the radio off and the windows open,

listening to the red-winged blackbirds shirring from fence posts, she struggled to stay awake. A John Deere tractor crawled across a field, swallows dipping and soaring in its wake while gulls circled and dropped to the rich dark earth. The warm air fingered her hair, lulling her to sleep as the car left the road.

She jerked awake, hitting the brakes when the vehicle bumped into the ditch. Adrenaline rushed alarmingly through her system. Putting the car in reverse, she tried to back out onto the road but her tires spun futilely. Getting out, she stood by the vehicle while the tractor veered off course and headed toward her.

The pounding of her heart slowed to normal, and she waved to the man in the cab as the John Deere slowly made its way onto the road. "You all right?" the farmer asked, swinging down from his high seat.

"I fell asleep. I'm sorry."

He nodded at the car. "I'll hook a chain to it and pull you out. Start it and put it in reverse, but don't step on the gas." Getting a logging chain out of a tool box on the tractor, he fastened one end to the plow on the back of the machine and the other to Peg's trailer hitch. Climbing back onto the immense tractor, he chugged forward slowly, dragging the car backward onto the road. After he unhooked the chain, she tried to pay him. He refused. "I do this a lot, but it's usually slippery out. Drink a cup of coffee before you get behind the wheel," he said with a friendly smile.

She thanked him and raised a hand from the open window as she drove away, wondering if she had narcolepsy or, worse, leukemia. Did she want to know?

At home, she found herself in a tangle of kids and puppy. The children talked at once, canceling each other out. "One at a time," she said, looking down at their rosy, excited faces. "Who is this fellow?" She picked up the squirming little dog, which licked her face. When she set him on his feet, he raced around in wide circles, falling over his large feet. She laughed.

"It's our new dog," Katie shouted. "His name's Rounder, 'cause he only goes in circles. That's what Mom says."

Annie came from the barn, pushing her hair back with one hand. "What do you think? Is it time for a new dog?"

They'd had to put Bert down three years ago. Renal disease. Even now, she hated to think of it. "I guess so. Here he is anyway. Cute. You can't take him back. He's a mix of what?"

"Hound and Labrador it said on the kennel. Probably should have gotten a herding dog."

"He looks like a keeper."

"Yeah!" the kids shouted.

"Are you coming out to the barn?"

"I can't. I've got papers to grade." She could do them later, but she was so tired. Plodding up the stairs to her apartment, she turned on the computer and read Charlie's message.

"Shipping out tomorrow. Will keep in contact. Am pretty nervous."

"Is it too late to change your mind?" she sent.

Then she turned to her long letter to Julie and added a few sentences. *Charlie comes back into my life and leaves for Iraq. Bert dies and Rounder comes to stay. Sophie boots me out and I'm relieved. I have to sleep now so that I don't drive off the road anymore.*

146

IX

Julie studied Sammy, thinking about how her changed looks seemed to have changed her attitude, or maybe it was the other way around. She only wore three tiny earrings, her hair had grown longer and turned a shiny brown, and her jeans were stylishly tight. "You look terrific. How's it going?" School had just started up after summer break.

Sammy grinned and the smile changed her face. "Awesome. Nicole and Patsy and I hang out together."

"Wow. When did that happen?"

The girl shrugged. "At the last meeting." She looked at her feet and mumbled, "I took out the rings and let my hair grow."

"Smart cookie."

"You told me to." There was the flash of blue eyes, now bright.

Julie laughed. "I wanted to see the young woman behind the

disguise."

It was the last appointment of the day. She dictated her observations after Sammy left and went out into a warm rain. After picking up Peggy, she made a quick stop at the grocery store.

"What do you want for supper?" she asked as they strolled down the aisles.

"Macaroni and cheese and hot dogs," Peggy said.

"That's all you ever want, kiddo. Tonight we're going to have a salad and homemade pizza."

"I don't want pizza."

"Hey, it'll be fun putting it together. Besides, I thought you liked pizza."

"I want Daddy to help make it."

She sighed. How to say that Daddy didn't want to help?

The For Sale sign swung in the breeze when they turned the corner onto their street. There was an open house Sunday. She and Peggy would have to leave for the afternoon. Joe's Lexus was parked on one side of the driveway. A surprise.

"Daddy's home!" Peggy shouted, her face and hands pressed against the window.

Joe got up off the swing on the front porch and walked toward them as she drove into the garage. Releasing Peggy from her booster seat, he held her to him, hiding his face in her neck.

Julie slid out of the car and stood rooted to the cement floor. She knew immediately. Charlie. Leaning against the roof of the car, she buried her face in her arms.

A stray shot, Joe told her when Peggy went to her room to get some pictures she'd drawn. "I have to go back to Washington tomorrow night, but I wanted to tell you in person." His red eyes revealed his pain. He swiped at them when Peggy reappeared.

"What's wrong, Daddy?" Peggy stopped running and looked worried.

"Uncle Charlie died," he said.

Later, when Peggy had fallen asleep and been put to bed,

Julie and Joe sat on the front porch swing.

"If I say it enough, will it become real, Julie? Does Charlie seem dead to you?"

"No. Yes. I don't know." The anger she'd felt toward Joe disappeared, punctured by Charlie's death. "Do you remember our discussions about what we wanted to do and be?"

"At least Charlie wrote his novel."

"He would have written more." She stared at the rain splashing on the sidewalk. "You're the protagonist in that novel. It's not always flattering."

"And you're the protagonist's wife. Do you ever talk to Peg?"

She shook her head. "No. I don't know where she's living."

"You know where her parents live. You should be the one to tell her, Julie, not me."

She stared at the downpour, knowing that he was crying too.

The rain continued steadily through the night. Like tears, she thought, as she squeezed her eyes shut hoping for sleep, for forgetfulness. She finally got up and took a sleeping aid. When she awoke, clouds scudded across a background of blue. September light was less direct than July. If the seasons were years in one's life, spring would be childhood and teens, July the twenties and thirties, September the forties and fifties. She was in the July stage. Her anger with Joe sprang directly from the fact that she'd not stepped out on him and wished that she had. She longed for the mellowness of September when maybe she would stop missing Peg.

She arose, still tired, and put on jeans and a T-shirt. She found Joe and Peggy in the sunny kitchen, making pancakes. Peggy stood on a chair, ladling the batter into the griddle, while Joe held the bowl. Both turned when she entered.

"We didn't want to wake you," Joe said. The skin around his eyes sagged. He forced a smile and she forgave him everything, if there was anything to forgive. She knew she'd withheld her love, hoarding it. Maybe they would remain friends.

She ate a few pancakes because Peggy had helped make them. "I'll be back as soon as I can. What time is your flight, Joe?"

"Eight. You don't have to be home till six. Call me if you're going to be later. Say hello to Peg." A wry smile tugged at his mouth, and she wondered if he always knew he wasn't number one.

"I want to see the other Peg," Peggy put in.

"We'll go somewhere exciting," Joe said. "You'll meet the other Peg, but not today."

She headed out of town, the sun in her eyes, the wind on her face, a vaguely sick excitement churning her stomach. Charlie's death rippled through her mind but wouldn't stick. In some ways she'd loved Charlie better than Joe. He was more patient, more understanding, more willing to listen. When she'd told him about Andrea, he'd said, "Are you surprised?"

She had been, though. She'd taken Joe's love for granted without ever trying to reinforce it, assuming it would maintain itself. It was Peg who ran elusively through her thoughts, always out of reach. Well, today she would see Peg, and she was quaking inside. What was the worse-case scenario? That Peg wouldn't want to talk to her? That she was happily involved with someone? It never occurred to her for some reason that Peg might not be there.

She recognized the place, although another had sprung up next to it and the barn had a long addition. With that sick feeling still working in her stomach, she turned into the driveway and parked next to the garage as she had all those years ago. Sitting in her Acura, she gathered enough courage to open the door and step out.

A large dog came bounding out of nowhere and planted huge paws on her chest. Staggering back against the car, she said, "You're not Bert." The dog had short black hair, long ears and a longer tail. Nose toward the sky, he belled like a hound that has found whatever it was chasing.

Annie panted after the dog, shouting, "Down, Rounder. Bad dog. Sorry. He's harmless," she said as the animal dropped to all fours. "He must think his name is Bad Dog." She stared. "Julie? Are you really here?" She ran toward Julie and hugged her hard. "God. How are you? Why didn't you call or e-mail?"

"I should have." She saw the truck and trailer were gone, that no one seemed to be around. "I suppose everyone's at a horse show." Her mouth twisted into a smile.

"Well, Jean and Rory are out of town." Peg's parents. "Listen, I'll call Peg's cell and let her know you're here, or better yet, we'll drive to the show. It's not far."

"Why are you home alone, Annie?"

"Perceptive as always. I'm done with what I stayed home to do. I'll put Rounder in the house and we'll go."

"I can't tell her at a horse show," she said.

"Tell her what, Julie? What happened?"

"Charlie was killed in Iraq." Joe was right. Every time she said Charlie was dead it became more real. Her lips trembled.

Annie's hand flew to her mouth, her eyes widening. "No! How?"

Julie shrugged helplessly. "A stray bullet, or so we were told. Friendly fire, I'm guessing." She started to turn away, but Annie grabbed her and held on. Julie buried her face in Annie's silky hair. "Goddamn stupid fucking war," she said.

Clinging to each other, they cried together. "I'm so sorry," Annie kept saying.

When they stepped apart, Julie said, "I'd like to see the barn again and the horses."

In silence, they walked to the stable. A light breeze followed them. Rounder ran ahead. If Julie closed her eyes, she could imagine Peg next to her and Bert ahead.

"How are you, Julie? Otherwise, I mean," Annie asked as they entered the cool building. "We sort of lost touch."

"I'm in the middle of a divorce. Our daughter is four. The house is up for sale. We just reduced the price. I'll probably move to a condo with Peggy. I'm a therapist and I love my job. Briefly, that's it." She looked at Annie, thinking that if it hadn't been for Peg and the fact that Annie was straight, she might have made a move on her. "How are you and Cam?"

"Good. We have a boy and a girl. Katie is four, Brian six. Cam loves training and judging horses. I enjoy teaching at UWO."

"Hey, I'm happy for you. I never should have married Joe. In a way, the divorce is a relief. And Peg? How is she?"

The stalls were empty, but Annie pointed out the additional eight stalls and the indoor riding arena. They walked outside to the pasture where Cosmo and Red grazed side by side.

"They look like they did the last time I saw them over eight years ago. I was afraid they wouldn't be here."

"Bert and Buck aren't. Hombre was sold. Cam's been through several horses since." Annie leaned on the fence, and Julie noticed the fine lines that had etched themselves into her smooth skin. She knew she had those lines in about the same places. "I'll call Peg. You should be the one to tell her about Charlie." She pulled a cell phone out of her vest pocket.

She put a hand over Annie's. "You tell her for me. If she wants to talk, she can phone me." She handed Annie her business card with her home number written on the back.

They talked for another hour before Julie went into Annie's house to use the bathroom. Before she left, Annie told her to keep an eye out for the truck and trailer. "I will," she said, turning around in the parking area and waving good-bye to Annie who held the dog by the collar.

Peg fumbled for her cell and put it to her ear. The kids were being silly in the backseat, their high, clear giggles startlingly loud. "Hush, you guys, your mom's on the phone."

"Hey," Annie said, "are you on your way home?"

"Yeah. We're almost to Omro. Why?"

"Julie just left. I thought if you were closer, you might cross paths with her. She's driving a silver Acura."

"What? Why was Julie there?" It's true that hearts soar and plunge, she thought with wonder. Hers had. Then it occurred to her why Julie might have been there. "Was it about Charlie?"

"She wanted to talk to you. She left her card with her number on it. You can phone her. I've got to go. The dog is running toward the road." Annie ended the call.

"Was that Annie?" Cam asked.

Peg nodded. "Yep. Julie was at the place this afternoon. She just left. Annie thought we might pass her before she turns south, but we're not even close."

"I can't go any faster with a loaded trailer."

"I know." Peg leaned forward as if that might speed them toward home. Knowing that she had missed Julie's visit made her feel slightly ill. After more than eight years, Julie shows up when she's gone. How ironic is that?

Her parents were still away when they drove up to the barn and unloaded the horses. Annie turned up as they were feeding. "Hey there." She spread her arms and the kids burrowed into her. "How did you do?"

"I got a blue ribbon," Brian said, showing it to her. He'd stuffed it in his pocket.

"Wonderful. We'll have to hang it up. How about you, Katie?"

"I rode around on Barney with Brian."

"We're going to have to buy another kid horse," Cam said, grinning at Annie.

Peg stood in the middle of the barn aisle, worried. Annie linked arms with her and led her outside, calling over her shoulder, "You guys can take care of the horses without us."

"Why was Julie here?" Peg asked. "Did something happen to Charlie?" Please, please, she prayed to no one.

Annie's voice shook a little. "Charlie was killed by a stray bullet."

"No!" Peg said as if that could change the fact. She dropped Julie's card when Annie tried to give it to her.

"Call her, Peg." Annie picked up the piece of paper and put it in Peg's pocket. "I'm so sorry. Do you want me to come with you?" But Peg pulled away and headed for the garage.

"No, Annie, not right now. Thanks." The cat waited at the top of the stairs, meowing for food. She picked him up and buried her face in his fur, but he squirmed and jumped to the floor where he wound himself around her legs. She fed him and went around the apartment, opening windows. Annie was still standing in the driveway, looking up at her apartment. She waved and Annie turned away.

She paced for a while, then sat down and stared out the window. The cat jumped into her lap. Squirming at the pain that wouldn't leave her alone, she got up suddenly. The cat emitted an indignant meow from the floor. "Sorry, Gato. I can't sit. I'll be back."

Walking out to the field where Cosmo and Red still grazed, she scratched Cosmo's withers until he wiggled his nose in pleasure. It almost made her smile. She hadn't told Charlie and now she wished she had. In fact, she hadn't told anyone. When she raised her face from the horse's warm body, she met Annie's worried gaze. "You don't have to follow me around, Annie. I'll be all right."

"Hey, you think I don't know?"

What did she know? That she was pregnant? That the baby was Charlie's child? That she still loved Julie? Afraid to ask, she assessed Annie's dark eyes for hints.

"Your mother knows, too."

"If you know so much, why haven't either of you said anything?"

"Because you haven't."

She nodded, her face burning. "There's no privacy around here." She walked hurriedly back toward the garage, arms crossed, eyes on the ground. It wouldn't do to fall. What a dope she was to think she could fool Annie or her mother. Of course they knew. She was thicker around the middle. She walked differently. Even her face looked fuller, rosier.

When Annie caught up with her by the gate, she said, "Will you call Julie and ask her when and where the funeral is going to be?"

"You call her for me. I can't."

"Why can't you?" Annie tried to catch her gaze, but she turned away.

She slept little all week and went to school tired and short-tempered. The kids seemed to sense her mood and were quiet and well-behaved. On Friday it rained all day, darkening her outlook even further. She sat at her desk, imagining Charlie's death, picturing him running and falling. Was it friendly fire that had killed him? One of her students brought her out of her black thoughts.

She'd set them to writing sentences using their most recent vocabulary. "You don't have to use the pronoun I with a verb? Right? You can say *voy* instead of *yo voy*?"

"Yes, but if it's she goes, then you have to use *ella va*, to differentiate between the female and male. When you're all finished, we'll read aloud your sentences." That helped them with pronunciation as well as grammar.

At the end of the day she went home and crashed. She knew now why she was so tired and hungry. She'd taken the over-the-counter pregnancy test twice in July and gone to a gynecologist. In her letters to Charlie, she'd started to tell him that he was going to be a father and then deleted it. Now he would never know. She cried a lot, like now, which annoyed the hell out of her.

Startled in mid-sob by the phone, she let the answering machine kick in. Julie sounded as if she were in the same room. "Hey, Peg. I have to talk to you. Will you give me a call at—"

She picked up the receiver. "Hi."

"You're there!" Peg had ignored the two previous messages.

"Yep." A silence followed and she thought of the long letter she added to every day. "Tell me about Charlie."

"All I know is he was struck by a stray bullet. Could have been ours. Could have been a sniper. Are you going to the funeral?" She heard Julie draw a deep breath. "I thought you could drive here and we could go the rest of the way together."

"With you and Joe?"

"No. Joe will fly in from Washington and rent a car. He's from Rockford too."

"I can't. I'm sorry."

"Oh." In that expelled breath she heard Julie's disappointment. "I know it's hard. I just think we three should be there. Charlie would expect us."

"Well, he won't know if we're there, will he?" She angrily choked back tears. She wasn't about to show up obviously pregnant and cry her way through the ceremony.

"This goddamn fucking stupid war has just taken one of my best friends. The least I can do is go to his funeral. Didn't you love Charlie, Peg?"

She was crying now, of course. "I can't talk about him right now." She hung up and went to the computer, adding to the letter.

I loved Charlie too, Julie. He was a talented man, another life thrown away in this fruitless war. He's also the father of my child and I never told him.

~

Friday Annie drove in behind Peg. They got out of their vehicles at the same time and Annie called over the roof of her car, "We're going on a trip tomorrow."

"Where?" Peg asked.

"To Charlie's funeral. You can sit in the back of the church and hide behind a tree in the cemetery, but you're going."

"You're going to make me?" she scoffed.

"If Cam has to tie you up and put you in the car, you're going. You have to do this, Peg." Annie's hair blew across her face, and she squinted in the sun, unaware of her kids barreling toward her. The dog caught up with them and all three hit Annie at the same time. There wasn't enough of her to fend off the weight. She fell into the car.

Peg laughed. Would her child greet her like this? The dog was jumping around her now. "Rounder, stay down." She didn't want her clothes covered with paw prints. "I'm going to change," she said to no one in particular and escaped up the steps to her garage apartment.

Curled into an orange ball, El Gato looked up from the sofa, his eyes half shut. No enthusiastic greeting from him. He jumped down and strolled over to twine around her legs, probably looking for food. She gathered him up. "I can't do this," she said into his fur. His loud purring reverberated against her.

The next morning she struggled into a skirt and blouse, hoping the jacket would cover her growing belly. Annie was waiting next to her Taurus wagon with Peg's mother.

"Are you going too, Mom?" she asked, knowing the answer was no. Her mother wore jeans and a sweatshirt. Except for her rapidly graying hair, she looked about the same as she had ten years ago.

"I wanted to say good-bye. I feel badly about Charlie. Tell Julie I'm sorry I missed her. She's welcome anytime."

Peg smiled wryly and hugged her mom. "You're so subtle, Mom."

"What does that mean? I always liked Julie."

"You used to like Sophie, too," she said.

"I did at first." Her mom pushed Peg's hair back and gave them both a hug. "Drive safe."

Annie drove west to Interstate 51 where she turned south toward Illinois. Peg put her seat back and tried to sleep. A disturbing mix of excitement and angst churned in her stomach. "I think I'm going to be sick," she said. Annie pulled over to the side of the road next to a field where sandhill cranes were gathering for migration. Some raised their long necks and watched warily as she retched a few times and got back in the car. A sickly pale version of herself looked back at her from the visor mirror.

"Get a hold of yourself, sister-in-law. You've hidden long enough." Annie was fond of calling her "sister-in-law."

"They're all going to know. I look like a dough ball."

Annie laughed so hard that Peg joined in. "*I* don't even know for sure. You haven't told anyone. Was Charlie the father?"

The "was" started her crying.

"Well, now you're really going to look terrific—red-eyed and doughy. It's all about attitude, Peg. Raise your head. Look proud. Quit sniveling."

Insulted, Peg laughed anyway at the "terrific" comment. She opened the window and the wind mopped her face. The day was warm and sunny. "Where do you get off talking to me that way?"

"I had to call Julie and get the details of Charlie's funeral. Why won't you talk to her?"

"I told her I couldn't go and now you're making a liar out of me."

"Is it because you're . . ." She gestured at Peg's middle.

"Pregnant?" she finished. "Yes, no, I don't know. Let's not talk about it. Okay?"

After a silence, Peg said, "You were so brilliant, Annie. Are you really happy? I mean, you probably could have taught at UW Madison. You used to talk about doing just that. Going to a big-name university."

"I've got everything—a job I like, a husband I love, wonderful kids and a home of my own and relatives close by."

"Oh yeah, lucky you, living right next door to your in-laws."

"Built-in babysitters. Hey, I love your parents. They never interfere."

"Wouldn't you rather live next to your own?"

"No. They do interfere." She threw Peg a look. "You know that Julie is divorced, don't you?"

"Yep."

"Wouldn't you like to . . ."

"You're just like Mom. What makes you think Julie is interested?"

"She loved you, Peg."

"I thought so, too, but then she married Joe."

"How can you hold that against her? Did you get pregnant on your own?"

"I didn't marry anybody."

"Well, maybe you would have."

"No and neither would he, not me anyway." She looked out the window again.

They'd copied directions to the church off Mapquest's Web site. An organ's rich tones swelled from the open doors, growing louder as they walked through the foyer and into the sanctuary. Peg recognized "Nearer my God to Thee." She straightened her spine and smiled at the couple that slid over to make room for her and Annie in the back row.

Julie took her seat next to Joe in the second row. She had looked for Peg right up till the service started. Charlie's family filled the first pew. She had met them on trips home with Joe, whose parents sat beside him. Earlier, Charlie's mother had asked if Peg was here, said she'd always wanted to meet her because Charlie talked so much about her. Julie had blinked and shook her head.

Joe took the podium after the Methodist minister finished speaking. She twisted her fingers, trying hard to cry quietly when she wanted to howl. Forcing herself to raise her eyes to Joe, she saw him focusing somewhere else in the crowded church. Andrea, she thought a little bitterly. She must be there, offering him support. But then his gaze fell on her and stayed.

He talked about his and Charlie's friendship, which had begun in grade school. He told of how in high school Charlie already knew he wanted to write books. Expanding on that, he talked about Charlie's novel and his bravery as a journalist. He said that Charlie despised the war that took his life. "We will never read the books that died with Charlie. His death is our loss."

As he talked, she saw how angry he was, how embittered, and hoped he used his rage to help stop the fighting that was taking so many lives, not just Charlie's.

When they exited the church into the bright sunlight, she shaded her eyes and looked at the vehicles in the funeral procession. In the car she took Joe's fist in her hand. Reaching out wasn't easy for her, not only because they were no longer a couple, but also because it let someone slip past her protective shield.

He glanced at her. "Peg is here with Annie. I saw them in the back of the church."

Her heart expanded and she put his hand in her lap. "I wonder if they'll come to the cemetery."

"Don't know," he said. "I asked Andrea not to come period."

The funeral car started to move. They followed, fourth in line with two policemen on motorcycles leading. "Your eulogy was moving," she said, choking back tears.

He shrugged. "Charlie made it easy. There were so many good things to say."

"Yes." She looked out the passenger window at the passing houses. When they reached the cemetery and stepped outside, she thought it was much too nice a day to be buried and chewed on her lower lip to keep from crying.

Joe escorted her to one of the chairs set up in front of the open grave and she said, "Did he ask to be buried?" She wanted to be cremated and sprinkled somewhere nice, like a field or woods or lake.

"What difference does it make?" Joe muttered. "He's dead."

People were walking across the grass toward the grave from all directions. She said, "I'm going to stand." She didn't want Peg and Annie to slip away unseen if they were here.

"Good idea. Give the old folks the chairs."

The minister said a few more words, which Julie heard but didn't hear. They all recited the Lord's Prayer and the minister invited everyone to join the family in the church basement for a luncheon. People began to gather in small groups. Julie's heels sank into the earth and she pulled them out one at a time while looking around.

Joe was leading Peg and Annie her way. When had he left her side? Her heart lurched into overtime as she watched their approach. Peg's short coat flapped open and Julie tried not to stare. Joe might not have noticed, but any woman who had ever had a child would. Was that why Peg refused to answer her messages?

"Hey, Annie," she said softly when Joe steered Peg toward Charlie's parents, leaving Annie with Julie. "Thanks for coming."

"I wouldn't have missed it. How are you?"

"I've been better. I depended on Charlie's friendship to get me through the bad times. It's hard for all of us." Her eyes followed Peg as Joe introduced her to Charlie's parents.

Annie took her hand and Julie blinked back tears. "At least you and Joe get along. It could be worse."

"It could always be worse. How is she?"

"Why don't you ask her? She's having a difficult time with this."

"She's pregnant." Surely Annie knew.

"Yes. She doesn't volunteer much information. She hasn't said who the father is."

"Charlie?" Julie asked.

"Probably. The timing is right."

"She won't talk to me." How long does it take to get over someone and why can't they at least be friends, she wondered, fighting a sudden urge to sit down and bawl. "Are you going back to the church?"

"Yes. Are you and Joe?"

"I will if you do. Joe has a plane to catch. God, Annie, whoever thought things would end up like this?"

"It's not the end, Julie."

"No, of course not. We all go our separate ways."

"Hey, it's never over till the last horse show."

Julie laughed, an incongruous sound. "Is that an Annieism?"

Annie smiled. "Charlie would want us to mourn him with beer and marijuana. Have you got any?"

She squelched another laugh. "I wish I did. I'd open a beer and light up right now, but he's the one who always brought the stuff." She saw Joe and Peg heading their way. "Oh, God." Why was she so nervous?

"It's only Peg and Joe. Cool it."

"Hi, Peg," she said softly when Peg was near enough to hear.

"Hey," Peg answered, her eyes darting to Annie.

Julie wanted to put her hands on Peg's cheeks and make her focus on her alone. "Annie said you're going to the church."

"Right," Annie said.

"I've got a plane to catch," Joe broke in. "Why don't you ride back to the church with Peg and Annie, Julie?" He kissed each of them on the cheek and winked. "What does a fellow have to do to hook his ex-wife up with her ex?"

Only Annie laughed. "That's either very gauche or very cool, Joe."

"You have to be a good loser if you're a politician. Fight like hell and then wish the winner luck."

Yeah, right, Julie thought. Who cheated on whom? It wasn't she. She walked with Annie and Peg to Annie's car. They followed the other vehicles out of the cemetery.

Peg said nothing at first. Annie effortlessly filled in the gaps in the conversation. She answered Julie's questions about Cam and the kids and asked Julie about Peggy. The divorce had been difficult for Peggy, Julie replied.

At a stoplight, Julie took a deep breath and said, "It would be nice if we could talk, even if it's only by e-mail, Peg. You haven't answered my messages. Did you get them?"

Peg looked into the rearview mirror, meeting Julie's eyes. "I've been writing back. I just haven't sent anything yet. It's kind of long and unfinished."

"I'd love to read it," she said, holding Peg's gaze in the mirror as hope swelled inside her.

X

"All right. I'll send it," Peg said and was immediately sorry. She'd edit the letter first, cut some things out.

"As is. Okay?" Julie persisted as if she read Peg's mind.

She nodded, looking away from the mirror, knowing she wouldn't.

In the basement of the church, cool and artificially lit, they filled plates at the banquet tables in front of the kitchen opening. Casseroles and green beans and coleslaw and cold salads and desserts made by the women of the church, some of whom must have known Charlie or Charlie's parents. When meeting Charlie's mom and dad, Peg had felt guilty for keeping the paternity of her child to herself.

She'd woken every night since hearing the news, disbelieving Charlie's death. It felt as if they'd met at the bookstore just days ago. The time she'd spent with him had seemed impossibly short to turn her life upside down as it had. Soon she'd have to talk about it to someone besides her gynecologist. When she started Lamaze classes, she would ask Annie to go with her. Before that, though, she'd do what she should have done a long time ago—discuss this with her parents. However, her greatest regret was not telling Charlie. She thought it might have made his last days happy ones.

They took their filled plates to a table with other people. Peg immediately forgot the names of those who introduced themselves. One woman around her mother's age asked if they'd gone to school with Charlie.

"Yes, he was one of our best friends. Have you read his book?" Julie asked.

"It's a best seller in this congregation," the woman replied.

"That's great." Julie turned to Peg and Annie. "What did you think of the book?"

"I recognized a few people," Annie said dryly, "but that only made it more interesting."

Peg said, "I loved it. I've read it twice."

"I have too," Julie put in, "and you're right, Annie."

Julie lifted one eyebrow and Peg's guard fell further. The familiar expression squeezed her heart into a fist. She'd told herself she liked being free of commitments. She was so glad to be rid of Sophie that sometimes she felt guilty.

If anything, maturity had made Julie more beautiful. She cupped her chin in her hand and smiled sweetly at Peg, who began to smile back, unable to resist the tug as Julie reeled her back in.

When they parted in the church lot, Julie reminded her. "Don't forget to send me the e-mail, Peg."

Clouds had gathered and a breeze kicked up debris on the ground. Peg held her hair back, taking one more look at Julie, wondering if the baby would fill the spot that Julie had vacated. "I will."

"Tonight."

"Or tomorrow."

"Tonight. Let's get together soon. I want to meet Kate and Brian, and I'd love for you to know Peggy."

"Just say when and we'll be there. Right, Peg?" Annie said.

"Right." Peg caught her upper lip between her teeth.

The drive home seemed long, partly because rain began to fall shortly after they left and partly because they had to stop twice for her to pee. She had barely made it through the funeral, hurrying to the bathroom in the church basement and going again before they left. The last fifty miles she slept, exhausted by emotion. When they got home, she said a quick good-bye, thanks for the ride and galloped up the stairs to her bathroom.

Sinking into the computer chair, she read her long letter to Julie. Editing it took her the entire evening. When she finished, she attached it to e-mail and sent it. Then she went to bed and lay awake worrying about what Julie would think.

She woke up in the morning to knocking. "It's me. Can I come in?"

"You don't have to ask, Mom. I'm still in bed, though."

"I think I'd stay there if I were you. It's cool and cloudy." Her mother took a seat in the only comfortable chair.

"Did Cam go to a show?"

"Yep. Brian went with him. Annie and Katie stayed home. Annie said yesterday was difficult for you."

"It was." A feeling of loss nagged her. She and Julie and Joe and Charlie had once been a foursome. Now they were three and split apart.

"Are you okay?"

"Oh, Mom," she blubbered, "I'm pregnant with Charlie's baby."

"I know," her mother said, moving to the bed and gathering

Peg in. "I'm so sorry about Charlie, but I'm thrilled about the baby."

The words stopped Peg's tears. She drew back to look at her mother. "You are?"

"Oh, yes. You're my daughter." As if that explained anything.

"You already have two grandkids, and I'm not going to marry anyone."

"I know." Her mother's eyes gleamed.

"What does Dad say?"

"He says if you're happy, he is."

"And what if I'm not?"

"Of course you're not. Charlie just died." Her mother ran a hand up and down Peg's arm and smoothed her hair back. "It will take time."

"I know, Mom." She picked at the quilt and felt cool air seeping through the window behind the bed. "I'm just so tired all the time, and this baby surprised me. One night. That's all it was."

"That's all it takes." Her mother's smile grew until she responded.

"I'm sorry I didn't say anything earlier. I didn't really tell anyone. You're the first."

Her mom laughed. "I think we all knew. It's hard to hide."

When her mother left, she went to the computer and logged on. A jolt traveled all the way to her toes when she saw an e-mail from Julie. Opening it, she read. *I loved your letter. I talk to you daily too. I just wish I'd written my conversations down. I'm coming next Saturday unless you tell me not to.*

She reread parts of her own letter over, the one she'd sent to Julie, skipping paragraphs and entire pages that chronicled her daily observations and actions, picking out bits and pieces to see what Julie had seen.

I've drifted through life. Maybe most people do. Not you and Joe and Charlie and Annie and Cam and Sophie, though. You all realized your ambitions. I became a teacher by default and joined the Peace

Corps because it was something you wanted to do years ago. Does that make any sense? You were in your first year of graduate school. I felt displaced that year, but I loved parts of Costa Rica—the ocean and rain forests and national preserves and the people. I'd like to go back again for a week or ten days, but not alone.

This baby took me unaware. I never expected to have a child. I haven't told anyone yet—as if I could make it go away, as if I wanted to, as if everyone doesn't know. Did you fall asleep at every chance when you were pregnant? The baby moves now. I think I won't ask the sex. What difference does it make? It is what it is.

Have I ever told you about Sophie? What Sophie wants, she usually gets. For some reason, she targeted me. Her pure soprano voice caught me in its web. I thought anyone who sang so beautifully must be beautiful inside. I think in the end I was afraid to trigger her anger. Is anyone what she/he seems to be? Sophie was my mistake, as I was hers.

The last paragraph read:

When you married Joe, I thought I let you go for good. Tomorrow Annie says we're going to Charlie's funeral. If I seem distant, it's for protection. I should have learned to stay away from straight girls when my best friend Cassie married right out of high school, and you were assigned to take her place as my roommate. By the way, I see her often. She works in a store, checking out groceries. We say hi and bye. You'd never guess we once talked for hours. I wonder if that's how it would be with us. Would we have anything to say to each other? You almost convinced me we were real. Maybe you almost convinced yourself. Remember Murray Street?

The letter ended there, all twenty plus pages. If Julie read it in its entirety, her eyes probably crossed. Embarrassed that she'd sent this compilation of mind-numbing events and ruminations, she shot back an apology.

Sorry. You must have been bored stiff. I'll be here next Saturday. If her response seemed a little cryptic, she'd poured her heart out in the letter. Maybe they could be friends again. Could she? Feeling about Julie as she did? She gave a mental shrug.

Later that day, she asked Annie if she'd kept any maternity clothes. She'd noticed that pregnant women seemed to carry their unborn babies out front like announcements. The students made her conscious of her condition. Sometimes she caught one of them staring at her belly and wanted to say, "Do you mind?"

Annie hauled out a few outfits tucked away in her closet. "I don't intend to have any more kids. I must have been thinking of you when I kept them."

"Oh, sure. You were as surprised as I was. Admit it." She held up a green outfit, slacks with elastic and a jacket. "This is great," she said as Annie brought out more pants and tops and placed them on the queen size bed.

"I was teaching part of the time when I was pregnant. I waddled around the classroom like a goose."

Peg laughed. "That's a good description of how I feel." She added as if an afterthought, "Julie and Peggy are coming to visit next weekend, or so she said in an e-mail."

"That's great, Peg. How did this come about?"

"I sent her the letter I've been writing ever since I saw Charlie." She pushed the clothes out of the way and sat down. "Charlie is fading already, and I feel terrible about that. They only buried him Saturday."

"And how often did you see him in these past eight years?"

"Once. This is the first I've seen Julie in as many years, but I never was able to get her completely out of my head."

"Charlie brought the two of you together again."

"We're not together, but maybe we can be friends."

"I couldn't be Cam's friend if we separated." Annie sat down next to her. "How about a fashion show?"

Annie clapped as she tried on the clothes. Katie came to the

169

door and jumped onto the bed. "Is that really a baby inside you, Aunt Peg?"

Annie raised her eyebrows, waiting for Peg's answer.

"Yes, sweetie. You're going to have a cousin."

"How does it get in there?"

"Your mother can explain that better than I can."

"The baby grows inside till it's big enough to live on its own, then it comes out," Annie said.

"How?" Kate looked wide-eyed.

"It comes out the birth canal."

"Where is that?"

"Between your legs."

"Where you pee? It's not big enough."

"It gets big enough."

"I don't want a baby. It would hurt terrible."

"Well, you're not going to have one till you're all grown up." Annie hugged her daughter.

"Those are funny pants," Kate said as Peg pulled on another pair. "They have a pouch like a kangaroo."

Peg wore the green pantsuit to work on Monday. It made her look less pregnant. Others might not even guess if they hadn't seen her before in her regular clothes. As she poured herself a cup of decaf in the lounge, the history teacher told her how nice she looked in the green outfit. No more liquor, no more caffeine. She missed the liquor more.

"Thanks." She seldom talked to her coworkers anymore, not even Kathy whose room was across the hall from hers. When she had a few spare minutes, she spent them in her classroom, cat-napping or grading papers.

"Are the kids giving you a hard time?" Kathy asked.

Peg blushed. "Why would they?"

"They're tactless and insensitive at this age."

"Insensitive, yes, but not necessarily tactless. They don't want to incur my wrath." She could play god with a student's grade, although she never would. She thought the kids were more curious than anything and she imagined their questions. Like why wasn't she Mrs. instead of Ms.? Was she really a lesbian? Maybe not since she was obviously pregnant.

Kathy nodded and washed her cup at the small sink. "Any time you need someone to talk to, I'll be glad to listen. I was in the same boat a few years ago. I felt like the elephant in the room."

Peg laughed at the image this projected, but she knew Kathy was married. "Thanks. There is one kid, Jonathon Wall, who snickers behind my back. You know him?"

"Oh yes. But he'd do that no matter what. He's the class comic who isn't really funny. A bunch of us are going out for fish on Friday. Want to come?"

The physical education teacher had already invited her. She guessed he had a crush on her, which she wanted to discourage without hurting his feelings. "I can't. Maybe next time."

The bell rang and Peg headed toward her classroom as the halls filled with kids, talking, laughing, shoving. She tried to stay out of their way but got bumped a few times anyway.

"Oops. Sorry, Ms. Kincaid," Michelle Peterson said. The girl was one of her best students. She hurried through the halls with her head down as if to avoid attention.

"What's the rush?"

The girl looked alarmed. "I wanted to go over some stuff before class." Michelle sped forward, books clenched to her chest, leaving Peg behind.

No teenager wants to appear chummy with a teacher. Peg understood that. Good grades alone made Michelle a butt of jokes by those less studious. The Wall boy sat next to her and farted, then held his nose and pointed at her. Peg moved Jon across the room where he did the same thing to another hapless girl. It sent the guys into hysterical snorting. She figured Wall's comedic attempts made him acceptable, like the court jester.

Once she had tried to talk to him but quickly realized from his furtive glances that he didn't want to be seen with her. Had she worried so much about what the other kids thought in high school? Her niche had been her friendship with Cassie. She and Tanya and Louise had been attendants to the queen. If the kids only realized this too would pass.

Michelle sat at her desk writing. Probably the sentences Peg had assigned the class.

"You work hard, Michelle," Peg said, wanting to sound encouraging.

Michelle looked alarmed at the acknowledgement as the room began to fill. How to reach one of these kids? It was like they were in different camps. She'd almost forgotten high school and its cliques before she started to teach. As a student, she had been friendly with a high school English teacher, Ms. Liston, whom the kids nicknamed Les, short for lesbian. She probably was a lesbian, Peg realized now, but she'd been a dynamite teacher. Peg had dared to stay after class to talk to her and had met the jibes of the jocks. "Is Liston a piston, Kincaid? She ask you out?" She'd denied the accusation, ducking her head and blushing furiously. She briefly wondered where Ms. Liston was now.

The week crawled by, her anticipation getting the best of her even as she fought it. Don't expect too much. Pieces of her letter to Julie crept into her mind at night, and she cringed at the intimacy of the written word. Don't care too much, she warned herself.

Friday after work she helped Cam get ready for a show, loading the trailer while he and Brian washed Dom and Barney. Clouds swept across the sky in front of a cool wind. Asters bloomed along the fence line. She paused to watch Cosmo and Red grazing on the pasture, moving in lockstep. Ginny Carver pulled up in an old Escort.

"Hi, Peg." Ginny had graduated from UWO in the spring

and was working as an assistant loan officer at a bank. Still horse crazy and finally able to purchase her own horse, Cam had found her a gray gelding in her price range. Cam took the horse to shows where Ginny rode the gelding in amateur classes, and he showed it in senior western pleasure. Ginny and Brian had taken Peg's place as Cam's right-hand people.

Someday maybe she would buy another horse and get back into the game, but right now she was taking a break. It seemed like work—all the effort that went into preparing a horse and its accoutrements to be competitive in the show ring. Even though she knew her place at Cam's side had been usurped, she didn't mind. She wanted to be outside with Rounder and Katie for company. Not to have any plans for Friday night no longer seemed pathetic. Instead, it was a chance to read with Gato in her lap.

Katie carried the show bridles and halters. Peg had to catch the reins and leads to keep them off the ground. "I'm staying home to meet Peggy," Katie told Ginny, who was carrying her saddle to the trailer.

"And who is this other Peggy?"

"She's my age and she's coming to visit Saturday. Right, Aunt Peg?"

"Right. She's the daughter of an old friend."

"So you're not going to the horse show?"

"Nope. We're staying home, aren't we, Katie?"

"Yep."

Peg held the trailer door open and gave Kate a boost inside the close quarters. A wave of nostalgia swept over her. She longed to be a kid again going somewhere with Cosmo. Only briefly, though. Julie was coming the next day. If it turned out all right, she might ask her to stay the night. No horse show could top that.

Night fell quickly now, the sun taking the heat with it as it sank behind the trees. Annie called the kids to supper. Cam would leave the barn when he was ready. Gato greeted her at the door, rubbing against her jeans, his body vibrating with purrs. "Hi, hair ball. You're hungry, aren't you?"

Noticing the telephone flashing when she filled the cat's bowl, she walked slowly toward it, knowing it would be Julie with some excuse about why she couldn't come. Maybe they'd hurt each other so much that neither was willing to risk the pain again.

"Hey, it's me, Julie. Peggy came home from daycare sick. Oops. She's retching again. I'll call back when she goes to sleep." A loud sound followed as if the receiver fell.

Well, she'd expected something like this to happen all week and now it had. She felt sick herself. Ignoring the mound of papers waiting to be graded, she made herself eat a sandwich and drink a glass of milk while reading a book Annie had given her. When the phone rang, she had moved to the chair nearby and Gato lay in her lap. She and the cat started at the sudden sound.

She barked a "Hello."

"It's me again. Peggy is finally asleep. She threw up until there was nothing left but bile. I'm so disappointed, Peg. I'd ask you to come here, but you might get sick and I might spend all day holding Peggy's head."

"It's okay. I've got plenty to keep me busy."

"I wanted to come, though. Can we do this next Saturday?"

Peg got up, dumping the meowing cat on the floor, and paged through her appointment book. "Next Saturday looks okay." Did she have no life?

"Oh, wait. I've got a conference that weekend."

A pause on Peg's end while she remembered how they'd tried and failed to keep a long distance relationship going.

"Hey, screw the conference. I'll cancel."

"You don't have to do that."

"I want to. Tell me what you were doing when I called."

"Reading."

"I was afraid you'd be out or have friends over and I wouldn't get to talk to you."

"Nope. The cat and I are home alone. Katie will be disappointed. She was looking forward to meeting Peggy."

"Tell her Peggy is just as disappointed. She was wild to see the horses."

"Next time." It was odd that she had so much to say via e-mail and so little on the phone.

"Peg? Do you really want me to come? Your letter made me think you do, but I'm not so sure when I talk to you."

She took a deep breath before answering. "I do. Too much, but not unless you really want to."

"Of course I want to. I miss you."

"As a friend?" Peg asked, embarrassed, but she had to know.

"Much more than a friend," Julie said with a little laugh.

"Why did you marry Joe?" She sucked in air and waited through the short pause that followed.

"Because I wasn't brave enough to be a lesbian? Because I wanted to have a child someday?"

"I'm having a child."

Julie sounded tired. "Look, Peg, can we talk about this when I see you? If Peggy is better tomorrow, I'll pack her up and come. I'll call in the morning."

Chastised, she said, "Don't move her if she's sick. I waited eight years. I can wait another week."

"Well, I don't know if I can."

When Julie hung up, she sat by her daughter's side and read until she was sure Peggy was not going to barf again. Gathering the girl in her arms she carried her to her bedroom, which had been the guest room until she and Joe separated. Placing Peggy carefully on the double bed, she changed into a T-shirt and slid in next to her.

She'd be glad when the house sold. The feeling of impermanency unsettled her. Joe had taken some of the furniture, which was good because no condominium was big enough to hold it all. The realtor had shown her several condos. When she walked through a place, she pictured her belongings in it and tried to imagine living there. She wanted a condo near a park and a school, one that welcomed kids.

An open house was scheduled for her home Sunday. She and Peggy would have to go elsewhere. Sending a hopeful thought for her child's quick recovery, she fell asleep. Around two in the morning she awoke and put a hand on Peggy's forehead. Cool. Maybe she had eaten something at daycare that made her sick. Perhaps she would be all right in the morning. Kids were resilient. The remainder of the night she slept restlessly, waking every hour or two. At first light, she got up. Peggy slept on. Her skin still felt normal.

Going downstairs, she started coffee and read the paper. Every day it told of more deaths in Iraq. Each loss of life infuriated her all over again. Charlie had put a personal face to the war. She read all the news, even the obituaries. When the phone rang, she jumped for it.

"Hi sweetie," her mom said. "Your dad and I were wondering when we were going to see you again."

"I should have called. I've been busy and I know you are." She appreciated her parents now that she was a parent herself.

"Any bites on the house?" her dad asked from another phone.

"Not yet. There's an open house tomorrow afternoon. I haven't found a place to move to yet anyway. How are you two? I miss you." After chatting a while, she put Peggy on the phone.

As she left the room, she heard her daughter telling her grandparents how she'd barfed and barfed last night. When Peggy hung up, they showered and ate.

"When are we leaving?" Peggy asked, slurping her cereal.

"Get your nose out of the bowl and stop smacking. If you feel good enough to go, I'll call Peg and make some sandwiches for lunch."

"I'm okay, Mama. I want peanut butter and jelly."

"What's the magic word?"

"Please."

"Want to make your own sandwich?"

"No. I have to get Magic." Black Magic was a stuffed horse that Joe had given her a year ago.

Julie put in Peg's number and waited for her to pick up. "Hey, it's me, Julie. We can leave within a half hour. Will you be there?"

"I'll be here. Want my cell number? By the way, I'd know your voice anywhere, Julie. You don't have to identify yourself."

"Same here. I'll give you my number too."

The familiar drive somehow seemed longer. Some trees were beginning to turn. In a few days it would be October. She hated the thought of winter, the cold and slippery roads that sometimes made travel impossible. When she turned into Peg's driveway, a humming in her ears shut out Peggy's running commentary and incessant questions. Parking near the garage, she sat in the Acura for a moment until Peggy got her attention.

"Mama, I want to get out." She'd managed to unfasten the seatbelt and climb out of her booster seat and was struggling with the door.

Julie pressed the unlock button and Peggy's door opened. Getting out herself, she picked her daughter up off the gravel and set her on her feet. Peggy grabbed her hand and pulled her toward the barn.

"Wait. We have to find someone to go with us. This isn't our place."

A little girl about Peggy's size ran toward them, followed by Annie. Peg's mom and dad emerged from their house. Peggy leaned against her mother, suddenly shy.

"How good to see you again," Julie said to Peg's mom and

dad.

They greeted her with a hug, saying she shouldn't be such a stranger. Out of the corner of her eye, she spied the dog barreling toward them. Shielding Peggy in front of her, she braced herself, but Annie grabbed Rounder by the collar and hung on.

Annie stooped to Peggy's level and introduced everyone, including Rounder. Peg's mom and dad solemnly shook Peggy's hand, and Annie pushed Katie forward. "You girls want to go to the barn?"

"How about a cookie first?" Peg's mom asked. She had them in her pocket.

Kate held hers with both hands as Rounder snatched Peggy's away.

"Bad dog," Katie said.

Peggy and Julie looked surprised, and then Peggy jumped up and down and laughed. "He likes cookies too," she said, turning to her mom.

"I guessed that might happen." Peg's mom took another cookie out of her pocket.

"Come on," Annie said. "Peg's in the barn, cleaning stalls." She linked arms with Julie.

"Thanks." Julie smiled at Peg's mom. "I think Peggy's forgotten her manners." The girls and dog ran toward the barn.

"See you at lunchtime," Peg's mom said.

Julie leaned into Annie, warmed by the welcome. Their daughters disappeared into the barn and reappeared with Peg.

Katie pulled on Peg's hand. "We wanna ride, Aunt Peg."

Peg put an arm around her niece. "You will. Who is this with you?"

"It's Peggy."

"Hi, Peggy." Peg touched the girl's shoulder.

"Hey," Julie said, taking Peg in with her eyes, noticing she wore sweats, realizing she probably could no longer zip her jeans.

"Hi. The kids want to ride the horses. Is that okay with you moms?"

"Well, I don't know," Annie teased.

"Come on, Mama," Katie said.

"Is this the Peg Daddy said I could meet someday?" Peggy asked.

"Yep," Julie replied, smiling at Peg. "You're named after her."

But Peggy wanted to ride a horse more than she wanted to know why she was named after someone. She followed as Kate dragged Peg into the cool barn.

Seeing her on Cosmo's wide back caused Julie to remember the first time she rode the horse. Peg walked beside Cosmo, holding the lead attached to the halter. Kate bounced around at a trot on Red. The horses' backs sagged with age.

"Katie won't fall off, will she?" Julie asked Annie who leaned on the fence beside her.

"It wouldn't be the first time. She can't sit Red's trot." Annie raised her voice. "Make him walk, Kate." Red put his head on Cosmo's backside as he slowed to a walk. "I don't know why horses have to be right on top of each other."

"It feels good to be here again. I wasn't sure anyone would want to see me."

"Oh, Julie. We all love you."

"Bullshit, Annie. I hurt Peg, and you all love her a lot more."

"You broke her heart when you married Joe. Why can't the two of you get past that?"

"I don't think she trusts me. I was in my denial stage, Annie. I thought I should try the acceptable way. Marry. Have kids. It's hard to say it was a mistake because otherwise Peggy wouldn't be here. Besides, I didn't see Peg trying to make anything work between us. It's difficult to explain." She gave up trying.

"Well, at least you're here at last. Katie, get Red's nose off Cosmo's rump," she yelled.

"She doesn't have much control," Peg called back. "It's okay.

She's not in a walk-trot class."

"Why don't you stay the night?" Annie asked.

A cool breeze swirled around them, competing with the warm sun. It carried the smells of earth and dry leaves and acorns. The dusty, nutty odors of fall.

"I haven't been asked."

"I just invited you. Cam and Brian are staying overnight in the horse trailer. It's a two-day show."

"We'll see how the day goes, but I didn't bring any extra clothes."

"I can find some for both of you."

As soon as Peg swung the girls off the horses, Annie herded them away. Julie watched Kate and Peggy run, little heels nearly kicking their tiny butts, long hair streaming—dark brown and blond. Tongue lolling, the dog ran circles around them. She smiled to herself and went into the barn where Peg was pulling the saddle off Cosmo.

"Can I help?" she asked.

"There's nothing to do really. We'll put them in stalls. The girls might want to ride again." Peg carried the saddle into the tack room.

When she came out, Julie said, "Peg, look at me."

"In a minute." Peg unhooked Cosmo and handed Julie his lead rope. "Put him in the nearest stall." Opening the neighboring stall, Peg released Red into it. Shutting the door, she turned and faced Julie. "It's harder than hell to look at you."

"You have such expressive eyes. I think you do want to look at me." She was taking the advice she'd given Sammy. Be gutsy, but her heart banged away. She stuffed her hands in the pockets of her Windbreaker.

"Do you want to ride?" Peg asked with a slight smile, nervously running fingers through her hair.

"Later, maybe. Right now I'd just like to talk to you. Maybe we could walk to the creek. Annie said she'd watch the girls."

180

Peg nodded. "Sure. It's a nice day."

In the pasture, Julie asked, "How are you doing with Charlie's death?"

"Trying not to think about it. How are you dealing with it?"

"It still doesn't seem real. I suppose in time it'll become bearable enough to think about."

"I don't want Charlie to fade away. Goddamn him for going over there," Peg said with sudden anger.

The grieving process, Julie thought. She wondered why she felt only sadness about Charlie and Joe. In a way, she'd lost them both.

They opened the gate at the far end of the pasture and crossed the stream on the log, arms out for balance. The woods on the other side enclosed them. Julie breathed in the odor of the pines.

Peg put her forehead against a tree. Her hands hung at her sides, and although she made no sound, the helplessness of her stance wrenched something inside Julie. She pinned Peg's arms with hers and leaned into her back. "Hey," she said quietly.

"I cry at everything." Peg's voice broke.

"You're pregnant. That's reason enough." Her own tears wet Peg's neck.

They ended up in each other's arms as if by default, comforting one another. When the tears dried up, they hung on, not sure how to let go or what to do next. After what seemed a long time but was probably only minutes, Julie lifted Peg's chin and kissed her on the mouth.

Catching her breath, Peg stepped back. "I can't do this again."

"Sure you can." She tried a smile, but it slipped away. Her heart was trying to escape her chest. It fell, it soared, it jumped around like a rubber ball.

Peg shook her head. "I feel like I was an experiment, that Joe was the real thing."

181

"And how do I change your mind?"

"I think I always thought you were straight."

Julie felt a twinge of annoyance. "You slept with Charlie."

"Only once. We had too much to drink and he was going to Iraq." She frowned. "Do you think it'll affect the baby, our drinking?"

"I doubt it. There'd be a lot of damaged kids out there if it did. You don't drink now, do you?"

"No, and I miss it."

Julie laughed. Although still short of breath, at least her heart had stopped its acrobatics. "Well, I promise not to imbibe in front of you if you'll stop hassling me."

"You're the one who kissed me."

"Yeah and I'd like to do it again. I'd like Peggy to have two mommies."

Peg was trying not to smile. "She's got a daddy and a mommy now."

"Every kid needs two mommies."

Peg laughed. "You always were annoyingly sure of yourself."

Was that the impression she gave? Really? She cocked an eyebrow as if she agreed and then grew serious. "I'm right about us. Look, I never gave Joe what he needed. I held it in reserve for you. He knew that and looked elsewhere."

Peg frowned, her eyes dark. "So he got hurt too."

"Hey, you went to Costa Rica and then you moved in with Sophie. Don't be so damn righteous." She was irritated now. "Didn't you ever want to be like just about everyone else in the world?"

"Not enough to marry some guy."

"Yeah, well, maybe you would have married Charlie."

"No, that wasn't going to happen. Look, I don't want to argue."

"Does that mean I can kiss you?" she asked, although she thought she heard Peggy's voice. "Damn."

182

"They've found us." Peg gestured with her chin as the girls yelled from the other side of the creek.

"I couldn't keep them away any longer." Annie smiled wryly.

"That's okay. Thanks for watching Peggy," Julie said.

During dinner at Peg's parents' Annie again extended the invitation to stay overnight. Being a mother, she had to know that Peggy would make it difficult for Julie to say no.

Later, when the three women were cleaning up, Annie said, "Peggy can sleep with Katie. You've got room for Julie, don't you, Peg?"

Peg's face burned, which Julie found interesting. What embarrassed her? Everyone here knew.

Peg wanted her body not to look as it did now, with no waist, a popped out belly button and swollen breasts. The first time alone with Julie in over eight years and she had to resemble a pear with legs. She mumbled, "Sure," and Annie laughed. Peg elbowed her. "Matchmaker," she whispered in her ear.

Annie laughed so hard she crossed her legs and ran to the john, which caused Peg and Julie to laugh too as if it were contagious.

Julie's hair glowed in the overhead light. She looked like she did the first time Peg saw her. Out of the sun, she hadn't aged at all. Still blond with wide gray eyes, a sensuous mouth and slender body, Peg wondered as before why Julie had chosen her. Maybe that's why she doubted Julie. Perhaps it had nothing to do with Julie and everything to do with her image of herself.

When Annie returned, Peg put down the dishtowel and went into the bathroom to look in the mirror. She brushed her short, curly brown hair, which fell back in place. She looked into her brown eyes and smiled at herself, checking her teeth for bits of food. She was cute, not beautiful by any stretch. She'd had a decent figure, toned by years of riding, but that was gone now.

Outside, the wind died, the air unseasonably warm. Peg walked to the barn, the kids following her like ducklings, the dog running ahead. Annie and Julie stopped to talk with her parents. She was going to turn Cosmo and Red out on pasture. Bouncing off the balls of her feet as if she were a kid again, she felt almost weightless. Julie was staying overnight with her after all these years!

Boosting each girl onto the bare backs of the horses, she told them to grab the manes. Then she took the lead ropes and started toward the pasture gate. Kate's little feet pounded Red's side.

"Giddy-up, old man," she said.

Peggy laughed and did the same with Cosmo who started to trot, causing the little girl to cant sideways. She looked frightened.

Suddenly, Julie was there, shoving Peggy back on the horse and taking Cosmo's lead rope from Peg. "Better not kick him if you don't want him to go, Peggy," Julie said.

Peggy hugged the horse, laying her head on his mane and grasping his neck with both hands. "I want a horse, Mama."

Julie made a face. "Where would we keep a horse?"

"We could move," Peggy said.

"Your mom can bring you here to ride Cosmo," Peg told her.

"Yeah!" Katie yelled. "We'll ride together."

"See what you started," Julie said in a low voice to Peg.

Peg smiled. "I'd say I'm sorry but I'm not." She lifted Kate down and then Peggy and opened the gate. She and Julie walked the horses into the field and took their halters off. Shaking free, the animals thundered off, kicking and farting.

Kate giggled. "They always do that," she said.

The alarm left Peggy's face. "They farted," she shouted and laughed when first one and then the other horse's knees buckled. The animals rolled, stirring up clouds of dust, then struggled to their feet and shook. Peggy pointed at them. "Look, Mama, look."

"I see." Julie took her hand. "They were scratching their backs."

Peggy groped for Kate's hand. "Katie is going to show me her room. Okay, Mama?"

"Sure, go ahead."

That left Peg and Julie standing at the gate, watching the horses graze side-by-side, their bursts of energy gone. "I guess you're staying with me tonight," Peg said.

"You don't sound enthused." Julie's gaze rested on Peg.

"I can hardly believe you're really here." She kept her eyes on the horses.

"Neither can I after all these years." Julie spoke quietly.

The sun was dropping toward the treetops. "Come on, let's go see what's going on."

After Peggy dragged her mother to see Kate's bedroom, Julie went with Peg to her garage apartment. "It's pretty basic," Peg said. "What you see is what there is, but it's big enough for me." She had stuffed the sofa back together that morning. Normally, she left it open and just pulled up the covers. "The sofa opens up."

"Hey, it'll seem like we're back on Murray Street."

Peg took the cushions off and pulled the bed out. "I have to change the sheets."

"No, you don't. I really don't care." Julie put a hand on Peg's arm, and Peg's hair rose under it.

"I have to wash my hands," she said, panicking.

"I do too. After you."

When Julie came out, Peg said, "Can I get you anything? I do keep wine for company."

Julie looked her in the eye and said, "Maybe later," the meaning clear.

A smile tugged at Peg's mouth. "You're so subtle." She locked the door, her heart beating so hard that she got an instant

185

headache. "You're going to be the death of me." She put Julie's hand on her chest. "Feel it? It's gone to my head. Bang, bang, bang."

"Mine too," Julie said, placing Peg's hand on her breast. "We better hurry up before we keel over."

Neither hurried, though. They shut the blinds and came together slowly, kissing, taking pieces of clothing off and dropping them on the floor until they were naked. Peg shivered.

"Under the covers," Julie said, pulling them back.

"It's not the cold. God, how I've missed you."

"Me too. I thought I'd never get you in bed again."

"You haven't yet," Peg whispered into her mouth and Julie walked her backward until her knees buckled and she fell onto the mattress.

Looking down at her, eyes hooded, Julie said, "I have now." She lay next to Peg and ran a hand over her belly. "You look like a piece of fruit."

Suddenly self-conscious, Peg said, "That's a nice observation. Who wants to look like a pear?"

"Ripe, luscious, tasty. What's wrong with that? Come here."

She rolled up against Julie, who tried to fit herself around Peg's belly. Peg laughed softly. "I wish you'd come back sooner."

Julie cupped a breast. "Wow! I like you this way."

"Well, I won't be like this forever. God, I can't wait to snap back in shape. What was it like for you, having Peggy?"

"Let's talk about that later." Julie's hand moved from Peg's breast over her belly and Peg opened up to her.

After, they lay propped up on pillows, quiet as if suddenly shy. Julie finally said, "Nothing's changed."

"What do you mean?" Peg asked, hopes sinking. She thought the lovemaking had been spectacular. Of course, she hadn't had any sex since the night with Charlie, and that she hardly remembered. Sophie she preferred to forget.

Julie turned toward her, one arm under her head, her hair

spilling over the pillow, a pale yellow in the light next to the bed. She traced Peg's collarbones with one finger. "It's like we're meant to be together. I stopped fighting that a long time ago."

"I didn't know it was such a struggle for you."

"I'm not sure I knew it either." Her smile looked sad. "You know, I'd open my mouth and I couldn't say I was a lesbian. I was brave enough to tell my mom once. She was ecstatic when I married Joe." She lay back.

"My mom was happy when she realized I was pregnant."

"Your mom and dad are just great." Julie laughed a little. "Annie got you going tonight, though."

"She forced me to go to Charlie's funeral. I wonder if I should tell his parents about the baby."

Up on her elbow, Julie looked with interest at Peg. "Do they have other grandkids?"

"I don't know. It seems like they have a right to know their grandchild."

"Peggy is closer to Joe's parents than to mine. Mine are still working obsessively." She sighed. "I think our parents shape our lives more than anyone else. We never stop trying to live up to their expectations."

"Do you like being a psychologist?"

"That's what I mean about our parents' influence on us. I'm a therapist. You're a teacher. Once in a while I get someone who nearly puts me to sleep, but on the whole, it's interesting. How do you like teaching?"

"Everything puts me to sleep these days."

"Me included."

"No, not you."

When they finally slept, it was well past midnight. The kids pounding on the door at nine o'clock in the morning caused them both to jump out of bed and into their clothes. When Peg turned the knob, the girls spilled into the room.

"Can we ride now?"

"Sure." Peg yawned and stretched.

Annie pounded up the stairs, breathless at the top. "I couldn't keep them away any longer."

Peg took hold of Katie's little hand. "It was time to get up. We're going to shower and eat something. We'll meet you in the barn. Okay?"

"Let's go, kids." Annie herded the girls out the door.

Peg squeezed into the small shower with Julie. "What's your cousin Jim doing these days?"

"You weren't pregnant when we got into his tiny shower. He's a computer programmer. I don't know what happened to Pete. I almost never talk to Jim." She kissed Peg soundly. "Want your hair washed?"

When Julie drove away that afternoon, Peggy's arm waved out the window at Kate who threw her kisses. Peg felt the emptiness she'd experienced years ago but not the helplessness. She knew that if Peggy were going to have two mommies, she'd be the other one. She and Julie weren't kids anymore. They were no longer in school. Both had jobs. There was nothing to keep them apart if they really wanted to be together.

Part III
2005

XI

She'd expected pain but not like this. No way was she going to have this baby naturally. She was gasping instead of breathing. Her mom had taken her to the hospital when she went into labor. Annie was at the university, teaching.

"God, Mom, I'm sorry," she said.

"Why, darling?"

"I did this to you." Another bolt of pain shot through her. There was no escaping it.

"Breathe," her mother said.

The doctor wasn't there yet. Her feet were in the stirrups. A sheet was draped over the mound of her lower body. She couldn't see past it. A delivery room nurse encouraged her to breathe, too, to control the pain.

"I want some painkiller. Put me out," she panted between contractions.

"We have to wait for the doctor," the nurse said.

"Well, where the hell is he?" she shouted as she thought she was about to be ripped apart.

Her mom said, "Yell as much as you want. I did."

Annie rushed in, dressed in the same greens as Peg's mom. "It's snowing like mad out."

"I'm not doing the Lamaze thing," Peg said. Her lower back was killing her. "Where the hell is the doctor?" she shrieked. "I'm not paying him either."

Her mom and Annie lifted her shoulders. "You'll want to see this."

A haze of sweat smeared her vision. Above the stirrups was a mirror. In it she could see what she thought was her crotch. Another contraction swept through her as the doctor entered the delivery room.

"Where have you been?" Peg asked angrily.

He laughed as he pulled on gloves and took his place between her legs. "They all ask that." After a brief examination, he said, "Do you want something to help with the pain? You'll still be able to see the baby born."

"Yes, yes," she said, gasping at the thing that had taken over her body.

The pain quickly became bearable. She was conscious yet sort of separated from her body, looking in the mirror as a fuzzy thing started to emerge. Then the baby turned and she saw its face.

"Here it comes," the doctor said. The shoulders emerged and the rest of the baby slipped out, covered with blood and mucus. "It's a girl!"

She lay back, feeling as if she'd lost her insides. The nurse cleaned the screaming, flailing baby, wrapped her in a blanket and put her in Peg's arms while the doctor stitched Peg's torn flesh. "Hold her," Peg said to her mother and fell asleep.

That night when Peg was alone with the infant in the hospital room, she undressed her baby and examined the tiny body. Every few moments the infant's arms and legs would shoot out as if not knowing what to do with all the space. Peg wrapped her tightly in the blanket and put her back in the little bed on wheels.

The phone rang in her room as she dozed off, and she fumbled the receiver to her ear. "Hey. I lived through it."

Julie laughed softly. "I heard. Annie called. Congratulations. Does Charlotte need two mommies?"

"She needs a different mommy. I think maybe I wasn't meant to be a mother."

"Oh, Peg, there's a name for this it's so common. It's called postpartum depression. I had it too. Tell me about her and you."

"I wasn't brave. I screamed and swore and begged for pain relief. The baby looks like a tiny old man. A high forehead, like she's going bald, a pinched face, wrinkled skin. She's so incredibly small nothing is going to fit her."

"Peggy is staying with Daisy tomorrow and I'm coming. I can't wait. You should sleep now. She'll be screaming for food soon."

It seemed as if Peg had been dreaming only minutes before Charlie jolted her awake with a thin, high-pitched cry. A nurse bustled into the room and handed Peg the baby to nurse. But Charlie hadn't caught on and pushed at Peg's breast with tiny fists, her eyes squeezed shut and her miniscule mouth screwed up in a breathless wail. Peg looked at the nurse helplessly.

"Put the nipple in her mouth."

Charlie, however, would have none of it. She flailed at Peg and screamed louder. When the nurse and Peg finally coaxed her to suck, Peg wasn't prepared for the surprisingly strong pull. She fell asleep feeling like a failure.

Crying babies woke her in the morning. Another woman and baby had moved into her room after the last feeding around four in the morning. She looked over at the other bed. The young, heavyset woman smiled tiredly back.

"My name's Rhoda and that's my latest singing a duet with yours."

Nursing had turned into an embarrassing struggle between Peg and this tiny person. Peg cringed from the humiliation of being rejected by her own baby.

It was Rhoda who butted in with reassuring words. "Hey, that happened to me, too. Don't take it personal. She'll catch on."

Rhoda had four kids. She was twenty-eight—Peg had asked—to Peg's thirty-two, which made Peg feel more incompetent. When Charlie beat upon her breasts with her tiny fists and screamed in frustration, Peg burst into tears. "She doesn't want to nurse," she said.

Rhoda climbed out of bed with her baby boy in arms—the nurse had left—and gave Peg a lesson on nursing. "It's painful," Peg said.

"It's going to hurt a whole lot more before you toughen up."

By noon when Julie arrived, Peg dreaded the sight of her own child. Charlie nursed like a pro now, but the pain was terrible.

"She's beautiful," Julie said.

"Liar," Peg shot back. "She's a torturer in the disguise of a wise little old man."

Julie laughed and turned back to her with a puzzled look.

Rhoda rose on her elbow. "She means it hurts to nurse."

Peg introduced the two women. "Rhoda's a pro at this. She has four kids and she's younger than I am."

When company came in to see Rhoda, someone pulled the curtain that separated the beds. "I'd kiss you, but I'm thinking they won't understand." Julie motioned with her head toward the closed curtain.

"Probably not. I'm so glad you're here and on a workday yet. How is Peggy?"

"She wants to see the baby, of course. We'll come on the weekend if that's okay. You'll be home then."

"Yes, me and my tiny tormenter." Peg smiled wryly. "I don't

know why anyone has more than one kid. First the excruciating labor, then the raw nipples."

"Just wait. The worst is yet to come." Julie put a hand on Peg's arm. As usual, the hair rose under it to meet her touch. "I'm kidding."

"Why did you just have one?"

"Because the marriage wasn't going well." Julie ran her hands over the edge of the bed. "May I hold her?"

"Please do."

Julie cradled the baby in her arms. Miraculously, Charlie continued to sleep. Julie smiled beautifully and whispered, "She's perfect."

"You're perfect," Peg said. "Maybe she'll grow up to be like you."

Peg went home two days after the baby was born. Her mother wanted her to stay at the house, and she did until Friday when she moved back above the garage. She wanted privacy when Julie arrived that evening. Peggy would be sleeping with Katie. Peg briefly wished she could send Charlie with her.

"I took your list and shopped for you. I figured you and Julie could eat with us this weekend if you like. Will that be okay?" Her mom stood over the crib where the baby lay sleeping. Charlie's skin was peeling and her umbilical cord had just fallen off. Peg thought about saving the cord and giving it to her on her thirteenth birthday, imagining the disgusted, "Oh, Mom!"

"Thanks, Mom. I don't know what I'd do without you." She remembered what a horrible teenager she'd been, often sullen and angry. She supposed she'd get the same treatment from her daughter. What comes around goes around.

"She looks like you did."

"I hope not," Peg said.

"There's something wonderful about reproducing yourself,

don't you think?"

"I suppose," Peg said doubtfully.

Her mom looked out the window. "Julie and Peggy just drove in. I'll go say hello. If you want time alone instead of coming for dinner tonight, we'll understand."

"Thanks. I'll call." What would she have done without her parents? Without Annie? She should be grateful instead of bristling because her mother gave her permission to be alone with Julie. There were things she and Julie hadn't worked out yet, like which one was going to relocate. They needed time to talk.

Peggy and Katie galloped up the stairs first, pushing through the doorway together. They rushed to the crib and the baby awoke. For some reason, though, Charlie didn't cry.

"You two must be magicians. She's not screaming."

"Can we hold her, Aunt Peg?" Katie asked.

"Sure." Peg got up and went to the crib. She still noticed the emptiness where the baby had resided so long. "Sit down on the bed and I'll give her to you." She settled the baby in Peggy's lap first. "Katie, you've already held her about a hundred times."

Katie ran a small finger across the baby's cheek and Charlie turned her mouth toward it and beat the air with her little fists. Katie burbled a high, excited giggle. "She wants to eat my finger."

Peggy laughed excitedly and Charlie started to cry.

"It's feeding time, I guess." Peg took the squalling baby out of Peggy's arms. "It's nothing you did, Peggy," she added when Peggy looked close to tears. "She's hungry."

"Why don't we go see the horses?" Annie said and followed the girls down the stairs.

Peg opened her shirt and winced when the baby latched on to her. "I don't know if I'll ever toughen up."

Julie smiled and sat down next to Peg. She traced Peg's breast to the baby's cheek. "So, what do you think of motherhood now?"

"Confining. Causes sleep deprivation. Demanding. How did you find it?"

Julie's eyes glowed, a light gray with sun shining through. Peg couldn't look away. She leaned forward and kissed her.

"The same," Julie said. "It'll change soon enough. You'll be chasing her around." She sniffed at the baby's head. "Babies smell so good."

"You smell good," Peg said, burying her face in Julie's hair.

When the baby fell away from Peg's breast, Julie changed her and put her to bed. "Have you thought any more about moving to Madison?" she asked, her back to Peg.

"Have you considered moving here?" She had a job too.

Julie turned and a shaft of sunlight exposed the fine wrinkles around her eyes and mouth. Peg thought of the years they'd already spent apart. Time was still on their side if they took advantage of it.

She pointed out the large impatiens plant hanging in the window. "From my students. They also gave me a gift certificate, as did the teachers. The cards are in the basket on the table." The note from Michelle Peterson said she was an experienced babysitter. It had made Peg smile. Jonathon Wall wrote that they were driving all the subs away so that she'd have to come back. She would return in six weeks and finish out the year, but would she sign next year's contract?

Julie put the cards back in the container and turned to Peg. "Looks like your kids miss you."

"Depends on who's subbing."

"I suppose."

Why hide the joy she felt at seeing Julie? "Maybe I have the post-natal blues. I feel sort of trapped." She patted the bed. "Lock the door and come over here. You can get close to me now." No belly.

Lying on the bed, face to face, Peg buried her fingers in Julie's hair and sighed. "I hope you never cut it."

"Funny, I was just wondering how I'd look with shorter hair."

"Not near as sexy."

"Oh well then, I better not." Julie took Peg's face between her hands. "What are we going to do, Peg? My lease is ending soon. I have to make a decision about whether to rent or buy and if I buy, I want to do it with you." The house had sold months ago.

Peg thought about summers in Madison, the smell of hot concrete instead of hay. She supposed she could bring Charlie and Peggy here for a few days at a time.

"Talk to me, Peg. How can I know what you're thinking?"

"You know I love Madison. It's a great city if you have to live in one. But it's two hours from here. Peggy could show with Katie and Brian if we lived nearby. The Fox Cities have everything a big city has, yet it only takes minutes to get out of town." She said these things in a rush.

"Hey." Julie kissed her gently. "Slow down. I don't know if Joe will let me move. We have joint custody, and he has an apartment in Madison."

She'd put Joe out of her mind. Peggy had only one daddy. Charlie had none. She would have to move if anyone did. Beginning a caress that ended up between Julie's legs, she put off the decision.

"It's too soon for you," Julie whispered.

"I know. Just relax and let me do this. Okay? I want to. A quickie, in case anyone pounds on the door. Come on. Help me."

Julie unzipped her jeans and raised her legs. A slight moan escaped from her as Peg slid her hand into the opening. "When we make love, I always think of the first time," Peg whispered into Julie's mouth. "What do you think of?"

"I think about you," Julie moved under the touch.

"What about me?" She nibbled at Julie's neck.

"What you feel like. How you're always so willing." Her rhythmic movements became stronger.

"What do I feel like?" Peg gently tugged on Julie's eyebrows with her teeth. She kissed her eyes.

"Like velvet. Like a horse's muzzle. Oh!" Her body became rigid, then fell back on the bed limply.

Peg laughed. "A horse's muzzle?"

Julie kissed her on the mouth. "That was just what I needed. What's silkier than a horse's nose?"

"Silk?"

"You still have to make a decision," Julie said, pulling her clothes together.

"Ask Joe if he cares if you move."

"Okay but he flies into the city on a day's notice and expects to see Peggy."

Sammy sank into what she probably thought of as her chair. Julie's clients invariably sat in the same place. To Julie's "What's happening?" Sammy looked at her feet.

"Life sucks."

"Why?"

"Nicole decided that she's straight after all. She said I was like a parasite that lives off other people, that I should find another friend. Patsy dumped her." Tears shimmered on the edge of her eyelids. She angrily snatched a tissue from the box Julie pushed her way.

"Have you thought of making new friends?" Julie asked, reflecting on her own major slip when she decided to go straight.

"Everyone goes around in cliques."

"Everyone?" Julie asked with obvious disbelief.

"I don't want to hook up with the kids no one wants to be with."

Julie lifted her palms. "They could say the same thing about you."

"They probably do." There was that flash of blue as Sammy

looked at her and quickly away.

"Sometimes those are the most interesting people, the ones who are a little different."

"Think so?" She met Julie's gaze and held it.

"Like you," Julie said.

"Yeah, sure." Sammy blushed and her eyes darted to the door. "There is this gay guy, though, a real femme, but smart and funny. I'd like to know him better. And there's a girl who is kind of cute but never says much."

"There, you see? Give a few people a chance and anything can happen. How's the rest of your life going?"

"Good grades. I signed up for a rowing class." Sammy's face came to life.

"I've always wanted to do that."

"Hey, maybe you could be in the same class. That'd be cool."

Julie felt ridiculously pleased. "You'd be the first one I'd choose for my team," she said, knowing that was impossible. She could get her license revoked for fraternizing with clients, especially one so young.

Now Sammy looked pleased. What a difference a smile made, Julie thought, responding in kind.

The session was the last one of the week, one Sammy had requested. She'd been doing well on her own. That's how it should be, Julie thought, putting work into her briefcase. There comes a time to let a client go. That's the whole idea, to help someone stand on her or his own feet.

Joe was flying in on the weekend. He wanted Peggy to stay with him, but he had scheduled a constituent meeting. He said Andrea would stay with Peggy while he was at the meeting, that she was looking forward to spending time alone with Peggy. However, Peggy announced flat-out that she was staying home because Peg and the baby were coming. She said her daddy could come see her at the apartment.

Peg was to arrive later in the evening. She was teaching again. Every weekend since Charlie's birth, Julie and Peggy had gone to Peg's. The drive back and forth tired Julie. She often had unfinished work from the week and only time on the weekends to do it and everything else that needed done. Although Annie protested otherwise, Julie feared Peggy might become an imposition, the ever-present weekend visitor in Katie's home.

After retrieving Peggy from daycare, she drove home to wait for Joe's arrival. He could argue with his daughter. Julie didn't care whether she stayed or went with him. She told herself she should be grateful to Andrea, not resent her as she did, but she couldn't seem to manage that yet. Despite their profession, therapists are subject to all the emotions they help their clients deal with, including pettiness and jealousy and possessiveness. She had to remind herself that Peggy was Joe's daughter too.

Joe was sitting alone in his car waiting in the apartment parking lot. It was a cool April day, spitting rain. Signs of spring were everywhere—green grass, flowering bushes and trees, new leaves. She loved it and the life it foretold—for her, for Peg.

Peggy dragged her feet, getting out of the car. She often seemed angry with her parents, especially when her parents were together. "Why, Mama, why can't Daddy live with us? Don't you love him?" These pointed questions Julie found difficult to answer without telling Peggy that Daddy loved Andrea more than he loved her and that she loved Peg more than she did Joe. She had done this once and Peggy had said, "Why don't you all live together?"

"Hi, pumpkin, give me a hug," Joe said and stooped for Peggy's onslaught, which didn't come.

"I'm not going," their daughter said, her lower lip pouting. "Charlie is coming to visit."

Joe got a funny, wondering look on his face. "What if we eat at Noodles and go see the new *Shrek*?" Noodles was Peggy's favorite eating out place and the first *Shrek* her favorite video.

"Can I come back and see Charlie before she goes home?"

"Sure." He looked at Julie questioningly.

"We'll call." Her heart lifted a little and she thought that it would be as if they were alone, she and Peg.

"Go pack your bag, darlin'," he said once the three of them were in the apartment.

"So, how goes it?" Julie asked after Peggy sprinted off to her room.

A little worn, but still lanky and good looking, Joe smiled. "Busy. And you?"

"Very. We're looking at condos this weekend." He had told her he didn't want Julie and Peggy to move away from Madison.

"Yeah? Does the baby look like Charlie?"

She put her briefcase on the couch. "Too soon to tell. She's a cheerful little girl." Was it better to never have a father than to share your father with someone other than your mother?

Peggy dragged a backpack into the living room. A sleeve hung out of the unzipped part. "'Bye, Mama."

Suddenly protective, Julie reached for her and held her close before setting her down. "Have a great time."

Joe took Peggy's hand. "See you Sunday."

"Aren't you going to kiss Mama?" Peggy asked, looking from one to the other.

Joe bent to give Julie a peck on the cheek, causing her to tremble at the unexpected sweetness.

After they left, she changed into jeans and got some notes out of her briefcase. She became so involved in work that Peg's knock on the door surprised her.

Julie took the carrier from her and Peg ran out to the car to get the rest of her stuff. "It's amazing how much baggage a baby has." The dark skies portended a stormy night, and the wind tugged at Peg's clothes and hair. Her cheeks shone cherry red.

The baby squirmed in the carrier and Julie took her out and held her against her shoulder. Babies smelled new, she thought, as Peg flew inside and pulled the door shut behind her.

She kissed Julie, making a sandwich of Charlie. "Missed you. I'll feed her and then we can eat. A baby is like having a horse. You always have to take care of it first. Is Peggy with Joe?"

"Yep. Andrea is going to watch her while he's meeting constituents tomorrow."

"Does that bother you?"

"A little, I guess. Selfish of me."

"I'll never have to worry about that."

"I just don't like Andrea much. She's a sneak."

"He's as much a sneak as she is."

"You know what I don't like about Andrea? She waited like a vulture, always available, after we were married."

Peg placed the baby in the playpen Julie had borrowed. "You sound like a jealous woman." She straightened up and looked at Julie. "I've been wondering whether I should contact Charlie's parents. How well do you know them?"

"Not well," Julie said. She had met them a couple of times when she and Joe were visiting his parents, but she had no clear impression to pass on.

"You don't think they'd try to take her away because I'm gay, do you?"

"No!" she said, stopped in her mental tracks. People surprised her all the time with their actions, though. Just the other day one of her clients forced his way into her office to talk nonsense. Scared her senseless.

"Mom thinks we should invite them up to meet Charlie. I suppose it's only fair."

"Sometimes I wish I were the only one with any say over Peggy."

"I suppose," Peg said vaguely.

"Come on, let's eat." Julie curled a tousle of Peg's hair around her finger. The pizza Julie ordered had just arrived.

"Tell me what you've lined up." Peg sighed, sitting down at the table.

"What's the sigh for?"

"I don't have a job here. Who's going to lend me any money?"

"I thought you'd want your name on the deed too."

"I don't care, Julie."

"You seem so reluctant. I want to come home to you, Peg." She sat across from Peg and pulled a piece off the pizza. "It's lonely without you."

"Hey, that's why I'm here. To look at places." Peg took a bite. "God, I'm hungry. I haven't eaten since noon. Do you have any milk?"

Julie poured her a glass and sat down again. "How long are you going to nurse?"

"I'm never stopping," Peg said. "It's so easy."

Julie laughed. "I seem to remember a time when you hated it."

"That was before my nipples got as tough as nails."

"Yeah? We'll see how tough they are later." Julie smiled. She loved Peg's lighter side.

"Hey, I'm ready for bed whenever you are. Driving two and a half hours after working all day is a bit much."

"Tell me about it."

"Okay, Julie, you don't have to ram it down my throat. I just dread looking for another teaching job. I hate the thought of moving."

The pizza turned tasteless and hard to swallow. Julie looked at the almost empty box. What kind of a life would they have if Peg didn't want it? Shrugging to herself, she got up and poured herself a glass of merlot. "I'm not nursing," she said.

In bed, though, everything turned warm and fuzzy again. Was

it sex that held them together? Did they have to mend their quarrels in bed? How long would that work?

"I'm sorry, sweetie," Peg whispered in her ear. "It just seems like such an effort, but you're right. We can't keep driving back and forth."

Julie loved waking up with Peg. Sunlight splayed across the bed. A cardinal sang insistently in the tree outside the window. The baby cried from the playpen, her head wobbling on her little neck as she raised it. Peg brought her to the bed to nurse.

"What a way to start the day, huh?" Julie traced a finger over Peg's breast to the baby's cheek as she had before.

"Yeah. We just need Peggy jumping on the bed. What did you tell her about us?"

"I told her I love you and her dad loves Andrea. She thought we should all live together."

Peg laughed. "I don't think so."

Toward the end of the day the baby was getting cranky from being carried in and out of the car. Even Julie was tired when the real estate woman, their old friend Chloe, unlocked the door of a two-story townhouse with high ceilings and tall windows, three bedrooms, a loft, a full basement and a two-car garage. The white walls gave the feeling of space and light.

Julie threw her arms wide and spun. This was it! She turned to Peg who looked a little dazed. Peg nodded and Julie said, "I love it."

Chloe's hair stood up an inch from her scalp. Her body was as emaciated as it had been years ago but she'd removed some of the piercings. She wore a nice pair of slacks and a blouse. She told them she'd reluctantly crossed the divide into respectability. They invited her over for a drink.

She was amazed that Peg had a baby. Emboldened by a gin and tonic, she asked if Charlie was a sperm bank baby, which gave Peg pause to wonder how to deal with such questions from casual friends.

Julie spoke up. "You can order babies now from an array of donors, you know. Were you looking to have a baby?"

"Not me," Chloe said.

"She's Charlie Schmidt's daughter," Peg said. "Do you remember Charlie?"

"Yeah, you and Charlie and Julie and Joe were a foursome." She looked closer at the baby in the playpen who was kicking her legs and waving her arms. Her dark hair and eyes could have come from either Charlie or Peg. "Didn't Charlie die in Iraq?"

"Not without leaving a book and a child," Peg said, sorry again that he never knew about the baby. "Do you ever see Tammy?"

"Yeah. She comes here or I go to Chicago. We have a blast. She's a CPA and works for a nursing home chain. We're starting a home for old lesbians when we're seniors. She said to say hello."

When Chloe left, Peg asked Julie if she knew Charlie's parents' phone number.

"No. Joe does, though. You can ask him when he brings Peggy back tomorrow. Think carefully about this, Peg. They'll become a part of your life."

"They already are." She snuggled close to Julie on the couch. "I am so lucky."

"How so?" Julie asked with a slight smile and that lift of brows.

"That you're you and not Tammy or Chloe or Daphne or Sophie."

"There are a lot of lesbians in town, sweetie. We'll have an open house if we buy this condo."

"We made an offer on it."

"Contingent on inspection."

"I remember thinking I couldn't live without you, that I'd follow you anywhere." She put a hand on Julie's leg. "Then I left and never really came back, not for good, not until now."

Julie covered Peg's hand with her own. "I know."

Jiggling the change in his pockets, Joe stood in the living room of the apartment while Peg quizzed him about Charlie's parents.

"I know them like any kid knows his best friend's parents. They're good people. They treated me like their own."

"Why don't you sit down, Joe?" Julie said.

"I can't. Andrea's in the car."

Putting aside her annoyance, she said, "Well, ask her in."

"She'd be uncomfortable," he said.

"We have to co-exist." Julie smiled slightly, painfully.

"Why don't you invite her in?"

She should, Julie realized, but she wanted to hear the conversation. Instead, she called Peggy away from the playpen where the baby slept and asked her to do it. Peggy slipped outside.

"I thought I should tell Charlie's parents that they have a granddaughter."

Joe perched on the edge of the couch and heaved a sigh. "I told them when I went to see them over Christmas. They were talking about Charlie leaving a part of himself, meaning the book, and I said there was something else he left."

Julie threw a glance Peg's way to see her reaction. She looked stunned but recovered quickly.

"What did they say?"

"They said they'd like to meet her but didn't want to intrude on your life."

Andrea and Peggy were at the door. "Come in, Andrea. I don't think you ever met Peg," Julie said.

"No. Hi." She looked flustered and retreated to the couch next to Joe.

"Hey," Peg replied with a friendly smile.

Joe's large hands hung between his knees and Julie stared at them, remembering their touch, at first fumbling but always gentle. Conflicting relationships and memories made any silence uncomfortable.

"You want to see the baby?" Peggy asked, tugging on Andrea's hand, taking her to other room where she could be heard saying, "She's awake. You can pick her up."

Andrea returned to the living room with Charlie in her arms. "Is it okay?" she asked Peg. "I love babies."

"Of course. She loves attention."

Joe stared at the infant and finally said, "How can she look like Charlie? She'll never have a mustache."

Andrea looked puzzled as Peg and Joe and Julie laughed shakily. "At least we hope she won't."

Joe scribbled on the back of a business card and handed it to Peg when he and Andrea left. "Call them when you're ready."

Peg met Julie's eyes when she closed the door. Sitting down, she opened her shirt to the baby. "I have to go soon. I want to be home before dark."

"That must have been a shock. It's just like Joe, though, to tell people something he thinks will make them feel better. It's how he gets elected."

"Now I *have* to call them. I was hoping we'd spend summer weekends at my place."

"We'll be moving, Peg." She thought how nice it would be not to drive back and forth.

The sale fell through. The next day someone made an offer higher than the asking price with no conditions attached. Who wouldn't take it, Julie thought as Chloe told her this over the phone.

"We'll find another like it. There are tons of condos. Maybe you'd like to consider a house?"

"No. We don't want to be tied down." How could they when Peg wanted to spend weekends at the family horse farm?

Peg took the news cheerfully. "There'll be another," she said as Chloe had.

"I thought you and the baby could move in with us when school is out even if we haven't found a place. You can job search better here."

"It will be hard for Peggy to show if we're there all summer."

"Who said she was going to show? She doesn't have a horse."

"We could buy her one."

"She's four years old. Can't that wait till she's a little older? I mean, we can split weekends between here and there if you want, but I want to live with you. Now."

"Sounds like an ultimatum," Peg said lightly.

"It's not. Don't you feel the same way?"

"Yes."

"Then why the hesitation?"

"I can't tell you over the phone."

"Try, will you?" She was becoming aggravated.

"I learned I could live without you and be a whole person. You sort of suck me up until there is no me left. I love you too much."

"What?" She searched her memory to see if this had ever been a problem for one of her clients and came up with nothing.

"I don't know how to explain it any better. I become your satellite like when we were at the university. We all were—Charlie and Joe and I. I lost my identity."

"Charlie loved you." She felt a little sick. "And I loved you too. I never saw you as anything but an independent person. I'm sorry if you think I take over your life."

"It's not you, Julie. It's me. I'll move there when school is out.

209

We do need to live together."

"I'm not Sophie," Julie said. "I'm not a prima donna."

"Sophie could never make me feel the way you do. I don't love her. I never did."

"Is that good or bad?"

"You can love someone too much, so that you can only take it in small doses, Julie, or you'll be swallowed up."

"I may taste you, but I won't swallow you whole," she promised lightly, pondering this view of love as a suffocating device. Did loving someone too much take away one's identity?

She walked around in a fog for a while, responding to Peggy's comments with noncommittal murmurs till her daughter stamped a foot and demanded to be heard.

"Okay. I'm listening."

"I want to go see Katie. Katie and the horses."

Two against one. She couldn't win.

XII

School ended the first week in June, springing Peg from the classroom. Teaching was probably less confining than most jobs, she thought as she took the baby to her mother before going out to the barn. At least she got the summers off. Her mom had said Cam wanted to discuss something with her.

Her brother beckoned to her as he unsaddled Dom and rubbed him down. The big stallion stuck his nose out and wriggled his upper lip in pleasure. Sweat made his dark coat glisten. With streamlined muscles, he looked like the athlete he was. Cam had points on him in halter and performance classes.

"Is he fun to ride?" she asked. She'd seen him spin on command, change leads with a touch of leg and then settle down to a rocking horse canter. At three, he was young for such feats.

"Ride him anytime. I wish you would." He ran a hand down the horse's sleek neck. Cam turned the animal out in the indoor arena and said, "Let's go outside."

They sat on the hay wagon. Cam had rented a nearby field where he grew alfalfa. He cut and baled his own hay in addition to judging and showing and riding and caring for the boarders' horses and his own. He looked down at his hands, dry and calloused.

She made a mental note to buy him some Bag Balm for his birthday. "Mom said you wanted to talk to me?" Picking up a piece of hay, she put it in her mouth. She loved the smell of it. "Do you want help haying?"

He glanced sideways at her, his eyes serious. "I want you to be my partner. The sign would read *Cam and Peg Kincaid, Horse Trainers.*"

Surprised, she met his gaze. "What?"

"Not because you hung around and took care of things when I was hurt. That I can never repay. I need two of me. I can't keep it together anymore and grow. Dad has offered to pitch in with the haying. What I need most is someone to give lessons, work the horses and show them. I've got two amateurs and two kids' horses in the barn. You're a good rider, Peg. I can't pay as much as teaching does, but I can offer a salary and insurance. I belong to a group policy."

"I haven't shown in months."

"It's like riding a bike. You never forget." He smiled slightly. He was thirty-seven—tanned, muscled, a little gray in his hair, eyes squinting under his ball cap.

"I'll think about it. I'm flattered, Cam. I don't know if I have the talent and drive, though." Even while she considered his offer, she thought how she'd told Julie she was moving to Madison. Why hadn't he asked her earlier? Would it have mattered, though, if Joe insisted that Peggy stay in Madison? "Meanwhile, I'll be glad to help. For free. What do you want me to do?"

She gave a lesson that afternoon to one of Cam's youth riders, an obnoxious eleven-year-old. When her horse didn't do her bidding, the girl jerked on the reins.

Peg had no patience with this behavior. "You're hurting his mouth, Cece. Would you like someone to jerk on yours?"

"It gets his attention," the girl snapped.

"It makes him throw his head up to get away from the pressure, and when that happens the judge marks you off his card. It also hardens his mouth so he's less responsive. Loosen the reins, sit up straight and cue him with your legs."

"Listen to her, Cece." The girl's stepmother spoke from the rail.

"You can't make me," the kid sassed.

Thoroughly annoyed, Peg said, "Don't waste our time, Cece. We're here to help you work with your horse. We don't have to do this. It's up to you, whether you want to learn or not."

Looking uncertain as if someone had called her bluff and she didn't know what to do, Cece did as Peg told her. The animal began responding after a few moments. He was a small gelding with a beautiful head and well-proportioned body. Peg thought that Cam would have bought him for Katie if his price hadn't been so high. She wasn't going to let this girl ruin him with her temper.

"Way to go," she said at the end of the lesson, eliciting a small smile from Cece who handed the reins to her stepmother. "Wait a minute. You have to put away your own horse."

"I have to use the john." Cece crossed her legs.

"Put his halter on and tie him in the aisle while you go. Then take his tack off and brush him down before you put him in his stall."

"I thought we paid for all this," Cece complained to her stepmother.

"We pay for board and lessons. You have to do your part," Mrs. Williams said as the girl led her horse away. When Cece disappeared into the bathroom, the woman said, "Thanks. She needs someone to be firm with her. By the way, my name is Vicki."

Thinking Cece deserved neither her stepmother nor the horse, she said, "I'm Peg, Cam's sister. That's a nice little horse."

"I know. It's hard for Cece, sharing me with her dad. Her mother's been out of the picture for years. It's not you she's mad at."

"It's not the horse either. I'll work with her. Maybe we can change her attitude."

"That'd be great. See you next week."

When they were gone, Peg went inside to nurse the baby. She hauled out a sweaty breast and offered it to Charlie who tasted it and turned her head away. "Okay, I don't blame you." She handed the squalling baby to her mom and quickly washed.

Her mother stood in the doorway, jiggling Charlie who quieted. "What did Cam have to say?"

"You know, don't you? Everybody probably knew but me." She dried off and took the baby.

"Well, we talked about it. I can watch the baby. You'd be right here and able to nurse her. Annie thinks it's a great idea."

She gave her mom a troubled look. "What about Julie? She thinks I'm moving to Madison. Joe doesn't want Peggy to move. He lives there when he's not in D.C."

Her mom sat down. "I don't know then. You two will have to work things out."

"Yeah." She'd left Julie when Cam was hurt. How could she do it again?

After lunch, she worked with Cam as he took the horses out of their stalls, one by one, brushed them and rode them in the outdoor arena. They spoke only a few words and none at all about his offer. Ginny showed up after work to clean stalls and get her horse ready for a show the next day. Peg had just put the next to last horse back in its stall.

"Is it that late?" She looked at her watch. Julie would be here soon, and what would she say to her about Cam's offer?

She remembered thinking years ago that maybe she could work with her brother if there was nothing else she wanted to do. Well, now that he'd asked her to do just that, there was nothing else she wanted to do. Would she tire of being outside in the heat, the rain and the cold? Maybe.

She'd mulled this over all day. Cam's horse business was booming year 'round. He traveled the show circuits. He judged on weekends when he wasn't showing. She could take care of things at the barn. Clients came in every day for lessons. Some clients left their horses to be ridden and shown by a professional. If she took money for working with animals that weren't her own, she'd lose her amateur status, but she didn't care about that. She could turn professional and if money ran short, she could substitute teach. There was always that ace in the hole.

Her angst about Julie's arrival transferred itself to the client's horse she was saddling, the one she'd saved to ride till last. As she pulled the cinch tight, the bay gelding kicked out with a hind leg. It was one of the bad habits that frightened its owner. She slapped him in the gut and he grunted. Then Brian ran into the stable and the horse jumped sideways, nearly stepping on her. She smacked him on the rump to move him away.

"You know better than to barge in here and startle the horses," she scolded. "People get hurt that way."

He skidded to a stop. "Sorry. Julie and Peggy are here."

"Already? I was going to ride Bay." The horse needed the exercise to get rid of some of its misdirected energy.

"I'll ride him," the boy said eagerly.

"I don't think so. He's not ready for you." She unhooked the gelding and led him into the sunlight. He was an elegant horse with a long neck and a well-muscled body. The client looked good on him.

"Can I lead him?" Brian asked.

"Sure." She ran a hand over her nephew's soft brown hair and handed him the reins. Julie was striding her way with long, sure steps and her heart leaped painfully. "Hey," she said, hugging Julie a little too long and hard. "Missed you."

Perceptive to any nuance, Julie searched her eyes. "Everything okay?"

"Look, you guys," Brian yelled at the girls who were rolling a suitcase toward the garage steps. Bay reared a little and the reins slid through Brian's grip.

The horse distracted everyone. He spun and trotted back to the barn, reins tangling around his legs. Peg went after him, cursing him for using any excuse to misbehave. The animal was eight, too old for this to be anything but a trick.

He stood in his stall, nibbling at hay on the floor. "Goddamn you, horse," she said in a calm voice, grabbing the unbroken rein. "Now look what you've done. Brian, get me another rein from the tack room. They're in the box."

Brian rushed to do her bidding.

"I'm going to have to ride him now. Do you mind?" she asked Julie.

"I don't want to keep you from your chores," she said with a dazzling smile that never failed to melt Peg's resolve.

"You are so gorgeous," she said.

"Well, thanks. You're kind of cute yourself."

"Here, Aunt Peg." Brian held up a mismatched rein. "I'm sorry."

"This horse took advantage of you, kiddo. You have to watch him every minute."

It was bedtime before Julie and Peg were alone. Julie had been acting like she had some great secret. She spilled it as they slid between the sheets. "I looked at a condo that's even nicer than the one we saw. Same sort of layout but bigger."

Peg listened with plummeting hopes as Julie talked. How could she tell her she didn't want to live in a condo and teach now that she had a way out? She couldn't, of course. She'd agreed to go, and after the years apart that started with her returning home following Cam's accident, she had no choice but to move. It was only fair.

"Sounds great," she said, trying to inject some enthusiasm into her voice.

"Should I wait for you to see it?" Julie's hand moved over her.

The baby stirred and emitted a tiny cry in her sleep. Did she sense her mother's distress? Peg looked over at her crib. A weight settled in her chest. She cleared her throat. "Go ahead and make an offer. I trust you."

"Are you all right, sweetie?" Julie's touch usually set off the passion between them.

Peg knew that Julie would guess something was wrong if she didn't respond appropriately and soon. She covered Julie's body with her own. Looking down at her she remembered their first time, their hesitancy, her disbelieving excitement. She could work herself into a state of desire just thinking of that improbable Thanksgiving when Julie had wanted her enough to take the risk of exposing herself to rejection and shame.

Julie rolled her off to the side and kissed her soundly. "We'll have a great life, Peg. Coming home to each other every night would be enough, having two kids would be enough, but then there are so many things to do in Madison. As students, we missed most of it—great concerts, wonderful places to eat, the two lakes. We could buy a sailboat or take up rowing."

Smiling at Julie's enthusiasm, she said, "Let's make sure we don't become stodgy and miss all the fun things."

Something was wrong. Julie knew it when she arrived. She read Peg's moods with remarkable accuracy and guessed the cheerful reaction to her news about the condo was forced.

The next morning Peg supervised Katie and Peggy on horse-back, then rode the horses in the barn and gave a lesson to one of

Cam's clients. Julie sat in a lawn chair in the shade of the barn, keeping an eye on the baby in the buggy.

At noon when they went to Peg's apartment, Julie said, "You know, I could spend the day reading at home."

Peg spread her arms. "The rest of the day is yours. What would you like to do?"

"Something that involves you."

"You name it."

"What's wrong, Peg?"

"Nothing. Just wondering what it's going to be like, you and me and the girls."

The door slammed open as Katie and Peggy rushed into the room and the baby began to cry. Julie lifted her eyebrows. "Like this?"

Peg laughed and picked up Charlie.

Julie made peanut butter and jelly sandwiches for the girls and sent them back outside. "Okay, let's talk. Be honest."

"I am being honest. Really. Why don't you believe me?" Peg bared a breast for the baby. "I feel like a spigot."

Julie smiled. The sight of Peg nursing moved her deeply. She guessed she'd have to get her answer from Annie. Maybe she could corner her this afternoon. "Hey, I'm okay watching the baby. I've got a good book. The kids will want to ride this afternoon. Maybe I will too. You do what you usually do."

Peg looked at her as if she suspected some ulterior reason for this sudden change of attitude. "What? I thought you wanted my undivided attention."

"Just some of it. It doesn't have to be undivided."

When they went out again, the baby asleep in the buggy, Julie parked under the huge maple in Peg's parents' backyard. Peg's mother came out as she hoped she would.

"Want me to watch the baby? I can sit out here and read and you can do something else."

Julie never knew what to call Peg's mother. "Thanks, Mrs. K.

218

Actually, I haven't seen Annie. I wanted to ask her something."

"You can call us by our first names, Julie. Annie does, so why not you? It makes me feel younger."

"Thanks for telling me that. It's been kind of awkward."

"I know. I never knew what to call my in-laws. I think Annie's home now. She was grocery shopping."

"I'll just go knock on her door then." The grass was spiky under her tennies. She made her way around to the side door of the two-story house where Cam and Annie lived, and knocked.

"Hey, it's you. Come on in." Annie backed away from the opening. "Where's Peg? Let me guess. She's out with the horses. Want a cup of decaf?" Annie started coffee without waiting for an answer and began unbagging groceries. "Sit down, Julie."

"Can I help?"

"If you knew where to put stuff you could, but since you don't, no. Talk to me."

"You're cheerful."

Annie paused to look at Julie, her eyes shiny with pleasure. "I think it's just great about Peg, don't you?" A frown appeared between Annie's brows as she studied Julie's face. "You don't, do you?" Annie sank into a chair, her chin on her hand. "I understand. You've got a profession and a clientele. What's the matter with me?"

"Wait. Slow down. I don't know what you're talking about."

"You don't? Well, it's not my place to tell you." Annie got up and poured them each a cup of coffee. "Ask Peg."

"I thought there was a distinct lack of enthusiasm over the condo I found. Tell me, Annie. I'll never let on you said anything." It was like they were kids, sharing secrets.

"Cam asked her to be his partner. He's overrun with clients and offers to judge." Annie stared at Julie. "What did you say about a condo?"

"I found a perfect one. When did this happen? Recently?"

"Yesterday. She didn't say anything last night, huh?"

"No." Julie took a sip of coffee and set the cup down. She sighed. "I know she doesn't want to move to Madison. She's pretending." She met Annie's eyes. "I do have a clientele and a profession. Don't let her know I know, Annie. I have to think about this." All the joy had left Julie and she slumped in the chair. Straightening, she gave Annie a troubled look. "Can you do me a favor?" Annie nodded. "Scare up some info on job opportunities in the area. I know I can look on the Web, but you might have insight into these places. Sometimes counties hire psychologists part-time. Maybe I could teach at one of the local colleges. I need an inside track."

"Sure," Annie said. "I was just so excited thinking both of you might be around that I wasn't thinking. I'm sorry, Julie."

"Hey, thanks for telling me. Nothing's ever easy, is it?"

"Seems that way."

"Keep it quiet. Okay? It might not work out and we would have to stay in Madison."

"Anybody would be lucky to get you."

Julie laughed softly, blowing coffee. "You're just prejudiced."

"Hey, I was your roommate once. Remember?"

The apartment was cool with the blinds closed. Julie hung up her keys and Peggy ran to the phone to call Daisy. Julie never completely unpacked her weekend bag. Either she or Peg was always on the go and now she wondered if it was always going to be that way. Depressing thought.

"Can Daisy go with us to see the horses?" Peggy yelled from the other room.

"We'll have to ask Peg and Annie," she answered absently. She made a mental note to call Chloe and tell her to stop looking. At least until she sorted this all out. She recalled thinking the horses were Peg's world and that she'd better learn to fit in if she wanted to be a part of it.

When she and Peggy left late that afternoon, Peg asked, "Are you going to make an offer on the condo?"

"Not till you see it." She slid onto the warm seat.

"I trust your judgment." Peg leaned in the driver's window while Katie hung onto Peggy's side of the car.

"I don't."

"How about I come Friday? I'll give you a call."

She'd said good-bye and put the car in drive when Katie and Peg backed out of the way.

You can't begin a relationship on a lie, can you, even if it's a white one? Julie wondered. The phone rang in the other room and Peggy picked up. Julie guessed it was Joe. He was another barrier to moving. She'd have to broach the subject to him.

"Mama, Daddy wants to talk to you."

She picked up the receiver on the bedside table. "Hi, Joe."

"I'll be in town next weekend. Will you be there?"

"What happened to hi, how are you?"

"Sorry. How are you anyway?"

"In a conundrum," she said and she began to tell him.

There was a long silence while he listened and apparently thought over what she'd said. Then, "I appreciate your confiding in me. You know, I don't think you ever did when we were married."

"Sorry," she muttered. Then she had hoarded her memories and thoughts of Peg.

"So when I fly in for a weekend, Peggy will be a hundred miles away? How is that supposed to work for me?"

"I could bring her here when you're coming." And pick her up? That would take tons of gas and time.

Joe sighed. "Have you got a job there? And why doesn't Peg move to Madison?"

"Not yet, and she's been offered a partnership with her brother."

"Doing what?"

She'd been afraid he'd ask that. "Cam is a horse trainer and a judge."

"Is this a real job, one that pays a living wage and offers benefits?"

"Yes."

"Let me see if I've got this straight. You want to move to where Peg lives and take our daughter with you. Peg is going to pay the bills while you look for a job."

"No, Joe, I won't move without a job. I'm only asking if it's okay for Peggy to move."

"I have to think about this. See if you can find work there and tell me where you'll be living and then ask me again."

"Okay. Thanks. Where are you anyway?" Maybe they could remain friends.

"In D.C., but I'm coming home on Thursday and want to take Peggy for a few days. I can pick her up at daycare and give you a call later."

"Sure."

Annie called her more than a week later on a Wednesday while she was testing a client. A very uncooperative kid, he was fourteen with a bad case of acne and an attitude that tried her patience. She thought maybe something to ease the skin eruptions might help him more than anything else.

She returned the call after the boy shuffled out, kicking the doorframe and muttering, "Bitch." She thought she'd give this kid to Dennis. He was rather good with tough teenage boys.

"Annie, hi, is everything okay?"

"Better than okay. One of the teaching psychologists at the university is going on sabbatical next year. I gave your name to the dean of the department as a replacement. They had someone lined up, but he took another position in California. Let me give you Jon's name and address."

222

She had already written to the Affinity Health Care offices in the area, but if she had her druthers, she'd not work for an HMO. There were a few private practices she'd sent inquiries to. She'd even tried the county mental health agencies, but really, she expected nothing immediate from these unsolicited probes.

"Thanks, Annie. What would I do without you?"

"I don't know, sweetie. Katie wants to know when you're coming back."

"Not this weekend. Too much to do."

"Even if this job is only part-time and temporary, it would give you a jumping off place."

"It would indeed." She didn't give it much hope, though. She'd taught as a graduate student. Labs. Testing. But that had been the extent of it. She'd gone into private practice. Nevertheless, she sent off the letter with her credentials the next day.

She told the head of the clinic that she was looking for another job in the Fox Valley area and asked to use her as a reference. Of course, all her coworkers found out the same day. Dennis hounded her for information. Where was she going? Why? She sidestepped his questions.

A week later Dean Jon Carruthers phoned her at work. His voice boomed over the line, momentarily stilling her heart when he told her who he was. "I have great respect for Dr. Kincaid." He was talking about Annie, she realized. "We received your letter and credentials soon after she recommended you. I'm wondering if you can come in Friday. Dr. Leyton, whom you would be temporarily replacing, is still here. He'd like to talk to you. The rest of us in the department would like to meet you." He'd already checked her out on the Web, talked with former teachers and her boss. "I have to be honest. We're in something of a bind, and your interest comes at a propitious time."

She glanced at her appointment book, amazed that this was happening, and said yes, of course. Three o'clock. After, she phoned Annie, her words spilling over each other in her excitement.

"Drop Peggy off here. I can't say I'm surprised, but I'm thrilled. We can ride to work together. When are you going to tell Peg?"

"After I talk to these people. I haven't got the job yet and it's not a permanent one. A zillion thanks, Annie. By the way, Dean Carruthers has the highest respect for you."

"He's a nice guy. Hey, I think I'm as excited as you."

Peg heard Julie drive in. "This is a surprise," she said when Peggy and Kate ran into the barn. "You're early, Peggy. Where's your mom?"

"She left. She had to go somewhere."

"Where?" she asked as the girls climbed on the fresh cut bales of hay. The barn was redolent with the odor.

"I don't know," Peggy yelled and then disappeared into the hay with Kate.

Peg was polishing tack for the show tomorrow and wanted to finish before she went in pursuit of someone to tell her what was going on. By the time she put away the saddle soap and silver polish, Annie was gone to the store and Peg's mother knew only that Julie had dropped off Peggy. Brian had left with his father to look at a client's horse.

She stared at her mother for a moment, thinking something was odd. "Will you tell Annie that I was looking for her?"

"If I see her, I will."

"Okay, Mom. Thanks for watching Charlie."

"My pleasure." Her mother smiled. "Go on now before the baby hears you."

She was giving a lesson in the outdoor arena when she saw Julie talking to Annie in the driveway. She heard their laughter clearly but not what they were saying. After talking to the girls, they walked toward Annie's house. Annoyed because Julie hadn't even said hello, she forced herself to concentrate on Cece. She wanted the girl to do well tomorrow. The kid was finally listening to her and not taking her frustrations out on her stepmother or her horse. She actually seemed like a nice girl.

When CeCe put her horse away and Ginny came in to clean stalls, Peg went looking for Julie and Annie. She stopped at her mother's for the baby and found all three in the kitchen, sitting at the table drinking wine.

"What is this?"

"It's five o'clock on Friday, cocktail hour," Annie said.

"Water or pop?" her mom asked.

"I'll get it." She poured a glass and sat next to Julie. "Are you celebrating something?"

"Should we be?" Julie asked, smiling at her.

"Did you find a condo? Get a raise? Win the lottery?"

"None of the above. So how was your week?" Julie asked despite having exchanged e-mails every day.

"You know what my week was like. What's happening here?"

"Your dad and I are going out to eat when he gets home from work, which should be soon. Then we're playing bridge with Ginny's mom and dad."

She looked at Annie. "And you and Cam?"

"We're going out too. The kids are going with us, all but the baby."

A night alone with Julie, except for the baby who didn't really count since she mostly slept. Relaxation flowed through her veins like wine.

After a dinner of tuna fish sandwiches and a salad with mandarin oranges, Peg apologized. "I didn't get to the store. I'll do better next time."

"I like tuna fish. Hey, I'd eat peanut butter or cereal to be with you." A quick flashback to Murray Street and they smiled at each other.

"I'll be so glad when I can drink a glass of wine again."

They had barely finished cleaning up when Julie said, "Let's go to bed. I've had an enervating day. I want to tell you about it."

"But it's not dark out. Don't you want to go for a walk or something? The baby can go with us."

"No."

"All right. I knew something was going on. What's the big secret?" Peg asked as they lay on the sheets.

It was quiet. No cars passing, no birds singing, no kids making noise. "First, tell me if you accepted Cam's offer."

"How do you know about Cam's offer?" Peg sat up. "Did Annie tell you?"

"More to the point, why did you keep me in the dark?"

Peg's figure was outlined in the dimming light. "You want to live in Madison, so that's where we'll live. I chose Cam over you once. I won't do that again."

Outside, the clouds and sky turned pink. A soft breeze brushed Julie's skin. She felt at peace with the past and looked forward with happy anticipation toward the future. "I wish you had shared that information with me. We can't make decisions if you don't include me in the process."

"I didn't think it mattered because Joe doesn't want Peggy to move." Peg settled back and put her hands under her head.

"Joe is willing to let Peggy go with me. I interviewed at UWO today. Annie recommended me to fill in for a psychology professor who's going on sabbatical."

Peg rolled on her side, facing Julie. "Say that again?" Julie repeated it as Peg kissed her face. "You're serious?"

"Would I tell you this if I wasn't?" She laughed and pulled Peg closer.

"You're going to be a professor?" Peg planted a few kisses on her neck.

"A temporary one. I have to look for a permanent job, but it'll be easier if I'm working here." More kisses.

"Why did you do this?" Peg asked, looking serious. "I would have moved."

"That's why. You would have moved even after you'd been offered the job you've always wanted. Years ago I knew you'd never give up the horses."

"But you're giving up your job."

"I'll find a job as a therapist, even if it's part-time."

"I'll substitute teach."

"There, see? It'll all work out," Julie said, her smile white in the darkening room.

"Where will we live?" Peg asked.

"Think we can build here?"

"Maybe in the hay field."

"I love you."

"I was thinking that. I'll never wonder again."

They made love quietly as the darkness wrapped them in its folds. Mouths and hands and damp skin becoming one.

Publications from
BELLA BOOKS, INC.
The best in contemporary lesbian fiction

P.O. Box 10543, Tallahassee, FL 32302
Phone: 800-729-4992
www.bellabooks.com

WITHOUT WARNING: Book one in the Shaken series by KG MacGregor. *Without Warning* is the story of their courageous journey through adversity, and their promise of steadfast love. 978-1-59493-120-8 $13.95

THE CANDIDATE by Tracey Richardson. Presidential Candidate Jane Kincaid had always expected the road to the White House would exact a high personal toll. She just never knew how high until forced to choose between her heart and her political destiny. 978-1-59493-133-8 $13.95

TALL IN THE SADDLE by Karin Kallmaker, Barbara Johnson, Therese Szymanski and Julia Watts. The playful quartet that penned the acclaimed *Once Upon A Dyke* and *Stake Through the Heart* are back and now turning to the Wild (and Very Hot) West to bring you another collection of erotically charged, action-packed, tales. 978-1-59493-106-2 $15.95

IN THE NAME OF THE FATHER by Gerri Hill. In this highly anticipated sequel to *Hunter's Way*, Dallas homicide detectives Tori Hunter and Samantha Kennedy investigate the murder of a Catholic priest who is found naked and strangled to death. 978-1-59493-108-6 $13.95

IT'S ALL SMOKE AND MIRRORS: *The First Chronicles of Shawn Donnelly* by Therese Szymanski. Join Therese Szymanski as she takes a walk on the sillier side of the gritty crime scene detective novel and introduces readers to her newest alternate personality— Shawn Donnelly. 978-1-59493-117-8 $13.95

THE ROAD HOME by Frankie J. Jones. As Lynn finds herself in one adventure after another, she discovers that true wealth may have very little to do with money after all. 978-1-59493-110-9 $13.95

IN DEEP WATERS: CRUISING THE SEAS by Karin Kallmaker and Radclyffe. Book passage on a deliciously sensual Mediterranean cruise with tour guides Radclyffe and Karin Kallmaker. 978-1-59493-111-6 $15.95

ALL THAT GLITTERS by Peggy J. Herring. Life is good for retired Army Colonel Marcel Robicheaux. Marcel is unprepared for the turn her life will take. She soon finds herself in the pursuit of a lifetime—searching for her missing mother and lover. 978-1-59493-107-9 $13.95

OUT OF LOVE by KG MacGregor. For Carmen Delallo and Judith O'Shea, falling in love proves to be the easy part. 978-1-59493-105-5 $13.95

BORDERLINE by Terri Breneman. Assistant Prosecuting Attorney Toni Barston returns in the sequel to *Anticipation*. 978-1-59493-99-7 $13.95

PAST REMEMBERING by Lyn Denison. What would it take to melt Peri's cool exterior? Any involvement on Asha's part would be simply asking for trouble and heartache . . . wouldn't it? 978-1-59493-103-1 $13.95

ASPEN'S EMBERS by Diane Tremain Braund. Will Aspen choose the woman she loves . . . or the forest she hopes to preserve . . . 978-1-59493-102-4 $14.95

THE COTTAGE by Gerri Hill. *The Cottage* is the heartbreaking story of two women who meet by chance . . . or did they? A love so destined it couldn't be denied . . . stolen moments to be cherished forever. 978-1-59493-096-6 $13.95

FANTASY: Untrue Stories of Lesbian Passion edited by Barbara Johnson and Therese Szymanski. Lie back and let Bella's bad girls take you on an erotic journey through the greatest bedtime stories never told. 978-1-59493-101-7 $15.95

SISTERS' FLIGHT by Jeanne G'Fellers. *Sisters' Flight* is the highly anticipated sequel to *No Sister of Mine* and *Sister Lost, Sister Found*. 978-1-59493-116-1 $13.95

BRAGGIN' RIGHTS by Kenna White. Taylor Fleming is a thirty-six-year-old Texas rancher who covets her independence. She finds her cowgirl independence tested by neighboring rancher Jen Holland. 978-1-59493-095-9 $13.95

BRILLIANT by Ann Roberts. Respected sociology professor, Diane Cole finds her views on love challenged by her own heart, as she fights the attraction she feels for a woman half her age. 978-1-59493-115-4 $13.95

THE EDUCATION OF ELLIE by Jackie Calhoun. When Ellie sees her childhood friend for the first time in thirty years she is tempted to resume their long lost friendship. But with the years come a lot of baggage and the two women struggle with who they are now while fighting the painful memories of their first parting. Will they be able to move past their history to start again? 978-1-59493-092-8 $13.95

DATE NIGHT CLUB by Saxon Bennett. *Date Night Club* is a dark romantic comedy about the pitfalls of dating in your thirties . . . 978-1-59493-094-2 $13.95

PLEASE FORGIVE ME by Megan Carter. Laurel Becker is on the verge of losing the two most important things in her life—her current lover, Elaine Alexander, and the Lavender Page bookstore. Will Elaine and Laurel manage to work through their misunderstandings and rebuild their life together? 978-1-59493-091-1 $13.95

WHISKEY AND OAK LEAVES by Jaime Clevenger. Meg meets June, a single woman running a horse ranch in the California Sierra foothills. The two become quick friends and it isn't long before Meg is looking for more than just a friendship. But June has no interest in developing a deeper relationship with Meg. She is, after all, not the least bit interested in women . . . or is she? Neither of these two women is prepared for what lies ahead . . . 978-1-59493-093-5 $13.95

SUMTER POINT by KG MacGregor. As Audie surrenders her heart to Beth, she begins to distance herself from the reckless habits of her youth. Just as they're ready to meet in the middle, their future is thrown into doubt by a duty Beth can't ignore. It all comes to a head on the river at Sumter Point. 978-1-59493-089-8 $13.95

THE TARGET by Gerri Hill. Sara Michaels is the daughter of a prominent senator who has been receiving death threats against his family. In an effort to protect Sara, the FBI recruits homicide detective Jaime Hutchinson to secretly provide the protection they are so certain Sara will need. Will Sara finally figure out who is behind the death threats? And will Jaime realize the truth—and be able to save Sara before it's too late?
978-1-59493-082-9 $13.95

REALITY BYTES by Jane Frances. In this sequel to *Reunion*, follow the lives of four friends in a romantic tale that spans the globe and proves that you can cross the whole of cyberspace only to find love a few suburbs away . . .   978-1-59493-079-9 $13.95

MURDER CAME SECOND by Jessica Thomas. Broadway's bad-boy genius, Paul Carlucci, has chosen *Hamlet* for his latest production and, to the delight of some and despair of others, he has selected Provincetown's amphitheatre for his opening gala. But Alex Peres realizes the wrong people are falling down, and the moaning is all too realistic. Someone must not be shooting blanks . . .   978-1-59493-081-2 $13.95

SKIN DEEP by Kenna White. Jordan Griffin has been given a new assignment: Track down and interview one-time nationally renowned broadcast journalist Reece McAllister. Much to her surprise, Jordan comes away with far more than just a story . . .
978-1-59493-78-2 $13.95

FINDERS KEEPERS by Karin Kallmaker. *Finders Keepers*, the quest for the perfect mate in the 21st century, joins Karin Kallmaker's *Just Like That* and her other incomparable novels about lesbian love, lust and laughter.   1-59493-072-4 $13.95

OUT OF THE FIRE by Beth Moore. Author Ann Covington feels at the top of the world when told her book is being made into a movie. Then in walks Casey Duncan the actress who is playing the lead in her movie. Will Casey turn Ann's world upside down?
1-59493-088-0 $13.95

STAKE THROUGH THE HEART: NEW EXPLOITS OF TWILIGHT LESBIANS by Karin Kallmaker, Julia Watts, Barbara Johnson and Therese Szymanski. The playful quartet that penned the acclaimed *Once Upon A Dyke* are dimming the lights for journeys into worlds of breathless seduction.   1-59493-071-6 $15.95

THE HOUSE ON SANDSTONE by KG MacGregor. Carly Griffin returns home to Leland and finds that her old high school friend Justine is awakening more than just old memories.   1-59493-076-7 $13.95

WILD NIGHTS: MOSTLY TRUE STORIES OF WOMEN LOVING WOMEN edited by Therese Szymanski. 264 pp. 23 new stories from today's hottest erotic writers are sure to give you your wildest night ever!   1-59493-069-4 $15.95

COYOTE SKY by Gerri Hill. 248 pp. Sheriff Lee Foxx is trying to cope with the realization that she has fallen in love for the first time. And fallen for author Kate Winters, who is technically unavailable. Will Lee fight to keep Kate in Coyote?
1-59493-065-1 $13.95

VOICES OF THE HEART by Frankie J. Jones. 264 pp. A series of events force Erin to swear off love as she tries to break away from the woman of her dreams. Will Erin ever find the key to her future happiness?   1-59493-068-6 $13.95